NOWHERE TO RUN

Anne's first warning was the smell, sharp and oily . . . and then the sound of a stack of fermenting grain igniting and bursting into a hill of flame.

"No . . ." The single word choked from her throat. It was the first time in her life she had seen an open fire. Smoke and heat in a biosphere had nowhere to go. For an instant, she was mesmerized by the look of it. And then a roar burst from within the mound of grain and an eruption of searing fire shot high into the rafters of the storeroom.

She screamed and ran for the door. The knob turned easily in her hand, but the door wouldn't open.

"Help!" she screamed. Would anyone hear? "Help me!" she cried again, then ran from the flames to the opposite end of the room.

She stared at the growing fire, a live and terrible force, trapping her. The air scalded her lungs, and black smoke was filling the room.

The fire would have her. It would have them all.

PINNACLE BOOKS HAS
SOMETHING FOR EVERYONE—

MAGICIANS, EXPLORERS, WITCHES AND CATS

THE HANDYMAN (377-3, $3.95/$4.95)
He is a magician who likes hands. He likes their comfortable shape and weight and size. He likes the portability of the hands once they are severed from the rest of the ponderous body. Detective Lanark must discover who The Handyman is before more handless bodies appear.

PASSAGE TO EDEN (538-5, $4.95/$5.95)
Set in a world of prehistoric beauty, here is the epic story of a courageous seafarer whose wanderings lead him to the ends of the old world—and to the discovery of a new world in the rugged, untamed wilderness of northwestern America.

BLACK BODY (505-9, $5.95/$6.95)
An extraordinary chronicle, this is the diary of a witch, a journal of the secrets of her race kept in return for not being burned for her "sin." It is the story of Alba, that rarest of creatures, a white witch: beautiful and able to walk in the human world undetected.

THE WHITE PUMA (532-6, $4.95/NCR)
The white puma has recognized the men who deprived him of his family. Now, like other predators before him, he has become a man-hater. This story is a fitting tribute to this magnificent animal that stands for all living creatures that have become, through man's carelessness, close to disappearing forever from the face of the earth.

FUTURE EDEN

J. M. MORGAN

PINNACLE BOOKS
WINDSOR PUBLISHING CORP.

To my children, Terry, Christopher, and Lisa Morgan, and all the children of our biosphere Earth. May they live in peace.

PINNACLE BOOKS

are published by

Windsor Publishing Corp.
475 Park Avenue South
New York, NY 10016

First printing: October, 1992

Printed in the United States of America

One

The day of the killing flood was a morning unlike any other. Heavy spring rains had soaked the desert for nearly a week, filling the rivers and narrow creeks to overflowing. The land bubbled like a pot of cooking meal, for the ground could hold no more.

The camp of the Outsiders, those people living along the Ware River valley of Texas, was below the climb to the high mesa and the glass peaks of Biosphere Seven. The sky had seemed to join the earth, for everywhere was a wavering gray. The heavens rippled, the land boiled, and the rivers churned with unleashed fury.

The once peaceful river which ran between the banks of flanking orange and lemon orchards, now pressed over the lip of the earthen embankments, spilling an uncontrollable surge of water onto the valley plain. The lemon trees washed down river. The orange trees were torn from their roots and joined the swollen flood channel. The earthen slopes of the Ware crumbled into the mad rumble of the storm's deluge.

And the rains went on, unceasing.

On the fifth morning, the clouds parted. A wedge of red-orange sky revealed itself like a portent from an angry god. Fingerlets of this fire bled into the track of gray above the heads of men, women, and children of the People, as if burning an opening through the hovering mist and vapor.

"What next?" asked Elizabeth Cunningham. She was standing at the doorway of her adobe house. The floor was a wash of sinking mud from the constant leak of rainwater through the lodge pole and thatch roof. "How will we live?" she asked. "Our crops are rotting in the fields. The river's taken the fruit trees, and even our houses are falling into the ruin of this constant rain. What else can happen?" she asked, turning to her husband.

The Indian nature of Josiah Gray Wolf wished she hadn't asked it. He was superstitious enough to believe that if you voiced such a question, the spirits of the land above and the land below would give you an answer. It was an answer he was sure they didn't want. "Come away from the doorway, Beth. It's too cold there." With an arm around her shoulders, he tried to urge her back to the warmth of the fire with him and their children.

Stubbornly, she shook off the comfort of his arm. "I want to see it." The words seemed bitten off, as if made of thin, brittle glass. "I've lost my family and my home once before. I was numb through that. I thought it was behind us, but it's happening again, isn't it? It's taking away the life we've made here, our home," she said more to the blood-orange break in the sky than to him. "This time, I want to see it. Everything we've struggled to hold together, everything we've worked so hard to build . . . gone."

Josiah went back to the small hearth fire where his four remaining children sat huddled beside the only heat in the damp house, two sons and two daughters: thirteen-year-old Una, Walker eleven, America—or Merc—nine, and six-year-old Tad. They were the four left to him. Four others—his daughters Sidra and Willow, and his sons Yuma and Jared—had gone north nearly a year before, to a colony of survivors living in Montana. The land of this place was less without them. He was less.

6

"Will the rain stop?" asked Tad. The boy was paler than he should be, thought Josiah.

"The rain always stops," he promised the child.

"Mama said God made it rain once for forty days and forty nights," declared Merc. She was her mother's daughter, a child who loved learning as much as food, and had a memory like a tight-fitting box. Nothing slipped away from her, or was ever forgotten.

"That was a story," said Josiah.

She looked at him doubtfully.

"Like a fairy tale?" Tad's eyes were ringed with worry.

Josiah took the boy on his knee. He could feel the cold living in this child, as if his small body could not hold enough heat to resist it. He rubbed a little warmth into the boy's arms and legs.

"The flood that story speaks of happened a long, long time ago," he told his son. "At the end, the story promises that such a thing will never happen again. You don't need to fear that."

Tad's eyes were gentle again, a sweetness that Josiah felt his own spirit returning to as he grew older. The old and the young were the innocents of life. He had once been what this child was, and was now going back to it in the fullness of his years. They shared this unity of spirit, he and his youngest child. In that, they comforted one another.

"The color of that sky. I've never seen such a morning," said Elizabeth at the open doorway, her voice sounding like a shudder on a loud wind. Something sudden whipped at the air beyond the four earthen walls of the house. And then, "Oh, God! Oh, dear God. Josiah, look!"

He stood, put the boy down, and moved the few steps to the doorway. A wall of water ten feet high raced behind the already swollen Ware river. It was coming toward them, the heel of its boot slamming into the crumbling embankments and flooding the adjacent valley, already crushing the first adobe houses.

"Children, run!" he shouted.

But it was too late to run. The weight of the water hit the front of the house, slamming one wall into the mudsink below. Josiah and Elizabeth were not buried beneath the collapsed adobe. Them, the flash flood carried away. Their bodies were swept into the tangle of trees and boulders. In an instant, they were crushed.

As quickly as the flood had hit, it passed by. Only now, the water of the Ware had become a dark, flat pool, shimmering in the broken daylight along the inundated wash of the valley.

In the aftermath of the flash flood of the year 2020, four were counted among the dead: Josiah Gray Wolf, called Sagamore and leader of the People; his wife, Elizabeth Cunningham; Skeet Hallinger, husband of Mary Logan and father of their two sons; and four-year-old William Wyse.

In all, there remained fourteen survivors in the camp of the Outsiders. Together, they were two men, three women, and nine children.

"We can't stay in this place any longer," declared Stephen Wyse.

The fourteen were gathered on the ridge overlooking the valley. They had taken shelter on the higher plain after the dead were counted. "The grain that was growing in the fields is lost. What little we had in the storage bins is gone, too. There's no reason to stay here now. Nothing to keep us tied to this desert."

"The biosphere's the reason we came here in the first place," Brad McGhee reminded him, reminded them all. He was the man the People called Prophet. "The men, women, and children inside that dome are like us. One day, they're going to find a way to

8

leave Biosphere Seven. We need to be here when that happens. To help them. There are so few of us on earth. We're part of them and they're part of us. We can't abandon each other."

"I can," said Wyse. "I won't wait for anyone else's death. A desert's no land for growing crops. We've been killing ourselves for years trying to squeeze out some kind of a life from this barren country. For what? For you, and some dream you have of the colony within the glass city coming outside? For Josiah, because he found us and brought us here?"

"We need to stay together," Prophet tried to warn them. "They can help us; we can help them."

"No more!" Wyse insisted. "I'll work, but I won't see all my efforts provide so little, not after what's happened. I'm taking my family and heading to Kansas or Iowa, any decent farmland for God's sake!"

"What about Merry, Crystal, and the children? Could you leave them behind?" Prophet tried to appeal to Wyse's humanity. "We need you, Stephen. None of us will make it unless we remain together."

But this appeal to Wyse's compassion seemed only to make the man more determined. "I'm taking all of them with me, those willing to leave. I won't abandon them to this desert. There's better land for us," he said. "We have the whole of the world. There's nothing to keep us here."

"I'll go with you," said Merry Logan. Her husband, Skeet Hallinger, had been one of the lives lost in the flood.

"Merry," Prophet tried to stop her.

"Don't say anything against this to me," she turned on him, a fury bringing a cutting edge to her words. "My husband is dead because of this country. It's a torment to the soul, this Texas. Summers that blister your skin and bake the breath from your lungs, winters so cold your fingers can't move, and spring rains that washed away four lives." Her voice

9

broke. "I won't risk any more of my family. My sons and I will go with Stephen and Emily."

"I'll go, too," said Crystal Rivers. "I want my daughter to grow up in a place where life is easier. "I'm sick of this camp, sick of never seeing a green woods or an ocean. There's a world full of houses out there," she said as if remembering them. "I want Grace to know what a real house looks like; I want her to live in one. There are cities with stores and clothes," she went on, speaking to no one in particular. "We could take anything we wanted. New clothes, makeup. Who's going to stop us?" Her laugh was hard, too sharp.

"The clothes will have rotted on the racks by now," Prophet said as gently as he could.

"Don't tell me that!" she yelled. "If I want to believe it, why do you care? I can't stay here, Prophet. I've had enough of death and desert. I can't," her words shattered into broken sobs.

Only Kipp Peters remained silent. Since his mother's death three years before, he had been adopted by all those in the camp. He was as much Stephen's child as he was Merry Logan's, Crystal Rivers', or Prophet's.

"What do you want, Kipp?" asked Prophet. "You have a vote in this."

Kipp was still a boy, only seven. His mother's eyes looked out of his small face, dark and solemn. He was nothing of Natalie Peters's image, other than her eyes, but Prophet remembered the woman clearly through her son. "I don't know what's right," he said, turning from Prophet to Stephen. "I want to make everybody happy again. It's so sad now, being here. I keep remembering the sound of the water coming over the houses. Sometimes, I think I can still see it."

"Isn't that enough for you?" Stephen asked Prophet. "Listen to the boy. Do you want him to go on remembering that everyday of his life? We've had

10

enough. He's seen too much death here. We all have."

Prophet's sense of loyalty was torn between what was best for the People — this small clan of fourteen which included his one-year-old son Andrew — and his commitment to the woman who had once been his wife, Jessica. For twenty-three years, they had been forced to live apart. She, within the fragile world of the biosphere. He, as Prophet and religious leader to the gathered camp of the People.

Jessie had made a new life for herself within the sphere. She had married someone else and had children. She had never asked that he stay in this desert and make his life a dim extension of her own, but he knew she needed him to be here . . . in case. For twenty-three years, he had remained in this hot, rough camp outside the biosphere, for the day when she might need him.

Now, it wasn't Stephen's words, but Kipp's, which would alter the course of Prophet's life. The boy could have been Andrew. Did he want his son scarred like this child had been scarred by the memory of the flood? Hadn't all of them been damaged enough? First by the manmade virus, which in its destructive force had swept the world of nearly all mankind. And now by the ravages of this flood. Hadn't they seen enough death?

Prophet's decision was the second most painful of his life. The first had been choosing to live in this valley, near enough to Jessica to see her and know of her existence, but forever parted from her.

The few survivors protected from the virus by the enclosed world of Biosphere Seven couldn't exist beyond the glass walls of the domed city, unlike the men and women of the Outsider's camp, those who called themselves the People. The People — Prophet, and the thirteen with him today — through some favored genetic inheritance, had either a natural immunity to the virus, or simply had never contracted it. Only one among them had ever become ill with the virus, and lived. That one person was Brad McGhee . . . Prophet.

"We need you," Stephen's wife, Emily Pinola, touched Prophet's arm. And then, in a voice loud enough for only him to hear, she added, "So many are depending on us. It would be safer if you'd come, too."

What did she mean, "safer"?

"You can't stay here with the baby," said Crystal. "I fed Andrew when you brought him to me as an infant, kept him alive on the milk from my body, as I did my own child. If you won't come with us for our sake, come away from here for his. He deserves better than this. He deserves to know women who'll love and care for him as he grows up. With us, he'll have three mothers."

"He has a mother, and she's here." Prophet tried to think what it would be like, waking up in a place where he couldn't look across the land and see the biosphere. Couldn't know that he was close to Jessie. Couldn't believe that he was with her still.

For himself, he never would have gone. For his son, for Andrew, he would have given up his life. "It'll turn cold in the north come fall. Traveling on foot with young children will be slow. If we're going to make it to a good stopping place before the first snow hits, we'll need to leave right away."

"We're ready now," said Wyse. "We've got nothing left but what we're carrying with us right this minute. I'm for starting out tomorrow morning, if the weather's clear."

The storm came back to harry them through the night. They made a crude shelter of a couple of ridge poles and stretched cloth, but it did little to keep out the cold or rain. By morning they were soaked and chilled. A weak sun glowed through the haze and mist, as the rains lessened and then stopped.

Like a tribe of desert nomads, they gathered their children and their possessions to them and started across the high mesa toward Biosphere Seven, heading north.

Two

"The needs of human life are simple," said Jessica Nathan, "clean air, pure water, and unpolluted land upon which to grow enough food to sustain us." The fifty-three-year-old leader and matriarch of Biosphere Seven stretched her tired back and stood among the children gathered around her in the field.

They were weeding between the rows of autumn crops in the ag wing. The children were lower to the ground, but she kept up with them, carefully hoeing unwanted grass and volunteer plants from between the new seedlings they had planted a month earlier.

"We've gained a precious understanding from living within this world, not on it," she told them. "When I was a little girl," she said, "my father read a story to me, about the Tree of Knowledge. I think, living here among nature, we've plucked knowledge from that tree again. It's understanding our place within nature that will give us life."

It was obvious she'd lost the attention of a couple of the younger ones. She saw them whispering. *Too philosophical*. Quinn was always reminding her to keep these lessons short.

"What shall we do after we finish weeding?" Her question was offered to the group as a whole. "Go for a swim? Have a picnic? Or a game of tag?"

"All three!" cried eight-year-old Dalton Innis, and the others shouted their agreement.

"Good choice. All three it is." She laughed at their high spirits.

"Let's go now," Maria Innis grumbled. "I'm tired of stupid weeding."

"We'll finish this last row," Jessica insisted, and bent her back to the labor again. If she could do it at fifty-three, they couldn't complain that the work was too hard for them at twelve and thirteen. At least, not too loudly.

She looked through the glass wall of the sphere to the glowering sky outside. So much rain. What must it be like for them in the valley? She thought of her one-year-old son, Andrew. Was he warm? Did he have enough food? She thought of Brad, Andrew's father, the man she had once called husband.

As if causing it to have happened by thinking of him, Jessica felt eighteen-year-old Lara Hunter touch her on the shoulder and say, "There's one of the Outsiders at the viewing port, Jessica. He wants to talk to you."

"Which one?"

Lara seemed reluctant to answer. The girl was old enough to have heard rumors, and of course with Andrew's birth last year, this was something even the youngest child would have talked about. "It's him, I guess. The one they call Prophet."

Jessica dropped the hoe in the field and walked quickly toward the viewing port.

"What about our swim and picnic?" Dalton Innis shouted after her.

"Lara, will you take them for me? I'll join all of you later," said Jessica. "A swim, a picnic, and a game of tag," she told Lara.

She heard their cheers as she walked away. The overcast sky made her uneasy. Another storm on its way. Three weeks of rain. Thinking of this, she hurried her steps. What could Brad be here to tell her?

By the time Jessica climbed the steps to the viewing port, lightning was striking in broken slats across the Outside sky. A few seconds later, the deep rumble of thunder shuddered through the biosphere like freight trains crashing head-on in the living air.

Brad was standing in the rain, waiting outside the viewing port. She saw him before she reached the top of the step. At first, she thought it was a trick of the light, the gray sky casting a darker tone to everything within its reach, but then she saw he was soaked through. His hair was dripping wet and plastered to his scalp. His clothes and shoes were caked with mud.

"Look at you!" The words couldn't be taken back, once spoken.

He looked up, and after she saw his face, she could have cut off her tongue with a dull razor. His eyes were beaten souls, and crying. "Brad? What is it? What's wrong?"

He didn't speak. Couldn't, it seemed.

She was almost too afraid to ask. "Is it Andrew? Where is he?"

"Andrew's fine." The words seemed to cost him. He sat straighter on the bench and visibly tried to draw up his courage and pull himself together. He obviously had something to tell her, and whatever it was, it wasn't good.

"Tell me what's happened." Her hands were trembling. She clasped them in her lap, a fist of strength to hold back the hurt she knew was coming.

"The rain," he began, "there's been so much rain. The ground couldn't hold any more water. The river was too high, and it spilled over the banks."

16

She stayed quiet, letting him tell it.

"There was a flash flood . . . and the camp is gone. Everything."

"A flood? Did anyone . . . were lives lost?"

Brad leaned forward, bowing his head into the cradle of his hands. "Josiah's dead, and his wife, Elizabeth."

"Josiah." The name came from Jessica like a torn breath, hard and painful. Her friend. For so long, he had been a part of her life. He had been the one to leave the biosphere and gather the survivors on the Outside. He had brought them back to live in a colony near the sphere, so that she and the others would know that the world was not completely empty of human life. He had risked everything, and now he was gone. She felt his death as a personal loss.

"Skeet Hallinger died too, and four-year-old William Wyse."

"We didn't hear it," she said. "We never knew anything had happened." Her voice sounded thinned and thready. "It could have been you," she said, trying to breathe, trying not to tremble, "or Andrew."

"Yes. It's because of Andrew that I can't stay here, Jessica."

"Can't stay?" Panic was making her heart race and skip.

"The houses are gone. The crops and orchards are washed away. There's nothing left for them. They can't live here anymore. Andrew can't live here. It could happen again. Another storm . . . another flood. It could be his life the next time."

"What are you telling me?" She knew. She knew, but the truth wouldn't stay fixed in her mind. It wasn't real.

"The others would go without me if I stayed behind." His words were touching her like fine cuts

17

with thin-bladed knives. "There's so few of us now, only one man besides myself, three women, and nine children. They need my help. We need each other."

She'd stopped listening to his words. "Don't take my child away!"

"Jessica—"

"Don't take him, Brad. He's my son. If you take him from here, I'll never see him again. I can't leave this place!" She struck her fist against the glass.

"And I can't stay," he told her. "Don't you know I want to?"

Her eyes were clouded by a swell of tears. A sleeting rain spattered the glass between them, or were those tears on his face?

"I've stayed in this desert for over twenty years, Jessica, only to be near you. I've been here all that time, without complaint, and I'd stay even now if it weren't for the others. If it weren't for Andrew. He deserves more of a life than the one I could give him in this land. Think what it would be like for him to stay here with only me. He's a child, Jessica. He needs to be with other people."

"I'm his mother!" she cried.

The words seemed to crush him. "If I could give him back to you," he said, "I would. He's all that I have . . . and I would give him back if it were possible, but it isn't."

Brad stood up to go. It was going to happen, she could see that. If she didn't say something to stop him, he would be gone. Andrew would be gone. She'd never see either of them again.

"No! Please, don't. I gave him to you. Don't take Andrew away. Brad, if you ever loved me—"

"My God, Jessie. I came to say goodbye."

"Brad . . ."

He looked at her then, and she knew he would do it. He was going. "I've always loved you, Jessie.

I never believed anything would make me leave. I thought for as long as I lived I'd be here for you . . . in case you needed me. It's not for my life." He put his hands on the glass between them and stared into her eyes. "Understand. It's for the others. I'm Prophet to them. It's for Andrew. We gave him life, Jessie. Now, we have to let him live it. Don't let my last sight of you be of your eyes staring at me like that. Please, God. Andrew's all we have of us. For him, God forgive me, I'm willing to tear my heart in half and leave you."

"Brad." Her fingernails were scraping into the glass.

"Goodbye, Jessie. I leave you to God." He turned, and started down the steps, moving out of her life.

"Brad!" she cried again. And then she was screaming his name, beating at the glass barrier, sliding to her knees and screaming over and over, "No! Brad . . . Brad!"

In the manmade world of Biosphere Seven, that day was lost to the mind of Jessica Nathan. She didn't know how she came to be in her bed, or how the night had closed over the day so quickly. The dark room was soothing, a well of peace to gain enough strength for another morning. It was silent here, a nurturing quiet, like the stillness of a mountain cave, or a dark and fertile womb.

For a moment she was safe, and still, and at peace.

And then she remembered.

Her cries shattered the chrysalis of this room, of her mind . . . and she was left wailing in the lonely weight of dark, knowing she had lost them both.

Brad and her son were gone.

Three

Hunting was a thing natural to the Inuit, John Katelo. In the north country, he had hunted with his father and his uncles. He had known the land and what it could provide him. Here, in Montana, he had learned the new tracks, new ways of bringing food to his family's table.

The moose was a wide-antlered buck. It stepped lazily into the water, bending its heavy head to bite mouthful after mouthful of the tender greens growing from the shallow banks of the river. By its size and weight, Katelo knew that it was a mature buck, still strong enough to be in its prime. Most probably, it was the breeding male in this area.

He felt an empathy for it. I'm like that, he thought: a mature man still strong enough to be considered in my prime, and the only breeding male in the area.

He had a wife and four children at home, the youngest only six. In some place far away from here, he had two more children, Seth and Jonathan, his eldest sons. They would be nineteen and twenty by now, if they lived. They had left the green Montana valley in hopes of finding survivors, people other than those of their own family. By John Katelo's reckoning, they had been gone two years.

20

He thought of these two sons as he focused the rifle sight on the back of the moose's skull, and squeezed the trigger. The buck dropped in lead-weighted immediacy onto the bank of the shallow water. Katelo rushed forward, and while the animal was still warm, its great heart stilled, he cut into the flesh. He hurried with the knife, knowing that the smell of blood would bring timber wolf, mountain cat, and bear.

Carefully, he wrapped each bundle of meat in a clean cloth and tied the bundles to the travois harnessed against the shoulders and back of his horse. While he worked in the thickening blood of the moose, he thought of his sons. Like the blood of this animal, their spirits were touching him. His thoughts were filled with memories of their faces, the too-brief glimpses from a time of childhood, swiftly flowing as a river across the hilled measure of his mind.

He remembered the time of Seth's birth. It seemed like yesterday, but it was twenty years ago. Thinking of it now, he remembered so well. . . .

Salena had waited throughout the long hours of increasing pain since early morning. She looked up at him with trusting eyes, squeezing his hand when the grip of agony was on her, and trying not to cry when each time of hurt ended.

"Will it be soon?" she'd asked.

Each time, he'd nodded, "Yes."

But it was not soon. The day had gone, the night came and went, and the howling shrieks at dawn pulled her into the next morning. Still, the child would not be born.

Now, she didn't ask, "Will it be soon?" Now, it was, "Oh God, help me! I can't—I can't. Please." And then the screams Katelo drew back from as

21

he would have from the boiling of his own skin.

She was no one he recognized, but an animal crazed with unending pain, her body thrashing on the twisted pile of bloody sheets beneath her. Her hair was wet and corded like rope. Her mouth gaped open, gasping air, muttering, "No, no. Please, no more," and then her lips drawn back over her teeth in the next hard scream.

He thought of cutting the child from her—reaching into the gaping flesh of her writhing body and cutting the unborn baby into pieces, and pulling the pieces from her. It was a thing the old Inuit grandmothers did when a birth went on too long. But he feared this, feared that Salena would die, too.

By night, she didn't pray to any God, or speak any words. She lay unmoving in the mass of her own blood, coming to life only when the grip of agony seized her, tearing her in two. Her voice was hoarse, and the sounds of her shrieks were inhuman howls of unbearable torment.

She didn't look up at him anymore. He was sure she didn't see him when he reached for the knife. He held it in his hand, wishing he could be sure. She'd lost so much blood. Cutting the child now might kill her.

Without Salena, he would be alone in the world. There was no one else. Since the virus, she was the only living person he had seen besides Jack Quaid, and now Quaid was dead. One other feeling held back his hand. He loved Salena. Together, they had talked about their child, waited the many months for it to be born. If it could still be born . . . if she could live.

He put the knife down and promised the spirit within him that he would wait until dawn. If by then the child had not been born, he would do whatever was needed. For those next hours, he prayed.

The child was born just as the sun's first peaks of daylight pearled the dawn sky. The infant was long, his head narrowed along the top of his skull from the force of the birth, but alive. Katelo used the knife to cut the birth cord.

Salena knew nothing of the boy, but fell into an exhausted sleep that was little more than death for the next two days. Alert enough only to take the water and soup Katelo spooned into her mouth, she collapsed back into coma-like stillness. He kept the child alive by feeding it boiled water and syrup. Salena did not wake from this death-like sleep until the third day.

It was then that she first saw her son. The infant's fierce redness was gone, and his head looked less pointed, now. Katelo laid the baby into the crook of her arm, and watched as the child's mouth searched for his mother's breast. In that moment, some source of life transformed Salena's face. He saw it happen.

"Seth," she said, and named their son.

Over the next few days, he saw that she willed herself to live, just as an animal will sometimes will itself to die. She struggled to drink the rich broths he held to her lips, and take any nourishment he offered, so that she might gain enough strength to feed the child. Each day, Katelo told her that he needed her, too. That they must bring up their son together.

She lived. Either for the boy, or for the love she felt for Katelo himself, he never knew. She lived, and they had gone on . . . as the only man, woman, and child they knew in all the world.

The wrapped bundles of meat were securely tied

to the travois. Katelo left the moose carcass for the scavengers of the forest. He rode the horse at an easy walk back to Mirror Lake. This fresh meat would give strength to his family.

The old Inuits had believed in taking on the strengths of the animals they killed and ate. He had laughed at such ideas as a boy, but now he understood more than the knowledge he'd thought he'd been so sure of as a child, that a man's survival often comes from the life stolen from an animal.

There was still snow on the ground; the grip of winter was longer in the Montana valley, sheltered by gray-black mountains. Spring grasses had broken through the cold earth, but the snows of winter were with them still, glistening in patches of ice along the forest-darkened trails. The horse picked its way slowly over the unsure path.

Katelo rejoiced in each new spring—life renewing itself in insistent spears of grass breaking through the snow, in the buds of new leaves swelling on the branches of trees, in the sounds of ice cracking in the river. Life returned each spring, and John Katelo watched for it, noticing the small events as much as the large.

He listened to the birds with their nests of young high in the trees. Their sharp, clear voices spoke to him, not in words he could understand, but in a sense of nature he felt a belonging with. Like them, he was part of the world they shared.

Something in the quiet of the woods reminded him of his childhood, walking beside his grandfather and his uncle in the white springtime of Alaska. The land had been quiet then, too. Along the Inuit hunting traces and in the winter-bound woods there had been a fertile silence. In such a silence, the mind can speak, and the thoughts of the young are forever changed by the sight of a tree limb bowed with a weight of snow, by the sound of ice crunching beneath the heel of a heavy boot, and by the feeling of kinship with your people, and the land.

Wisps of gray clouds flitted in wind-driven gambols across the sky. The clear blue thickened and disappeared beneath the dark strands of a coming storm. With the clouds came the cold, and with that, the memory of another day of threatening storm, another dark gray canopy of sky overhead, and the strong recollection of an Inuit man teaching the ways of his people to a young boy.

It had been clear to Katelo since the days of his children's youth, that not Seth, his firstborn, but Jonathan his second son, would be the inheritor of the Inuit awareness and knowledge. As the two boys grew, it was Jonathan, who at the age of twelve, saw the yellow ring around the moon as the pale face of the ancient grandmother of earth; Jonathan who kept the small black feather of a raven with a wide splinter of rose quartz in a secret cache of rocks, and a smooth river stone the color of blood. It was Jonathan who followed the track of the sky, watching the groups of stars move over the face of the heavens.

It was to this son that John Katelo told the story of his escape from the biosphere in Siberia where the virus began, and of his lonely journey across the lands of ice and snow, hearing the accusing voices of the dead following him.

"There were spirits who wanted my life," he told the boy. "I felt them with me as I crossed the tundra, and with me as I tried to sleep. They touched me, and I heard them weeping. Old and

25

young, I heard them cry out, for they were no more."

Katelo taught the boy stories of the Inuit people. This child was the continuance of all those who had gone before. His square face, dark chop of bangs, and black onyx eyes were the same as Katelo's, the same as Katelo's uncle's, his father's, and his grandfather's. The boy's way of seeing the world was Inuit, too.

"Why do you keep these?" Katelo had asked, expecting Jonathan to tell him they were treasured finds, tokens of boyhood to mark some remembered day, or simply small objects that a child might think pretty. But Katelo had been wrong.

"These are the stories you told me, Father."

"Tell me of them," said Katelo.

The boy held up the pink quartz. "When Great-grandmother of the Inuit people cast down her comb of stars from the sky, it fell to a place of swirling heat and became Earth. The pink of this quartz holds the color of that heat," said Jonathan. "In its clearness, I can feel the stars of Great-grandmother's comb flying across the heavens as she combs her long black hair."

Katelo had never told Jonathan such a story; the boy had dreamed it wholly from his mind. But wasn't that, Katelo wondered, where all such beliefs came from? "Tell me of the river rock," he urged his son.

Jonathan picked up the smooth red rock and rolled it in the palm of his hand. "When the moon, our Grandmother, made the first people, she sent her light to touch the world and waken the sleeping life in it. But the highest place on Earth were mountains, and so Grandmother's light touched them first.

"The stone-people became alive, but could not

26

move to the rhythm of Grandmother's song. The rivers and oceans moved to the songs, the seasons came and went by the touch of her soft light, but the stone-people could not move. They were fixed to the cooling core of Great-grandmother's comb."

Jonathan touched the red stone to his cheek, as if feeling a kinship with it. Katelo felt the same drawing in that he had known when listening to his grandfather's stories. Listening to his son, he knew these were stories from the heart of an Inuit; there was no doubt of that.

"The Grandmother called her first people to move to the rhythm of her moonlight. The mountains tried. They pulled at their stone feet until blood came to their surface. They rumbled and cracked from the star comb, rolling their great boulders down from the high cliffs and into the deep canyons and river valleys. There, the waters washed them, smoothing the jagged edges from the stones until they began to roll and move in the water. They felt the pull of the water, and moved with it to the slow rhythm of the Grandmother's song.

"Later," Jonathan went on, "when Grandmother saw how hard it was for the stone-people to obey her, she lowered her hair, the yellow stretch of living moonlight, taking it from these oldest brothers and letting it touch the softer ground of earth. From this softer ground, she made the first men and women."

"And the stone-people?" asked Katelo.

"They remained fixed to Great-grandmother's star comb. Only sometimes, they still try to walk. They crack free and fall, still wanting to move across the face of the earth, following Grandmother's song."

Jonathan held the river stone out to his father. "It's still red from their blood. Can you see?"

Katelo saw the red in the stone and nodded, but he saw much more in the words of his son. "Tell me of the feather."

The boy's fingers moved to the small black feather, hesitated as if he didn't want to touch it, and then between his forefinger and thumb plucked it from the cache of rocks.

"Is that from the wings of the Sky Father?" asked Katelo, guessing his son's mind.

"No." Jonathan's eyes were dark worlds held in the face of a twelve-year-old child. These eyes that had seen so much, now held tears. "Black is for the death of man from the earth," Jonathan said, "and the feather is for the hovering spirits of their wandering souls. I feel them too, Father. In the air, in the sky. They touch me, as you said they once touched you. I feel it like that feather, their touch. I hear them cry."

Katelo had comforted Jonathan, then. But the boy's strange words had comforted Katelo, too. They told him the Inuit people were not gone from the earth. Their stories and their wisdom were branches taken root in the mind of a twelve-year-old boy.

"Have I made you sad?" Jonathan asked, touching Katelo's cheek. The boy's fingers came away wet with tears. Katelo hadn't known he was crying.

"No, not sad," he told his son, "but brushed with the strokes of life. Your stories have made me feel a closeness with all the earth," he said. "For a moment, I felt the people lost from our world, too."

They said no more about it, but John Katelo never forgot that this son was the most like him.

He loved all of his children, but through this one boy he felt the unbroken link of the Inuit people.

Now, as he rode toward home, hearing the sounds of the horse's hooves on the icy trail, and the drag of the travois in the snow-crusted earth behind him, he watched the darkening sky and remembered his two sons, far away.

Four

John Katelo had gone high into the range of forest to hunt the moose. This was a wide stretch of woods loggers had never cleared. It was old growth, a shaded world thick with the smells, colors, and tastes of trees. The forest had dominion over this land. He was the trespasser here.

To Katelo, the world had become a more mystical place. In the twenty-three years since the virus made man an endangered species on the earth, Katelo had come to accept a kinship with the land as a living being. It nurtured him and his family, and if they didn't abuse it, provided them with the means of sustaining life.

This acceptance of himself as a child and the earth as his mother, was an old belief. He had come back to it as a child will return home after a long wandering. It was part of his heritage, the remembered knowledge of his people. In this place, he felt as much a part of the world as the trees, and the water, and the land . . . but no greater than they.

Above the filtered light of the forest, storm clouds swelled into a line of menacing gray metal shields across the sky. When the shields met and clashed, the first white splinter of lightning pierced the hovering clouds, and struck the trees.

Katelo saw it hit. A tall pine exploded, its crown bursting into a sudden torch of burning pitch. The needle of flame was somewhere lower on the ridge, near the treeline where the valley met the forest.

At first, Katelo wasn't afraid. It was so far away, and he was on horseback. There seemed little danger. The skies were heavy with the threat of rain; the downpour would put out the small blaze.

It wasn't until he felt the loud thumps like cannon fire shudder the ground, and saw the living torches of four or five more trees in the curving stretch of woods nearest the valley, that he began to understand what might happen.

The quick-burning, oil-laden pines were exploding like the branches of Christmas trees tossed into a well-kindled fireplace. The sticky sap ignited, and the fireball each tree became set off four or five others. The single blaze had become a reddened mouth, widening like a piece of burning paper, devouring the towering green pines like match sticks.

The wind was carrying it his way. He could smell the ash in the air.

Already, the narrow cut through the mountain pass to the valley below was sealed off to him. Fire had claimed that escape, and sent shaft after shaft of red-orange heat into the sky. On one side of him was a sheer drop, a rocky cascade down the boundary of the woodland range. He wouldn't have wanted to try descending it even with a sturdy rope and climbing gear. Without the right equipment, it was suicide.

A smothering heat billowed up from the flames. Katelo heard a chain of loud popping as the narrow trees caught and exploded into streaks

31

of brilliance, sounding like his memory of fire-crackers on the Fourth of July.

His skin began to sting with the heat, and his eyes burned from flying ash and smoke. The horse whinnied, stumbling at the verge of the narrow cut in the mountain. All of Katelo's soothing would not urge the animal any further into the raging inferno. The stallion's hooves skittered over the ice in a skidding dance of spirited panic.

If there was no way down, then going higher into the forest range was the only choice left to Katelo. The fire would climb, too. He knew that. The fire would eat the trees with its bright mouth. Behind it, only scorched earth would remain. And the higher the flames climbed, the more trees would catch and burn in the blistering wind. He would be trapped in the middle of it. Like the trees, he would burn if the rain didn't break from the heavy clouds. If the storm didn't put out the fire and save him.

The travois made the turnaround that much harder. It would have been better to cut the wooden poles free and leave the heavy bundles of meat behind than to have the weight of them dragging at the horse's steps. But Katelo was afraid to come down from the stallion's back. He could feel hard fear ripple along the horse's strong neck and flanks. Riding the frightened animal gave Katelo some control over it. He knew if he swung his leg over the saddle and came down at the moment another tree exploded or a crack of lightning shot across the sky, the horse might bolt. The fire would move faster than he could walk, or run.

He didn't want to burn. That would be a hard way to die.

The stallion must have felt the same fear, must have sensed the fire coming for him, too, reaching for his smooth flesh with torch hands, for the whinnies became screams, and the screams broke above the roar of the holocaust. Burning embers flew through the air, singeing all they touched, igniting new sparks.

Katelo bent low over the stallion's neck and hung onto the thick mane. Ash and smoke choked the breath from his lungs, and he could see nothing. The terrible heat was coming closer, searing through his clothes, into his hair, scalding away his life.

He didn't want to burn.

"Over here, Chukchi!" The voice came at Katelo from behind the black smoke to his left. It was louder than the roiling bellows and hard clap of the fire. It was louder than the stallion's screams, too. He heard it clearly, over the sound of everything else.

"This way, Chukchi!" it called, again from Katelo's left.

"Who's there?" he shouted, but the voice was gone, and he had no answer but that from his own heart. Some part of him knew, and understood.

With a hard tug on the reins, he turned the terrified horse to the left and urged the animal forward with soft words in his ear. "Now, boy. Now!" A touch of his heel against the stallion's flank sent them scrabbling over the ice at the edge of the mountain's rib. The hooves slipped where the ground tilted and fell away. Off the icy ridge . . . over the crumbling lip of the broken promontory, and down into the snow-draped valley below.

The stallion turned over and over, hooves catch-

33

ing the air and then rolling under again. The travois twisted and broke, spilling the cracked wooden poles and the tied bundles of meat down the rock face of the mountainside. The fire had not touched where they fell. Only the soft crush of snow, and the hardness of unyielding rock.

The horse was dead before it hit the jagged boulders at the bottom of the cliff—the travois pole had pierced its heart. Its dark body lay cushioned against the white snow, and ash fell in gray rain, like a shroud settling over it.

John Katelo was higher up the mountain. His neck had been broken in the horse's first fall against the rocks. He'd been flung clear of the tangle of horse's hooves and splintered poles, thrown onto the level arm of a jutting precipice, and there remained.

Above him, the fire raged. The rain clouds held back their heavy burden, keeping the water which might have saved the forest. The mountainside burned. The old-growth timber was left charred, the earth blackened. All life within it died.

John Katelo's eyes saw nothing more of this place, but opened onto the living dream of a new land. His mind was not troubled with grief or pain. With his people who had called him, he crossed out of this awareness, and moved over the white hill to the rich valley beyond.

Salena Cross saw the burnt-orange color dress the sky above the mountain. It was the mark of a fire. She knew John was there. She'd heard the thunder earlier, and seen the lightning strike, feeling a sense of dread come over her with each jagged spear of white across the darkening canvas of storm clouds.

Although he wasn't her husband in any way that was legal, or even religiously sanctioned, she had lived with John Katelo for twenty-three years. He had become as much a part of her as her eyes, or the fingers of her hands. She believed that she could feel what he felt, know what he knew. They had a history together.

For a time, they had been all there was for each other. Couples in love always said that, but for them it had been a cold truth. They had literally been the only ones for each other. The virus had taken everyone else.

Salena watched the color of the sky redden and rise into the night. It would be a big fire to throw such light into the sky. She'd thought John would be home by now. If he could come home. If the fire hadn't trapped him.

"Oh, God," she whispered, pressing a knuckle to her mouth.

"Mama," said Salena's twelve-year-old daughter, Lacy. The girl had come outside so silently, Salena hadn't heard her until now.

Lacy Katelo was thin as a sleek young deer, and fawn colored, too. Her hair was soft, golden brown, and her eyes were a shade between green and brown. She had her father's long eyelashes, and his ready smile. But she wasn't smiling now.

"What is it?" Salena asked.

"I think I heard something a minute ago. Down by the river. I think I heard horses coming. And I thought I heard somebody say—I know I didn't—but I thought I heard a man say, 'Up by Mirror Lake.' "

Salena listened for any sound. Could it be John? But who would he be talking to? The child would know the sound of her father's voice. No, it wouldn't be him.

"Come on," Salena said, taking her daughter by the arm and walking quickly in the direction of the house, "we'll wait inside until we know who's out there."

It never occurred to Salena Cross to doubt what Lacy had said she'd heard. There had never been any reason for Salena's children to lie to her, or make up stories. There was no one here to impress with such tales. If they said something happened, it had.

They were on the porch of the house when the sound came again. "There, Mama! Hear that?" asked Lacy.

This time, Salena heard it, too. More than one horse, she was sure, and although she couldn't make out the words, she could hear the voices of people talking. One of them said, "Almost home." And she knew.

She ran, arms reaching out before her into the dark.

"Mama, where are you going?" cried Lacy, fear wrapping around the high pitch of her words. "Come back! Mama, please come back!"

But Salena kept running. The soft sound of the horses' walking was moving toward her, coming up from the river crossing. She knew the voice of her firstborn, clear as her own heartbeat thudding in her ears. It was Seth who'd said, "Almost home."

Her two sons had been gone almost two years. It could be no one else. They had come back! "Seth!" she called. "Jonathan!"

Dark surrounded her, blanketing sight. Noises filtered through the stretched seams of it, coming at her from layered points: the rustle of something moving in the nearby brush, the lowing of a cow on the hillside, the steady clip of horses' hooves in the distance, and the voices of her sons calling, "Mother! Mother!"

She saw them, gray shadows moving against a darker plane of ashen slate. Their faces were masked by the night, but she saw from the shapes of their bodies which was Seth and which was Jonathan. Seth had always been the taller of the two. Even sitting, his back rising in a straight line from the saddle, he was a head higher than his brother. Where Seth was more like her, thin and angular, Jonathan was Inuit, wide-shouldered with a blockier build, with a squared box of a body, slightly dented at the middle for a waist.

Seth came off the horse and ran to her, tightly hugging her in his strong arms. Her head barely touched the center of his chest. He had grown in the two years since she had seen him. She put her hands to his cheeks, trying to read the lines of his face beneath the mask of dark.

For a moment, she couldn't speak. Her voice was swollen within her, trapped by the flood of feelings which rose and would not bridge the soundless world between them. She could only touch Seth's face, his arms, see that he'd returned, and wait for the pulse of her heart to slow.

Then Jonathan was there, too. The little air in her lungs was crushed from her in his embrace. She sensed in him a man so like his father.

His father . . .

The vision of the red sky above the mountains came back to her, and she found her voice. "Your father must see you," she said to them. "Your father must know you've come home."

"We'll go to the house together," said Jonathan.

"No, he's away—hunting." She turned her head

37

to face the bleeding rust above the mountain. "There."

A broad band of pain circled Salena's chest. Her two sons were home, and that was a terror she had lived with, that they might not return. Now, the fear she had carried for two years, like a growing child with her, had become joy. Oh, she was happy! But, John wasn't here, and the red furnace glowing just below the leaden clouds frightened her.

"Mother." Jonathan's hand touched her arm, turning her back to them. It was then she realized that the other horses had riders too, vague shapes silhouetted against the wavering panel of trees and uneven ground of the sloping riverbank.

Her eyesight was poor. It had gotten worse over the years, but she managed to see the things she needed. Now, she had to squint and strain the muscles to try to capture the blurry vision before her, and make it clear enough to allow what she was seeing. How many others were there? Six? Seven?

Jonathan moved away and helped one of them off a horse. She saw two shapes walking toward her, close together shapes. "Mama," he said, calling her the remembered name from his childhood, "this is Willow, my wife."

"And this is Sidra," said Seth, bringing forward another woman.

One by one, the others were led to her, their names given. One by one, she felt the confines of her world stretch and widen. Everything was changing. Her sons were home. They had found people and brought them here. Wives. There were humans in the world besides themselves.

It was a beginning of things.

But the burnished light from the cored black of

the mountainside bloomed through the night like an unfolding flower. It was a heated rosiness that spoke of blood and suffering. In the stinging smoke of dawn, with the smell of charred wood in the air and the taste of smoldering ash on the tongue, it spoke of death.

In that indefinable language of the heart, Salena Cross knew her husband was dead.

Five

Since the day a tornado lifted a teen-age Willow Gray Wolf from the camp of the Outsiders—those living in the Texas desert near Biosphere Seven—and carried her miles away, releasing her to earth unhurt, she had been known to the People as Spirit Woman. Once, she had been as unremarkable as any of them, but the will of the Great Spirit had changed everything.

After the tornado, Willow sometimes heard voices the others didn't hear, and without warning, she knew things of the future. It was because of this, and because the People feared her, that she chose to leave the camp of the Outsiders. She chose to make her life with Jonathan Katelo, and follow him and his brother Seth to this place of green hills, clear rivers, and blue-black mountains.

Montana. It spoke of the range of peaks which surrounded her. Land of mountains. Land of visions, too.

She had been warned of John Katelo's death, seen it in the wide sweep of her mind, long before the night of the fire. She had seen it before she left the camp of the Outsiders.

The visions had come to her in quick images, a burning land, the cracking of trees and the loud bursts of timber exploding into flames. She had seen terror in the eyes of animals trapped by the heat and blazing forest, and knew their fear. At first, she had seen no one in the blinding smoke, but knew the vision was a message of death.

She had believed the flames were for her.

It was during the long journey to Montana with Jonathan and Seth Katelo, with her brothers Yuma and Jared, her half-sister Sidra Innis, and the Wyse brothers, Nolan and Martin, that Willow saw more of the vision and understood who would die in the fire. Long before they reached the house by Mirror Lake, she had known Jonathan would never see his father again, and that she would not meet John Katelo, except through the terrifying and unforgettable images of her mind.

She had known, but said nothing. Silence too, could be a gift.

In the end, it was Katelo's wife, Salena, who had seen the truth of her husband's death and insisted that Seth, Jonathan, and her other children stop their search for him. Willow saw something else in Salena Cross.

Instead of retreating into a silence as Jonathan had feared she might—for she had done this when her ten-year-old son Cody had died two years before—Salena had stepped out of her role as wife to John Katelo, and became the mother for all of them. She became the one to whom they turned for understanding, and also for a remembrance of what it was like to live on earth before the virus. She was the keeper of that knowledge, the only one among them who had lived in the old world.

For Willow, Salena Cross became the eyes Spirit Woman needed to see into the past.

"What were the big cities like?" Willow asked.

"When a river is clogged with rocks," said Salena, "and the water is forced to flow over the

41

stones, pressing and churning into a white-water rush," she said, using her fingers to show how the water would spill over the rocks, "that was what the big cities were like. We spilled over one another, like fast-running water. We broke on the stones, and we pressed forward in a surge. The cities were exciting, like a wild river, but hard to live in."

"Why didn't the people of Old Earth work together, like we do now?"

Salena's lips curved up at the corners, but her smile was painful to see. "We forgot that we were a family. All of us were individuals climbing for a place at the top. Only, there had to be those on the bottom, in order to support a top. Still, we scrambled up."

"What was it like to be a nation?" asked Willow.

"Do you see that cluster of stars?" Salena pointed to a spot.

"I see it."

"To be a nation was to say that one cluster of stars was separate from the others in the sky. We told ourselves we were separate, too. We were the United States, or Europe, or Africa—separate. But we weren't. The virus taught us that. It claimed mankind as one, and never saw a difference between us."

"What should we do now?" asked Willow.

"Know that we're all one family," Salena told her. "And know that we're a part of the earth."

In the nights, when Jonathan slept with his body curled against hers, Willow felt a belonging to these people and this place. The land was rich beyond her imagining. An abundance of fish were the food of the water, and the land held game of every kind. Ducks and geese winged their way across the sky, and the earth gave them crops to ease their hunger.

In the summer of that year, when the grass dried to a dull brown and the heat turned the valley to baked clay, Willow knew she was carrying a child. It would be born in the spring, in this place of such beauty. Like Salena, and like the generations of women who had gone before her, she would give birth to sons and daughters. She would gather them to her in a family like this one, and she would no longer be called Spirit Woman, but Mother.

While Willow and Jonathan had become a family, Seth and Sidra knew a distance between each other. It grew as the child in Willow's womb increased in size. In place of a new life, it was a swelling discontent.

The trip to Montana had been hardest on Sidra. In her memory was not only leaving her mother and father, brothers and sisters, and all the close family of the biosphere, but leaving Cameron's grave too. She felt as if she had abandoned him to that hard Texas earth. He was truly apart from everyone, now.

He's dead, she reminded herself. *Staying to die with him wouldn't have changed that.*

Sidra felt apart from everyone here. Salena was the mother to all of them, and Willow was Jonathan's wife, and Spirit Woman. *What am I?* Sidra wondered.

Is it enough to be Seth's wife?

She knew the answer to that was no.

She had gained a freedom in leaving the biosphere with Cameron. She hadn't left for that freedom, but for love. Still, by doing so, the whole of the earth was now hers to claim, if only she had the courage. This place in Montana with Seth's family was like another cage, another biosphere. She felt it closing in on her with unseen walls, crushing her spirit.

By summer, she knew she must leave.

In secrecy, she began to store things she would need for the journey: a sharp knife, a box of matches, warm clothing, and food. She would go alone, and she would tell no one, not even Willow. Seth wasn't a violent man; she didn't fear him. She did fear that he would try to talk her into staying, or tell the others, and leaving would be that much harder. She couldn't stay, not and want to go on living.

She didn't love Seth. For a time, she had believed she could love this tall, dark-haired boy. In Texas, she'd tried to tell herself that her feelings would change and grow stronger for him as they lived together, but that hadn't happened. She saw him always as a boy, one who might never grow up. She didn't belong here with these people, in this place that was so much their home.

She was more afraid of staying than of being alone.

On a summer night that was brightened by a full moon, she took from the corral the mare they had caught and ridden up from Texas, tied a blanket and pack behind the saddle, and without a parting word to anyone, rode away.

From her place at the window, Willow watched her sister leave. Only she, of all of them, had known this would happen. Willow had kept her silence, protecting Sidra with it, and loving her enough to let her go.

Sidra was heading south.

There would be many hardships for this strong-willed woman, and times when she would regret leaving this place of safety—Willow knew. She feared for Sidra, but let the fear go, with the woman.

Each of us must take our chance and risk all for our own happiness, she thought. Her sister could never have been happy here, could never have loved Seth. What she was daring was right. Live or die, it was right.

But Willow would miss her. They had grown close in the two years they had known one another. They were more than sisters of the same father; they were alike.

She thought of their father, Josiah Gray Wolf. His courage had been bred into them both. His determination, too. Neither sister was much like the woman who had given birth to her. Both Elizabeth Cunningham and Cathe Innis had been content with a life of motherhood and survival.

If Willow was right about Sidra, she knew both of them wanted something more.

She watched her sister leave the boundaries of the house beside Mirror Lake, and said nothing to stop her, not even goodbye. She turned back to her bed and came into the arms of Jonathan, who had stirred into wakefulness.

"Can't sleep? What were you looking at?" he asked, his arms wrapping her closer to the warmth of his body.

"The life I carry keeps me awake," she answered, not lying. She knew he would believe she meant the child, but she had meant that second source of life, the one born in her after the tornado. She had become a seer that day. Now, too often, the things she saw caused her pain. Pain was a living

45

part of knowledge, she understood.

She felt peace spread through her as she lay beside this man. She loved him as she loved no one else, not father, mother, sister, brother, or child.

"You're not worried about the baby, are you?" he asked. He smoothed the hair back from her face.

"I'm not worried."

"And you're not unhappy here with my mother and family?" His hand rode the curve of her side and hip, coming to rest on her thigh.

"Your mother is our child's grandmother." She moved his hand to rest over the small curve where the life they had started grew inside her. "Your family will be its uncles and aunts, and maybe cousins one day."

He laughed softly at the thought.

"You're all I need," she said to him quietly. "My life is here with you."

His eyes were serious now. "I'll never let anything bad happen to you, Willow. I'd give my life to protect you—you know that."

A terrible certainty coursed through her at his words. Not for the first time that night, she was sorry she was a woman who could see into the future.

"You're shaking," he said.

"Hold me," she told him, trying to block out the sure image that was there. "Closer," she whispered. But the image remained, burned into her consciousness.

I'd give my life for you, he'd said.

And she knew.

She knew one day he would.

Six

Summer grass lined the valleys between the mountain peaks. Sleek-legged deer footed the soft meadows, their young trailing behind them like shy children. The days were luxuriant with bright, cloudless skies, warm weather, and the heady scent of an abundance of life growing from the earth.

Sidra's mare picked her way easily over the cushion of grass. Heavy winter rains and melting snowpack had produced a thick carpet of life-giving grasslands in the valleys. In places, clear pools of that water remained. She and the horse stopped and drank from those pools.

For the first time in her life, Sidra Innis was alone.

She'd been born inside Biosphere Seven, a separate world much like a small planet, enclosed by the glass walls of the sphere. She'd been part of a family: her mother, step-father, brothers and sisters, and the other Insiders who called the biosphere home.

For love, she left the safety of the biosphere, and came into the less-sheltered world of the Outsiders. But love had died, there among the first real breezes she had ever felt. A part of her that wanted to be with people had died, too. She'd needed time to be alone, to grieve for all that she'd lost: her parents

47

and family, her friends within Biosphere Seven . . . and Cameron.

Instead, she had tried to make a life with Seth, and failed.

Now, in these first days of riding south across green summer meadows, she was free. It was exhilarating, like nothing she had ever felt before. There was fear for what might happen, the unknown that touched her like a second skin, but the loneliness felt good. She was living life on her terms, finding her way.

In the evenings, she would hobble the mare the way Seth had taught her to do, gather wood for a campfire, and cook whatever food she had been able to find that day. Most often, her supper was a stew of wild vegetables grown in fields that once had been productive farmland, coarse bread shaped into a flat pancake and cooked directly over the lid of the one cooking pot she'd brought with her, and a few berries she'd picked from bushes along the way. The mare lived on the sweet grass of the valleys.

She had killed an animal for food twice in the ten days since she'd left Mirror Lake: a rabbit stunned by a thrown rock, and a wild prairie hen she'd managed to catch in her bare hands.

She'd killed animals before, those raised in the biosphere for food, and the chickens, pigs, and even cattle living in the camp of the Outsiders. She knew what must be done, but her appetite for meat was less. If she could find enough food from the abundance of this land to sustain her, she preferred not to take any animal life. Something had changed in her thinking, something which now saw animal lives as important, too.

At night, under a ceiling of countless stars, Sidra slept and dreamed of a stone tunnel, snaking out from the face of the mountain, and burrowing deep within it. There were no stars in this tunnel, for the cave roof sealed them out. She felt their loss. Something waited for her there. She heard voices from the walls, strange and urgent words she couldn't understand, and saw a brilliance of colored lights.

When she awoke from the dream, the stars were fading from the early morning sky. At first, she thought she was still in the hollow hill of the tunnel, but the sight of sheltering trees told her she was awake, and free of it.

Seth and Jonathan had told her of this place. They had seen it on their journey to Texas, and the strange man living there. Seth told her that he thought of this man often, that he had found a place in Seth's mind, and would not leave it. When he described the man to Sidra, the image stayed. She imagined him as clearly as if she had seen him herself. At night, she dreamed of the stone tunnel, and the man called T. J. Parker.

Seth had tried to lead them back to him, on their journey to Montana. Jonathan had been against it. "He nearly killed you the first time. Have you forgotten that?"

"I haven't forgotten," Seth had argued, "but he was afraid of us, I think. His mind was troubled. Remember how he talked to his dead wife and children? We should see if he needs our help. He might be hurt, or starving. He's all alone in that place."

Because of Seth's concern, they had tried to find the place called NORAD, but days of heavy rain flooded the river crossing. They were forced to ride west for two days before they found a safe crossing. By then, the trail Seth remembered was lost.

"We can't risk the others by searching for a trail that you might never find again," Jonathan told him.

49

"I hate the thought of leaving Parker there," Seth had said. "I'd hoped we could bring him with us."

"Forget the man," Jonathan said. "He was lost when we found him, and he's still lost. Nothing we could have done would change that. Let him go, Seth. You can't save him. No one can."

Now, waking from the dream, Sidra wondered if she could let him go. She'd had this dream before. Haunting images of a place she had never seen, of a man she had never known. Seth's story about T. J. Parker touched her. She saw him in her dreams. It was as if Parker was calling to her, and she was following.

When she had saddled the mare and scraped the last of the night's fire into cool ashes, she put the dream away . . . but rode south, toward the place of a stone tunnel called NORAD.

In the house by Mirror Lake, Seth realized Sidra was gone. He had known it the first moment when he awoke and found her place beside him empty. He had known it then, but kept the truth of that thought from the others. He had let them search for her, never admitting that he knew she was gone. She had left more than this place; she had left him.

Sidra had cared for him, he knew that, but she hadn't loved him enough to stay. All the love he had given her had only made her unhappy, made her want to run from this place, and from him.

Jonathan would have gone on searching. He would have pressed them all into riding into the burned mountain, or into the lands far west of Mirror Lake, but Seth had kept them from it.

"She doesn't want to be found."

Jonathan reeled back as if struck by a fist. "Doesn't want to be found? Are you crazy? She's lost, Seth, like Cody."

"No, this isn't like it was with Cody!" Seth heard the unfamiliar sound of his voice, flat and hard. "Our brother was lost and hurt. It's not like that with her."

Jonathan leaned closer. "Then, what is it like? Tell me."

"I saw her leave early this morning," said Willow. "She saddled the white mare and rode away."

Both Seth and Jonathan turned to her.

"You watched her go, and you didn't tell Seth? Didn't tell any of us?" Jonathan's face was darkening with anger.

"Jonathan . . ." Seth tried to stand between Willow and his brother's building fury.

Willow was calm, seemingly unafraid. "Is this place a home," she asked, "or a cage? Was my sister not free to go, if that was what she wanted? Like Seth, I love Sidra, but I didn't stop her, because I knew she needed to leave us."

Jonathan's anger was visible in the rigid line of his jaw, and in the way he stood, unbending to what he clearly saw as their weakness.

"Sidra's searching for something, Jonathan." Willow touched his arm. "She has had little peace since Cameron's death. She tried to find it among us, but couldn't. It wasn't Seth; it wasn't any of us. It was her. You were right when you said she's lost. That's true. Sometimes, we need to let people be lost, in order for them to find themselves. We couldn't keep her," Willow laid her hand gently on Jonathan's cheek. "It's wrong to hold any creature who longs to be free. Love her enough to let her go."

"Why are you telling this to me?" Jonathan pulled back from Willow's hand. "Tell him," he said, moving his arm in Seth's direction. "Both of you are fools. You want to let her go." He turned

51

away from Willow and walked out of the house.

"He doesn't mean what he said to you," said Seth. "It's my fault, anyway. I'll talk to him, make him understand."

"No," Willow stopped him. "Say nothing. Jonathan's anger is quick to burn, but it will cool. When it does, he'll see the truth of what we've said."

"What's he got to be so mad about? I'm the one Sidra left."

"He loved her, too." Willow was standing at an angle from Seth. He could see the rounded shape of the child she carried below her waist. Her body was thickening with the pregnancy.

"You mean as a sister?"

Willow's faint smile was painful to see. It turned up the corners of her mouth. "No, Seth. Jonathan loved her as a woman. I think she knew that. I think it might have been one of the reasons she left without telling me."

"You don't mean he—"

"No, nothing happened between them, I'm sure. But it might have, if she'd stayed." She laid her hand over the roundness of her skirt. "I'm not pretty to Jonathan, now. He looked at my sister, and could see me the way I was before the baby. Sidra and I look so much alike. It was natural, I think, that he loved her a little."

"Natural!" Seth's hurt turned to an anger of his own. "I would have killed him if he'd touched her."

"Would you?" Willow asked gently. "Could you have done such a thing?"

Seth didn't answer, because he didn't know. It was a question he hoped he'd never have to answer. "Don't you hate him for feeling that way about another woman?"

"No," Willow said. "I love him, and I know he

loves me. Some things you must let go."

And some people, Seth thought. *Sidra.*

It would be hard for him, he knew, living here without Sidra. Maybe he wasn't meant to stay in this place, either. Maybe this land was for Jonathan and Willow, and their child to come. In that moment, Seth felt a little of the sense of being trapped that Sidra must have felt. She had needed to be free. He couldn't wish any less for himself.

"You still see things that are going to happen, don't you, Willow?"

"Yes."

"What do you see for me? What happens in my future?" he asked.

She looked away for a moment, as if deciding whether or not to tell him, and then glanced back again. "I have seen so much for you, Seth. To tell you might change the paths I have seen. Know that you will be strong, and have only begun your journey. It will lead you far away from this place, this green valley."

"Will I ever be with Sidra again?" His voice was strangled with longing.

"No." Her voice was flat as the nothingness he felt upon hearing the word.

"Then, I'll be alone."

Her words followed him as he walked away. "No, you won't. I'm sure of that." She started to tell him more, "I see someone—" she began, then stopped.

"Tell me," he urged her.

"You'll find what you're meant to find, Seth. My words won't bring your future to you one day sooner. Your path is there for you, if you choose to take it."

"But . . ."

"No more questions. It may be that I've already said too much."

53

She left him standing in the rich grassland before the house. To the north were the gray-black mountains rising like shields around the valley. Beside him was Mirror Lake, holding in its reflection the mountains, valley, and even the tall wooden house in which he had been born.

He would leave this land, but where would he go? He stood in the field turning, turning, and found no answer. The burned scar on the mountain to the north reminded him of his father's death; he would not go that way. The trail south reminded him of Sidra; he would not go that way, either. To the east was a blue corral of more mountains, pressed back to back into a wedge of solid rock.

Your path is there for you, Willow had said.

He turned to the west. The grasslands stretched as far as he could see. It was an open track of land, wide and inviting. To the west was an ocean; he had heard his mother speak of the Pacific. The thought stayed in his mind. All that day, he imagined it. That night, when he closed his eyes to sleep, he knew.

He would follow this open pathway to the west. At the end of his journey, he would come to a place whose name was the word for peace . . . Pacific.

Seven

On the planet Earth, little over five thousand people had survived the first devastating effects of the pandemic virus of 1998. The initial loss was overwhelming to the population of mankind, separating the few survivors into isolated pockets, camps of humans ignorant of each other's existence. All forms of communication beyond language ceased. There were no telephones, letters, books, or television to inform mankind about the world which was left to it.

Now, in the year 2020, a great change was seen on earth. A flourishing of nature brought forth abundant life, once hidden by the cities of man. The constant flow of chemicals and pollutants into the seas and rivers of earth stopped. Cars were still as tombstones, the air no longer choked with the carbon monoxide from their exhausts. Chlorofluorocarbons in the atmosphere were diminished, reducing the size of the holes in the ozone layer. The numbers of cattle and other methane-producing animals decreased as animal life returned to natural selection in breeding. Once again, the wildlife of earth was governed by the hard rule: survival of the fittest.

Many of the animals once tamed into pets or beasts of servitude to humankind perished with man. Few small cats remained. Most were eaten in the first months by coyote, wolves, and packs of hungry dogs. Many toy breeds of dog perished. Not strong enough to become predators, they were soon considered prey. Larger dogs quickly learned to form packs to protect themselves from predators, who now freely came down from the mountains and hunted the vacant streets for carrion, or prey.

In downtown Los Angeles, rats made their nests on all floors of the First Interstate building, and in all abandoned buildings of all big cities. The lights of the cities were dark, and within that dark, rats scurried over the ruins.

The cities, most of all, became dangerous places. The rank smell of carrion drew predators to these areas in the first months of the virus, and many packs of dog, coyote, and mountain lion remained, hunting in these concrete and steel canyons.

In National Parks, where animals such as the grizzly bear and wolf were once allowed a controlled and limited existence, their population rapidly multiplied. Bears now ranged a wide sweep from Montana to California, and wolves roamed the cold, northern states, venturing south in large aggressive packs only in the winter, when deep snows made food scarce.

On the open grasslands of Texas, herds of wild mustang fattened on the sweet pastures of former cattle ranches. Stallions with harems of twenty or more mares ran freely across state lines which no longer existed, claiming the rough plains as their pasture.

These herds were not composed of the starving mares and abandoned foals once seen in the regulated populations of mustangs. They were sleek stallions and well-nourished mares, many whose sides were swollen with twin foals. They had flourished on the abundant grasslands of America, and once again claimed the open range as their own.

A curious change slowly emerged across the face

of the earth. In the initial absence of man, a profound silence had hung in the air like threatening clouds, heavy with dark portent. Man had been the voice of the planet. The sounds of man, from his cities, from the unending span of houses where he lived, and from the roads where he traveled, had echoed like living thunder over the land. With the death of all but a few humans, the sounds were stilled.

For a time, this silence frightened the animals, keeping them in hushed quiet. They waited, as if for the shot that would ring out in the forest from a hunter's rifle, for the trap that would catch the unwary in its jagged teeth, for the whirling flap of a helicopter in the sky, to chase and corral them into pens of waiting death. To control their numbers. They waited for the sounds of man to return . . . but the silence remained.

With the next breeding seasons came the birth of animals who had never listened in watchful fear to the overwhelming sounds of man. Instead, the many voices of wildlife were heard in joyful freedom over the plains of earth.

In the small places of human refuge, it was man who listened at night to the howling wolves, the roar of a mountain lion, grizzly, or a pack of wild dogs, and waited for dawn in that guarded quiet called fear.

Sidra Innis heard the snarling. It came at her, hard sounds through the sieve of night. The growls were either from timber wolves, or a pack of feral dogs. She threw more wood on the campfire, building the size of the flame. Sparks splintered up and out from the burning tinder. In the flare of light, she saw the white mare stomping a small tattoo on the earth with her hobbled forelegs.

To be alone was a wider dark than Sidra had imagined night could be. She felt the heat of the fire sweep against her like a feverish touch, and wondered, *Will they come for me?*

In a city, a place with no name, she had found a gun. The cities with their streets of hardened black ground and flat white rock growing before their houses like grass . . . the cities frightened her.

The gun had been lying on a blue cloth behind a wall of glass. She had broken the glass, the shattering a loud crash of slivered fragments of that wall. She had cut her wrist reaching in for the gun. The weight of it had been heavy in her hand, comforting. The weight of it pressed back her fear.

And then she'd remembered bullets.

With the butt of the gun, she'd broken the rest of the glass wall. It cracked into splinters which nested in sharp points on the wooden ledge and on the rock-covered earth below. With her hand, and with the gun, she scraped the glass shards out of the way and crawled through the window, into the dim hollow of the gun shop.

It was a long while before she found the right boxes of bullets, and days of missed shots along the trek south before she was able to bring down her first kill with this weapon. The small antelope had eased her savage hunger, and the gun had eased her thin terror of the lonely night.

Now, beside this fire, with the whinnying mare as her only companion, Sidra held the gun in both hands and waited for the snarling pack to break through the cover of trees. She thought of cutting the mare free, to give it a better chance of escape in case the pack came at them, but decided against it. Sidra knew what her chance of survival would be without the horse. She needed the mare, and kept it hobbled.

The thought came to her of saddling the mare and

riding away from this danger, but the dark was too deep, and other hunters watched the night. No, she decided, unless the pack came for her, she would stay beside the protection of the fire. If she was lucky, the heat and light of the flames would keep them away.

The night had edges, black and cold, dangers where Sidra's eyes could not see. She listened for the rustle of movement in the trees, for the rasped breath of an animal panting. She listened for the soft pad of wolf or dog, circling her camp.

When it came, the snarls and excited yips were as sudden as unseen knives. In the distance, behind the break of trees, the pack had found its kill. There came one long cry of an animal in final torment, a shriek, and then the sounds of the pack fighting over the torn pieces of flesh.

Sidra waited through the night. Sleep was a promise she could not give, even to herself. When the stars faded into a gray wash of morning, she covered the burning embers of her fire with sand, and rode out of this clearing.

All that day, the land fell steadily lower. Jewel-like meadows glittered in the bright sunlight, their grasses spreading like lush green carpet over the low hills and valleys. The trees were different, too, not always coniferous pine, but often birch and aspen, with small, rounded leaves dancing in the wind. A music played in sleepy rhythms in her ears, of spinning leaves blowing to that wind. She heard it, and saw the flat gray-green leaves twisting on thread-like stems, turning in the sun, moving in a sweet harmony of light, and air, and open space.

She knew she was near the place where Seth had wanted to take them on the journey up from Texas — to see the man called T. J. Parker. It was this direction. They hadn't been able to go there the first time, but now, she wanted to see this cave called NORAD,

59

and the man who lived there alone.

By mid-morning, the need for sleep lulled Sidra into a trance that came over her in a warm blanketing layer. Her chin sank to her chest, her hands gripped the pommel of her saddle. Her body slumped over the saddle horn, unconscious of when the mare stopped and grazed lazily on the sweet grass, or of what path it followed.

Until the jarring movement woke her. Her eyes opened to a streak of silhouetted forest, tilted at an impossible angle . . . and then she fell. Her back hit the ground, and she rolled downhill, loose-jointed as a doll. She heard the horse fall, too, a heavy thud above her, and then a shrill scream as the animal pitched recklessly over the edge and down the mountainous ravine.

The ground was rocky and speared with narrow trees. Her shoulder hit the slender trunk of one. Her head struck a boulder, and pain flashed into her mind like a slant of blinding sunlight. Then the sky came in at her . . . a dark net . . . and she knew nothing more.

The man had been sitting on a boulder in front of the tunnel when he heard the horse's scream. The shrill noise jerked him upright, as if a rope had been yanked through his body. He ran into the forest toward the sound.

He found the white mare at the bottom of the slope, standing on a narrow road. One foreleg was held off the ground. The mare didn't shy away when he approached her, but let him rub her trembling flanks with soothing strokes of his palms. He led the white mare for a few yards, and watched how she put her weight on the injured foreleg in halting steps. If she could walk on it as well as that, the leg wasn't broken.

The saddle told him she wasn't one of the wild horses he'd seen grazing on the rich grasslands below the foothills. If there was a saddle, there had been a rider. If the horse fell, the rider might be lying hurt somewhere on the hillside. He tied the mare's reins to an aspen trunk, and started up the rough ground.

The trees were more thinly spaced here than those higher up the steep incline. It didn't take him long to find the fallen rider; the deep blue of her clothes was visible as a dark bruise against the pale aspens.

From where he stood, he could see where the horse had slipped over the edge and fallen. The earth was dented by the weight of the animal, and marked by the sliding efforts of the mare to right herself. He saw that the horse had come dangerously close to falling directly on top of the woman. It's weight would have crushed her . . . if she wasn't already dead.

The woman was lying on her side. He stepped closer to the still body. All he could see was a tangle of long, dark hair. It was twisted around her head and neck, covering her face. There was blood in it. His hands came away with her blood when he tried to brush back her hair. The woman's eyes were shut, and the right side of her forehead was swollen and clotted with reddened dirt.

She was the first woman he had seen in years.

He stared at her with the same amazement he might have felt for a shooting star. She was just as unexpected and inexplicable. Looking at her brought a rush of feelings to him. Seeing her awakened him into life. A surge of memories flooded his mind. As he watched, he saw her take one shuddering breath and realized with surprise, that she was still alive.

A wide boulder in the ground had stopped the woman's fall. The slant of the hill dropped sharply from here. If the boulder hadn't caught her at this spot, he realized, she would have slipped over the edge and fallen another two hundred feet to the bottom of the ravine. He was careful not to lose his footing when he lifted her. If he did, they would both fall down the canyon.

It was hard work, carrying the unconscious woman down the soft-packed earth. Her body was a slack weight. It blocked his visibility of the forest floor. She was unable to help by putting her arms around his neck for support. Once, he stumbled and fell, dropping her. Her body skidded a few feet down the ravine on the carpet of pine needles, but his hand caught her arm, and pulled her back to him. After that, he carried her over his shoulder.

He didn't burden the injured mare with the woman's weight. Instead, he led the willing animal behind him as he made his way along the forest track toward home . . . back to the entrance of the tunnel.

The first sense Sidra recognized was pain.

She tried to move. Her back responded by all the muscles along her spine knotting into clenched fists, pummeling her. The effort was excruciating, and her body held in that casing of brilliant torment, as if paralyzed by it.

The second awareness was a shimmering of colored lights. Around her on all sides were flashes and steady beams of bright red, green, orange, and blue. She remembered the fall . . . slowly, the recollection came to her . . . the horse stepping off the narrow path, that moment of feeling suspended in mid-air, hitting the ground hard and tumbling down the rocky face of the hill. She remembered her shoulder striking the tree, and felt again the terror of seeing the boulder loom up before her. There had come a smothering darkness . . . and now, she was surrounded by pain and colored lights.

A loud, insistent hum reverberated from somewhere nearby. She felt the throb of it in her ears.

I'm badly hurt, she thought, fearing that the recurring flashes of lights and the strange humming were signs of a serious head injury. She turned her head slightly, struggled to see where she was, and a wedge of pain cut through her from neck to ankle, making her gasp.

Sidra's eyes shut tight against the grinding agony. The hurt went on . . . it went on until dark sparks filled her vision behind the crush of closed eyelids . . . and she felt herself slide into the relief of soothing blackness.

When Sidra opened her eyes again, he was there. A man with light-colored eyes, partially hidden behind an unruly mass of shaggy, graying hair and thick, reddish beard, sat next to her. A naked man.

"Where . . . ?" She tried to speak, but the effort cost her. She felt the rush of pain come in splintered points along her head, neck, and back.

He reached across the space between them and touched her forehead. His fingers were gentle, a comforting brush of warmth against her cold skin. The gold-red hair on his arms and chest shone in the light. He was burnished as a copper pot. Unable to speak, she could only stare at him.

When he stood, she saw that he was bare from head to foot.

The colored lights remained, and the strange humming noise was still there, but it was the man who claimed Sidra's complete attention. When she looked into his eyes, she forgot the torment of pulled muscles and bruised spine. Before her was a man clothed only in the sorrow of his eyes.

Now, she knew exactly where she was. Seth's description of this place came back to her: a rock tunnel beneath the Colorado mountain, chamber after chamber filled with lights and humming sound of machines, and a naked man living in a place called NORAD Communications Center.

She had found T. J. Parker, or he had found her.

She remembered what Jonathan told her. Parker was capable of violence. He talked to his dead wife and children. He'd tried to kill Seth. Now, she was alone with this man, unable to make a single move to protect herself. If he was dangerous, there was nothing to keep him from killing her.

Strangely, she wasn't afraid. Parker's eyes, pale blue oracles of truth, told her she was safe with him. He didn't speak, but his eyes were eloquent. The expression in them told Sidra he wouldn't hurt her, and that he'd do whatever he could to help her to heal from the fall. A sense of being protected and cared for came over Sidra, and she felt the strain of fear and tension slowly fade.

Under the watchful gaze of the man called T. J. Parker, she felt a calmness of spirit, and rested.

Eight

Eleven-year-old Walker Gray Wolf was aware of every bone in his body. They all ached. Like everyone else, he had been walking the roads leading north for so many days, he couldn't remember how long, or how many. The road seemed endless, a black band that stretched farther than he could see, and when he got to the end, there was always more. They had been walking for weeks.

Stephen was leading them north, but Prophet was the one all of them turned to when they needed food or shelter for the night. Prophet carried the youngest children on his back, and insisted that the group not travel too far each day, for these youngest ones' sake. Because of him, the pace was kept slow. Prophet was always ready to offer a word of comfort, or patience. In his strength, he kept them all together.

Shepherd Hallinger ran a few steps to catch up with Walker.

"Where've you been?" Walker eyed him curiously. They thought of themselves as lookout scouts, sometimes running ahead of Stephen to be the first ones to discover an interesting area. They were the same age, and made up of the same daring nature. If Walker didn't want to try something, Shepherd was sure to give it a shot. And if Shepherd thought anything was too dangerous, Walker felt compelled to risk it. They were like that, the two of them. Closer than brothers. They were friends.

"I was at the back," Shepherd told him, "walking for a while with my mother and the babies."

Walker knew that meant Shepherd had been *carrying* the babies. Everyone took a turn carrying the youngest ones, but Shepherd often took the burden from his mother when it was her turn.

Sometimes, it seemed to Walker that Merry Logan was lost. She stumbled as if she couldn't see where she was going, and she never talked to anyone. Lost in her own head, he thought. They'd all noticed how odd she'd become since the flood, and since Skeet Hallinger's death. The woman who had been Shepherd's mother had disappeared that day. This woman who was left in her shadow was nothing like the mother Shepherd had always known, or the Merry Logan the rest of them remembered. Walker thought all of this, but said nothing of it to his friend.

"There's a city up ahead," Walker tried to distract Shepherd from thinking about how changed his mother was, and interest him in a little adventure for them both. "We could take off for a while and scout around a little, before the rest of them catch up. Go through some houses," he suggested, knowing this was the scariest thing they could do. "Let's see what we can find."

It was a test of bravery by which they judged each other's courage. To go into one of those houses alone, that was worse than facing a rattler. You could pin down a rattler with a stick, grab it behind the head and throw it away from you, but an empty house was always a new threat. Anything could be in those dark rooms: hungry rats, wild dogs, a whole nest of vipers, or death.

It was the gap-eyed skulls that scared Walker the most. He was pretty sure Shepherd felt the same way. "You take the left side of the streets, I'll take the right?" Walker offered the usual challenge.

"I don't know," Shepherd seemed to hesitate. "Maybe we should stay with the group. It's getting late. They'll be looking for a place to camp for the night. I don't want them to have to look for us, too."

Walker wanted to get away from the group, he could feel the need for freedom stinging him like a nettle from inside his skin. He was tired of hearing babies cry, tired of Stephen Wyse grumbling at everyone to keep up. He wanted some excitement to mark this day, before they had to bed down in some empty building for the night. By the time they got settled and had something to eat, everyone would be too worn out for anything but sleep. No, if he and Shepherd wanted some adventure, they'd better get it now. Any later, and Stephen wouldn't let them out of his sight.

"They won't have to look for us," Walker encouraged Shepherd. "We can be the ones to find a place for all of us to stay the night. That'll save Prophet and Stephen the trouble. We'll be helping them, really. C'mon," he urged. "I'm so bored with moving along like some damn cow, I'm gonna start mooing pretty soon. Don't you wanna do something?"

"Okay," Shepherd agreed. "I'll take the houses on the left. But, we'll keep track of each other, right?"

"Sure, right. Let's go." Walker was already fast-footing it down the road. "Come on, let's get outta here before somebody notices we're gone. The faster we're there, the more houses we can get into before dark."

For a few seconds, Shepherd's eyebrows angled into an uneasy V, but then Walker called to him again. "Hurry it up!" Shepherd's brows smoothed, and he ran to catch up with his friend.

The town was a flat graveyard, square-box houses standing like markers where the dead were buried. Mostly, that's where the families of Old Earth had died, in their own beds. Walker and Shepherd had found enough of them to know.

Walker Gray Wolf remembered the stories his father had told him about the time of his journey, when his father—the man their people called Sagamore—had searched the land for survivors. His father had been alone. He had entered the houses, hoping to find someone alive. Walker tried to think of his father's courage, and feel it become a part of him, as he stood before the tall, bone-white house at the end of the narrow road.

He couldn't see Shepherd anymore. They had separated when the street became a divided branch. Shepherd took the houses on the right branch; Walker had taken those on the left.

He tried to convince himself that it wasn't almost sunset, but he knew that it was. He should go back to the others. They would be wondering about him. The house waited. He stared at it, feeling an uneasiness jiggle his insides from just looking at this place. Some houses were like that; they made him want to curl up and stay put.

His father hadn't stayed put. His father had gone into every house, looked behind every door. His father had been a man. Walker needed to think of himself as a man, too. He was Josiah Gray Wolf's son. He could go alone into this grave marker. If it was bigger than the others, or seemed a little scarier, then he could count himself braver for going into it. He was sure this one would beat anything Shepherd might find.

The front door wasn't locked. Sometimes, he needed to break a window to get into the houses, but this one seemed to be inviting him. Walker moved out of the lingering wash of sunlight, and stepped into the darkness of a wooden cave.

The windows were too dirty to allow even a hope of light. A smell of mold was in the air, and the chalky taste of dust. Walker tried not to take too deep a breath. It was the unclean center of a tomb.

In this core of darkness, Walker heard the sound of singing.

He froze. The voice filtered down through the open slats of the ceiling. Walker's head arched back, and he stared at the unrelieved black. Nothing of life could live in such a place.

"Is somebody there?" he called.

The singing stopped.

Get out of here, he thought. *Run to that door and get out of here right now.*

He heard the floorboards overhead creak and groan as weight was pressed on them. Something moving. *Someone.*

"I heard you!" Walker shouted, the chalky dust settling in his mouth with every word. "Come down," he called, and then began side-stepping backwards, cautiously moving closer to the front door.

It was cold, but sweat was making his palms slick. God above, this had been a fool idea. Nobody was around to help him if there was trouble. Nobody even knew he was in this place. He wished he'd stayed with Shepherd. At least, they would have been together. They could have helped each other. But, Shepherd wasn't here.

He should have gone outside, found the others, and brought them back with him. He should have . . .

The staircase was only a few feet away. Whoever was hiding in the dark of this house was up there right now, and might be gone when he came back. Nobody would ever believe him. He had to see for himself.

"I'm Walker Gray Wolf," he said in a loud voice, as he climbed the first tread of the staircase. Above him, the floorboards creaked again and he heard a hurried shuffling across them. "I'm not alone. There are others with me," he called into the pulsing silence. He wished it were the truth.

He was at the head of the stairs before the thought came. Was someone playing a trick on him? Was it Shepherd? Could Shepherd have raced ahead of him and come into this last house on the lonely road to hide?

If it was Shepherd, he would be crouched down, waiting in the dark to jump out at him. Shepherd would tell the others how afraid Walker had been, how he'd run from the house screaming, and they would laugh. The thought made Walker angry, and anger pushed him forward into the dark, uninviting rooms. Anger pushed him past a place of safety, and into the center of the room upstairs.

Walker flinched when the door to the room swung shut.

He couldn't see. Even the soft glow of the moon was useless through the dirt-caked windows. Nothing of light could enter this room. He felt the hidden presence, before he heard the scuffling sound.

And then Walker knew — Shepherd would never

have done this to him. The boy was his friend.

"Shepherd!" Walker screamed, just before the cold fingers reached across the lightless space and touched him.

Shepherd was tired of searching through abandoned houses. This one would do fine for the People to sleep in tonight. It was a lot bigger than the others on this road, as if the smaller houses were children of this larger one. He liked thinking of it like that. The idea made him smile—little families of houses clustered together on a street. It was better than thinking of them as boneyards.

Walker had introduced that idea. It took a lot of effort, but Shepherd was trying to erase it from his mind. Walker liked things to be exciting. He was always looking for something to do that would be a little dangerous, or scary. That was why he was here right now, going through these houses by himself, because Walker liked being scared. Or maybe what Walker had said was closer to the truth: he was just bored.

It wasn't as if they hadn't found any skulls and bones. There were always bones. Since they'd left the Outsider's camp, he'd seen too many remains of the people of Old Earth. They were everywhere.

Some had died in their houses, some in their cars, some even in the streets. At first, he hadn't looked at them. The faceless skulls had frightened him. Now, he'd seen so many, they just made him sad. Each one was a life which had died. Each one had been a person. He never touched the skeletons, or took anything from them. Not because he was afraid, but because he felt a bond between these dead and himself. They had been children of the

71

living earth, like him.

Thankfully, this house didn't hold any reminders of death. Shepherd opened the windows to let the clean air blow through. His mother would like this place. She could rest here. One room upstairs had a wide bed. He would bring her to it, and stay with her in the dark. She cried out, sometimes. She needed him to hold back her fears. Since the night of the flood, his mother had changed.

Shepherd remembered that night, too. He thought of the water coming over the planted fields, over the adobe houses, taking his father's life. The flood wave had lifted Skeet Hallinger from the ground and carried him at its crest for a few seconds, before his body was crushed beneath the weight of the water.

That day, the flood had taken a second father from him. In ways which could not be counted by inherited traits such as eye color or ethnic origins, Josiah Gray Wolf—the one called Sagamore—had become a closer meaning of the word *father* to Shepherd than the man who was his true parent. Now, with both men gone, Shepherd felt a sense of guilt at not grieving for Skeet Hallinger as much as he mourned the loss of the man called Sagamore.

Everything had changed when Sagamore died. They were no longer the Outsiders, for the world of the biosphere was far away. They were The People, the wanderers of earth, seekers of the new Eden. All that had gone before had passed away with the flood, that time of beginning, but Shepherd was old enough to know he would always remember it, and the man who had led them.

As a river of rushing water leaves it mark on a canyon, Sagamore had left such a permanent mark on Shepherd. In that way, he would never be without him.

The pearled light of late afternoon had slipped away, and Shepherd saw that he was standing in the dark of this room, and that it was night. The others would be searching for him, worrying that he might be lost. He hurried from the empty house . . . and from his memories, too.

Nine

Prophet held Andrew in his arms. His son was hungry and crying to be fed. The baby wasn't wrong, thought Prophet; it was time all of them found a place to stay for the night, and had a meal. Instead of that, they'd spent the last hour searching for Walker and Shepherd.

"Would you give Andrew his supper for me?" Prophet asked, handing the one-year-old to Crystal Rivers. "I need to keep looking for Shepherd and Walker, but Andrew's about to fall asleep from exhaustion, without being fed. Could you take care of Andrew for me while I keep looking for them?"

Crystal accepted the child into her arms. "Andrew's always welcome to stay with me," she offered, then added, "and so is his father."

This was an invitation for more than a warm supper, Prophet understood, but he didn't have time to deal with it right now. He would think about what it meant after he'd found the missing boys.

"I'd like to stay," he began, trying to leave without hurting her feelings. He liked Crystal; he always had. She was a woman who'd been independent and self-sufficient since the first days when Josiah had gathered the survivors together. She'd never asked for anything. Of all the women, Crystal was the only one who remained alone. She had lived by herself for years, and now shared her life with Grace, her fourteen-month-old daughter.

"Go on," Crystal said. "I know you're anxious to find the boys. We can talk later. I just wanted you to know what I'm feeling, that's all."

Prophet left Andrew with Crystal, the seduction of her words staying with him as he walked in the direction of the dark streets which fanned away from the road. Somewhere in this maze of empty houses and narrow streets, Shepherd and Walker were hurt, hiding, or lost.

Stephen Wyse stayed with the others. With only two men in camp, it was better for one of them to remain with the women and children in case there was trouble. Prophet chose to be the one to continue the search, instead of Stephen, because he knew how angry Wyse would be when the boys were found. More and more often on this journey, it was clear that Stephen had a dangerous temper.

A breeze ambled through the night air, slight as a whisper against his skin. He walked with a purposeful motion that belied his fear. There was fear in the cities. It had remained when the people died. Fear bloomed among the stones, among the empty houses and abandoned buildings. Once, the welcome lights of the cities had been places to hold back the night. Now, the seeded dark prevailed. It was as if all that man had been and done was unimportant, unrecognized, and swallowed up by the vast and hungry night.

He didn't call to the boys. He was alone and didn't know what waited in the blind alleys. Predators hunted these graveyards of man. It was better not to call attention to himself.

When the scream came, Prophet felt it in the marrow of his bones.

He didn't know which of the boys had cried

out. The sound came so suddenly, he only knew it was from somewhere ahead of him. It hadn't been a cry of hurt, or sorrow. It had been a scream of terror. Fear pumped an energy like fuel through Prophet's veins. He ran through the harrowing dark, forgetting his caution and shouting, "Walker! Shepherd! Where are you?"

From somewhere close by, he thought he heard a whimper. Then it was gone.

"Here!" came a shout from farther away. "Over here!"

Prophet knew the sound of Shepherd's voice. He started to go toward it, then stopped and called for the boy to come to him. He didn't want to move from where he'd heard the faint whimper.

Shepherd ran the distance. He was breathless, but seemed unhurt. "It got dark so fast," Shepherd tried to explain. "I tried to find my way, but I started looking for Walker and got lost in these winding streets."

"Shhh, not now." Prophet was listening to something else. The sound was soft as a leather moccasin on a wood floor. Coming near him. Was it *breathing?* "Come on," he said to Shepherd, grabbing the boy's arm. "Stay right beside me."

Keeping a firm grip on Shepherd's arm, Prophet started forward. Walker's cry had come from somewhere up ahead of them.

"We were looking through the houses," said Shepherd, ignoring Prophet's warning for silence.

Inside the houses. Oh, God. Prophet's fingers dug into Shepherd's arm. He tried not to think about what might have happened to Walker—what could be happening to the boy right now. Instead, he tried to concentrate on staying ahead of the scuffing sound behind him . . . and getting to the place where he'd heard the scream.

76

He listened, and was sure; it was breathing behind him.

"I'm getting you out of here," said Prophet. "We'll come back with the others in the morning."

"I'm not leaving him. Walker!" Shepherd shouted. He tore loose and ran ahead. Only a few steps, but against the curtain of dark, Prophet lost sight of the boy immediately.

"No! Come back!" He could hear the eleven-year-old's footsteps running away from him, into the night. And he could hear the shuffling noises surge around him like water rushing around a boulder in a river, chasing after the child.

"Shepherd!"

Prophet rushed forward, knowing that he was moving into danger. To stay behind was intolerable. To go back, impossible.

Shepherd rushed through the vacant houses. Inside them, he felt the walls of his chest begin to tighten on his lungs. It was hard to breathe. Fear did that. Going into each night-blackened house was like entering a sealed tomb. Terror surrounded him . . . but Walker was in one of these houses. The memory of Walker's scream kept coming to him in the dark.

He was almost at the end of the road, only one more house, when he heard the sounds behind him. He twisted back, wishing for a candle or bright moonlight, but the night sky was hidden by clouds. He couldn't see. "Walker?" he said into the wavering black. "Walker, is that you?"

No one answered.

"Who's there?" Shepherd's voice fell to a whisper, now. Fear pressed at his throat, like fingers squeezing.

77

He turned and ran the few remaining steps to the last house on the road. The size of it dwarfed the others. He'd been afraid before, but he felt different about this house. What he felt was panic—that going inside would change things forever.

"I'm too afraid," he said out loud, as if explaining why he couldn't move. To Walker, to Sagamore, to himself. "I'm afraid."

A shout burst from the window above him. Walker.

He carried his fear with him. Holding it to his body like a shield, Shepherd ran into the house, arms stretched out before him. Seeing with his hands to find his way through this cover of night, Shepherd found the stairs. The shout had come from the second floor. He knew if he waited, his courage would die. He rushed the stairs, calling, "Walker! Where are you?"

"In here."

Shepherd followed the sound. The stairs ended. It was so dark, he couldn't see if the floor was beneath him. He couldn't see his hand before him. He could only see his fear. It was glistening as the head of a snake. More than anything, he didn't want to go into the room at the top of these stairs.

"Here!" Walker shouted.

His friend's voice was like a spur; it carried Shepherd beyond his fear. He crossed the hall, opened the door, and stepped inside the room.

"It's okay," said Walker. "You don't have to be afraid."

"I'm not afraid," Shepherd said, denying the sweat that soaked his skin.

"Not you," said Walker. ". . . Kara."

For the first time since entering the house,

Shepherd took a breath that didn't end in a strangle grip just below his throat. He noticed what he hadn't stopped to think about before, that his heart was beating as fast as galloping horses. The tightness in his chest began to relax, and his legs felt weak.

"Aren't you going to ask me who Kara is?" asked Walker.

"No." Shepherd's legs started to buckle, and he sat on the floor. He couldn't get enough air. Either the room was getting blacker, or he was dying. His blood was pounding so hard, he felt like it was lifting him off the floor.

"C'mere, Kara," said Walker.

In a moment, Shepherd could feel the thump of Walker's knees on the hardwood floor, next to him. Another thump sounded, too. Someone else beside him in the dark. And then . . . a touch.

He hadn't expected the feather-touch of fingertips on his face. He gave a startled grunt and jerked back, scuttling like a crab over the floor.

"What's the matter with you," Walker loomed over him. "Are you trying to scare her?"

"Something touched me," Shepherd shot back, angry in his own defense. "Felt like a big spider on my face."

"Shut up. Don't be so stupid." Walker was the one who sounded angry now. "It was Kara; she touched your face."

This was too much. Coming into these houses by themselves had been Walker's idea in the first place—a dare. They were both going to get into trouble for that. Scaring his mother and the others, getting lost in those winding streets, and running away from Prophet just to save Walker's scrawny neck . . . and for a thank you, Walker was calling him stupid.

"Maybe I am stupid," said Shepherd, getting to his feet, "stupid to have looked for you in the first place. Prophet was right. We should have let you rot out here until morning. I'm going back."

"Hang on." Walker grabbed his arm. "Look, I'm sorry I called you that. It's just . . ." his voice dropped to a whisper, ". . . I didn't want you saying anything else about the way Kara touched your face feeling like a spider. She can't help it. She's blind."

The thought horrified Shepherd. Being like this all the time, pitch black. Never being able to see more than he could see right now. "Blind?"

"Yeah." Walker was still whispering. "It's her way of seeing us, by touching. It scared me, too," he admitted. "You should have heard me yell."

Shepherd remembered the scream.

"She's more scared of us than we are of her," said Walker. "I didn't want you saying things that would make her feel bad—like calling her some kind of spider."

"Well, how was I supposed to know?" Shepherd was still mad. "You could have told me. And why'd you stay here? Why didn't you bring her back to camp?"

"Don't you think I tried? She wouldn't leave this room. She kept saying, 'No, no,' like she was afraid of something."

At that moment, Shepherd felt a shifting of weight on the floorboards beneath his feet. He was suddenly aware of something moving in the hallway outside the room.

"I don't know how she finds anything to eat," said Walker. "I don't know—"

"Shhh." Shepherd was listening to the creak of the floor. He whispered, "There's something in the hall."

80

Without another word, he took hold of Walker's arm and pushed him back, until they were standing flat against the wall. From there, he could barely see the vague outline of four shapes moving into the dark.

"Who the heck—"

Shepherd yanked on Walker's arm, silencing him again.

"Kara?" The name was a question from the black cage of night.

Kara didn't answer.

"Come on," said Walker. "I think she's in trouble. I'm not leaving her over there by herself." He started across the floor.

"Wait!" Shepherd called softly, but Walker had moved out of grabbing distance.

A lot of things happened all at once. It was hard to figure out which came first. Shepherd heard a noise like something going *thwack!* Walker yelped. A heavy weight thudded to the floor. The downstairs door banged open, and Prophet was shouting, "Shepherd! Walker!"

"Up here!" Shepherd called. "Hurry!"

He could hear Prophet rushing up the stairs, hear the panicked scrambling around the dark room, and that unfamiliar voice crying, "Kara? Kara?"

And then Prophet was there, holding a burning torch in his hand. The light from that torch lifted the cover of darkness, and Shepherd saw three little children and an older boy. The girl called Kara was huddling at the window. And on the floor in the center of the room lay the motionless body of Walker Gray Wolf.

Ten

Walker wasn't dead, just knocked unconscious by the sycamore bough swung by the teenager at the center of the room. From where Prophet stood holding the wavering light of the torch, he could see all of them: the young man with the club, the girl in the corner, three smaller children, and Shepherd kneeling beside Walker.

"I don't know who you are, or how you got here," Prophet directed his words to the older boy, "but don't move."

Walker groaned and made several struggling efforts to sit up. A line of blood trickled down his forehead. His eyes were open, and he blinked at the glare of the torch, then glanced around the room. "God above," he said, loudly enough for Prophet to hear.

"Are you all right?" Prophet asked, bringing the torchlight closer to Walker's face. He couldn't see the boy's pupils clearly, but he seemed alert. That didn't mean there wasn't a concussion, or that they wouldn't have more trouble later as a result of this knock on the head. All it meant was that for right this minute, Walker was okay.

"Ohhh," Walker groaned. "My head feels like somebody kicked it."

"Somebody did," said Shepherd, and pointed to the one with the club. "Him."

"Why, you—" Walker was up and charging head

82

first like a bull. Before anyone could stop him, he knocked the older boy off his feet, and was kneeling on his neck, cutting off air and hammering the boy's face with both fists.

Prophet waded into the fray. "Get off!" he shouted, yanking the eleven-year-old back by one arm around his waist. Walker had enough fight in him that Prophet doubted he was seriously hurt. "You're even, you hear me? No more of this. It's over."

Walker was throwing hateful glances Prophet's way, as was the boy picking himself up off the floor. The club had fallen in the scuffle, and the older boy started toward it.

"Leave it!" said Prophet.

The young man stepped back. The three younger ones moved in closer to him. It was clear from the way they behaved now, the children saw him as their protector.

"Where'd you get the torch?" asked Shepherd, breaking the uneasy silence.

"I made it after you ran off," Prophet told him, giving blame where it was due. Then he turned his attention back to the older boy. "I don't much like things rushing past me in the dark, either. That was you, wasn't it?"

He received no answer.

"Tanner," said the girl at the window. She stood, and Prophet saw that she was older than he had thought at first. He guessed that she was about twelve or thirteen, because she was taller than either Shepherd or Walker, but still slim as a boy. She was a pretty girl with a sweet-looking oval face, and a cropped cap of blond hair. When she held her arms in front of her and walked across the room, he could see that she was blind.

"Tanner?" she called, a tremble of fear in her voice.

"Over here, Kara," said the young man. He walked the distance between them and took her outstretched hand. The girl's arms roped around the boy's neck, and she buried her head against his shoulder.

"All right, let's all calm down," said Prophet. He could see that there was a genuine tenderness between these two, and between the younger children and the boy. It seemed that the one called Tanner was some kind of leader to them all.

The shock that these five children were alive, that they were on their own, hit Prophet with a force that left him feeling stunned. "Where are your parents?" he asked.

"Dead," said Tanner. "We're alone."

"Alone?" The thought was incredible: children surviving like a pack of animals. The youngest one looked about four years old. Perhaps the mother had died giving birth. Could children have fed and cared for an infant?

"When did your parents die?" asked Shepherd.

Prophet could see that Shepherd was thinking of his own mother.

"Opal's mother died last winter," said Tanner. "She was having a baby . . ." his voice faltered, ". . . and she got sick. She died with the baby still in her."

Clearly, they had been witnesses to the woman's death in childbirth. Prophet imagined the scene, and was filled with compassion for these children. Opal, the only girl among the four littlest ones, was black. The other children were white. "Weren't there any other adults?" he asked. "What about the rest of your parents?"

"Mine died a long time ago. I was little, like Dillon," said Tanner, pointing to a boy of about six. "I don't remember my mother," he said, "but my father had some kind of pain in his side. It got worse, and he got sicker . . . till he didn't know me anymore. One morning, I woke up and he was dead."

It sounded like appendicitis, thought Prophet. If so, the man had died in agony. What else had this boy seen, he wondered. "And the rest of your parents?" he asked. "Are all the adults gone?"

"Kara, Jamie, and Dillon are one family," said Tanner. "Their mother cut her arm open on a fence wire. Couldn't stop the bleeding. It kept on till she was empty, I guess. That was when Dillon was just starting to walk. That same year, their father took off one day—hunting. He was Opal's daddy, too. We never heard what happened to him. Something got him, I guess."

Prophet flinched at the hard way the boy listed these events of their lives.

"Opal's mother was the last. She cried for us when she was dying," said Tanner. "She cried for her little girl. After a while, the cries turned to screams," he said, "and I stopped listening. She left us, like the others."

Prophet tried to imagine it: five children left on their own in a world that was empty of humankind. How had they lived?

"Have you been here since then?" he asked.

For the first time, the boy looked confused. "This is our place," he said.

"Why didn't you leave?" asked Shepherd. "Why didn't you look for others?"

"Till tonight," said Tanner, "we were all there was."

The boy's words stayed with Prophet. These children were a world unto themselves. They had lived with only the knowledge of each other. Now, their world had changed. If Walker and Shepherd hadn't been exploring through the empty houses, these children might never have been found.

85

Prophet felt a certainty that this was the Spirit at work; God had a part in bringing all of them together. "I want you to come with us," he said.

"Come with you?" Tanner's eyes narrowed. "Where?"

"First, back to our camp for the night. You'll meet the rest of us: another man, three women, and seven children besides these two." He waved a hand in Shepherd and Walker's direction. "Tomorrow, when we're rested, we'll keep heading north. We plan to settle on good farmland. I want all of you to come with us," said Prophet.

The three younger children were wide-eyed, but silent. Only Opal betrayed her feelings by a pleading touch on Tanner's hand. He glanced at the little girl for an instant, then looked away, as if he hadn't seen her — or the look in her eyes.

"We're fine right here," he said. "You go without us."

Prophet tried to think how to convince him. The boy was so proud and stubborn. It was clear that he liked things the way they were, being the leader among them. Prophet knew it would be hard to persuade Tanner to let strangers make the decisions for awhile, and, without Tanner's agreement, none of the rest of them would come along, either.

In the end, it was Kara whose words made the difference. She had been silent the whole time, except for calling the boy's name twice. Now she spoke up. Her voice was no longer trembling. "I want to go with them," she said.

"What? Be quiet, Kara."

"Tanner, listen. Opal is too little to go hunting with you all the time. I can't take care of her. It would be good for Jamie and Dillon to meet other children. All of us have been getting sick, lately. We need help."

"We're all right," he argued.

86

"I want to go with them, Tanner," she insisted. "I want us all to go."

"My mother knows how to bake biscuits," Shepherd tempted them.

"Biscuits!" said Dillon. "Oh, Tanner . . . biscuits!"

"All right! You want to go with them, we'll go. I don't care. We're leaving our home, that's what. We're leaving the place where your mama is buried," he said to Dillon. "For what? Biscuits!"

"Don't you say that, Tan. Don't you hurt him like that."

"I'm not hurting anybody," he said, defensively. "You're hurting us, and he's hurting us. I'm just trying to keep us together."

"It's all right, Dillon," said Kara. "I think Mama sent them to us. I think she wanted this to happen."

Prophet didn't wait for them to change their minds. "Let's go," he said, and led the blind girl down the stairs.

Like chicks racing after a broody hen, the others followed.

It was clear to Prophet from the start that these new children were going to be a blessing—and trouble. The eldest, Tanner, was used to having everything his own way, and had been the leader of these five for so long, he bristled at attempts from any of the Outsiders to so much as feed the younger ones.

"I'll take care of them," he'd say.

The children obeyed like scared little puppies at first. He had only to call them, and they would run to his side. For the first few days, he lorded it over everyone in camp, demonstrating his control and power in sometimes cruel ways. Once, Dillon was eating a hot meal cooked for him by Merry Logan, and Tanner called the boy away, long before the child was finished. Dillon had cried, but no one could convince the six-year-old to leave Tanner's side.

Such dominance lasted for about one week; then, it was as if a siege of war had broken out in camp. Tanner's shouts for the children went unanswered. Dillon remained with Merry Logan, Jamie stayed with Crystal Rivers, Opal was with Elizabeth Pinola, and Kara was with Walker. When Tanner shouted for them, no one came rushing to him.

The boy sulked about camp for an afternoon, and then he left. No one stopped him. No one followed.

It was two days before any of them saw him again. He followed them at a distance. On the evening of the fourth day, he returned to camp. Prophet offered him food, and he took it. The children remained shy with him, and no one spoke of the time he was away.

In many ways, Stephen was an example of what Tanner might have become: a demanding leader who held his people together by unyielding strength, need, and fear. Stephen wasn't liked, but he was followed. He was better at hunting than Prophet, and provided the camp with fresh meat to sustain life along the trail.

Prophet didn't interfere with Stephen's rough ways. He knew the People needed a man like Stephen to get them to a permanent settlement. He would drive them harder than Prophet would have had the heart to do, but his insistent urging of them further than their strength would allow might get them north and settled in shelters before winter set in. Because of this, Prophet watched Stephen bully them, and said nothing.

Each day, they moved north. Stephen was relentless with those who complained that they were exhausted, or too sick to go on.

"Grace is hot with fever," said Crystal. "She can't keep food down for more than an hour. She needs to rest, Stephen. We all do."

"Stay behind, if she's too sick to keep going," he told her. "Catch up with us when she's stronger."

"You'd abandon us?" she asked, horrified.

"I'd abandon anyone who stands in the way of us getting to our permanent settlement before winter. If we're stuck on this prairie without a shelter when the first blizzard hits, we'll all die."

"But she's too sick to walk," cried Crystal. "What am I supposed to do?"

"Make yourself a sling," he said bluntly, "and carry her on your back. I'm not going to let you slow us down. Make up your mind to either keep up with us, or stay behind."

Angry, Crystal turned to Prophet for help. "Are you going to let him do this?"

"He's right about winter," Prophet said. "We've got to get to where we're going, and have our shelters built before the first snow falls."

"You'd leave me behind?" she asked. The words, *after everything I've done for you?*, weren't spoken, but he knew she was thinking them.

"I'd have to go on with the others," he admitted. "We'll need everyone's strength to get the shelters built in time. It seems hard, I know," he struggled to explain, "but —"

"I understand." The words were the first bricks of a wall between them. Crystal did as Stephen told her. She fashioned a sling from a wool shawl, and tied the sick child to her back. Each time he offered, she refused Prophet's help. She never mentioned living with her again.

Eleven

Jessica Nathan's dreams were full of images of Andrew. Her son haunted her sleep like a subconscious ghost. He was there when she closed her eyes; there, just before she awoke. He was the soul of her other life, that one which her mind couldn't control. Through the gift of her dreams, she filled her need of this child, and so was able to continue living through the days which followed, after Brad and Andrew went away.

The biosphere claimed her alert mind. There was always work to be done. The ag wing had to be planted with a rotation of crops all year. Pest control meant long hours of washing away insect infestation with buckets of onion-scented water, and introducing large numbers of ladybugs to control aphids, predatory beetles for spider mites, and colonies of wasps to control white flies. Maintaining a dominance for the food supply over the insect population of Biosphere Seven was a battle that all of them fought on a daily basis. If they grew careless, the insects would take over. If they eliminated the insects, the food chain would die.

In addition to maintaining the ag wing, the gas chromatograph in Biosphere Seven must be monitored to prevent too high a buildup in carbon dioxide levels beneath the glass dome. The temperature and salinity of the ocean must be monitored and regulated, and a chemical analysis continually supervised of their drinking water. There was food to be gathered and prepared each day, animals to be fed and cared for, children to be educated, and all the working functions of the biosphere to control and safeguard.

Jessica could fill her waking hours with work. There would never be enough time to do it all. She could keep herself so busy with the hard labor of maintaining the biosphere and the lives within it that she didn't think about Andrew. That she didn't think about Brad. But eventually, the heavy chain of sleep would drag her down, and her dreams would once again betray her.

If Jessica was honest with herself, she would have to admit that Brad's leaving, going north with the rest of the Outsiders and taking their child with him, had divided her in two. Part of her remained in the world of this biosphere, living as a wife to Quinn and a mother to their children, continuing in her duties as the leader of these people and this place, and chronicling the history of all their lives within the sphere. This was reality. Only reality wasn't always truth.

The truth was, another part of Jessica had fled from this world with Brad, and with their son. With them, she was set free of the glass and steel dome. At night, she dreamed of a pale horse which would come for her. It would stand outside the biosphere and wait. She would leave this place, and climb upon the white saddle on its back, and it would carry her to the place where Brad and their son waited.

"Can't you sleep?" asked Quinn. He had rolled onto his side in the bed they shared. He was staring at her.

"No, I want to stay in this world a little longer," she told him, and moved closer.

Quinn slipped one arm beneath her neck, and cradled her against him. She laid her face against the warmth of his shoulder. His skin was always hotter than Jessica's. She moved into the heat of him, and felt a comfort in the warmth of his love. The wealth of hair on his chest tickled her nose, and she was aware of the familiar male scent of him. He was as constant as the reality of the sphere. Quinn was her husband, the father of two of her children, and parent to five of the others. He loved her.

In spite of the way she had always felt about Brad, the yearning to continue to be a part of his life, she loved Quinn, too. There was no denying her feelings. Quinn was her husband, the man who held her in his arms each night. The truth was she loved them both.

In Quinn's embrace, with the heat of his kisses on her mouth, she felt an urgency of life rise up within her.

"Come back to me," he said. "It's as if you've been gone somewhere, and I haven't been able to reach you."

She was responding to his touch. He was gentle, easing her body into a well-remembered longing. She could feel the course of her own needs building, a low roaring in her ears as her heart beat faster and her blood rushed through her veins, as the needs she had been denied so long now raced into being. Her body was heat, and touch, and points of pleasure that now awakened from the calm.

"Jessie . . . I love you."

She turned away, trying to close out the feelings that surrounded her.

"Don't," he whispered, and drew her back. "Don't shut me out. Jessie." He kissed her ear, her neck, her mouth . . . a longing burning all resistance from its path. His broad hands stroked her skin until she felt the heat of life spark and flame. "Come back to me, Jessie. Come back to the man who loves you."

She cried as she clung to him. She cried, and kissed him eagerly, answering his enduring love of her with a desperate passion of her own. "Hold me, Quinn," she cried. "Hold me." She couldn't get enough of his arms around her, of his body pressed against her own. "Don't let me be lost again. Don't let me go."

"Never," he promised, and pulled her to him, tighter still.

Half a world away, in the French coastal city that was once called Coquelles, an army of three hundred men, women, and children gathered on the quiet shore. Here, the morning was just lifting into the sky, and the doubts of night fell away, as fearful as shadows in the light of dawn.

At the head of the horsemen and their families, was the man called Zechar al Maghrib. He was the leader of this multitude, the Berber nomad who had led them: first from the High Atlas mountains in Morocco to the Sahara, and then in camel and horse caravans across the countries bordering the Mediterranean Sea.

The lands they crossed were wide corridors of uninhabited earth. For three years, they had followed the curving promise of the coast, through the desert countries, across the hard plains of the lands north of the sea, and then west, to the shore of this green valley. Along the way, they had gathered this company of survivors.

They were a people of many races. Men with

broad Slavic faces stood beside others with narrower cheekbones, and eyes dark as pools of oil in the desert. European farmers were now family to their Bedouin brothers. Blacks and whites were children of the same house, survivors of the family of man.

These few had lived, when the rest of the world had died. Some were children of those first survivors, as was Maghrib, himself. Some were the survivors of that time—the last generation of Old Earth. Maghrib had found them.

From the desert he had led them, the Berber, Zechar al Maghrib. His children were as numerous as the women of the camp. His horses were the finest stallions. And his wife, Rhissa, was the matriarch of this band of nomads who called themselves the Travelers.

Now, stopped by this arm of the sea beyond the coast of France, Maghrib gathered his finest riders to him. They sat around the morning campfire and spoke of the lands which lay across the channel.

"Beyond that water is the countryside of England," said Tadeo Valdez, the best horseman of Maghrib's camp. "There is fine grazing for horses and cattle. Our sheep would fatten on the gentle hillsides, and clear streams flow in a richness that brings life to the land."

Maghrib stared at the stretch of turbulent water. His people were too many to cross this channel of the sea in small open boats. With them were herds of sheep and cattle, camels and horses. With them were little children, many still at their mother's breasts. "The risk for loss of life is too great." Maghrib placed too high a value on the people of his camp to take such a chance.

"There is another way," offered young Phillip Boussard. The boy was thin as stretched bones, a

94

tall youth with the first stubble of a beard like a bloom of golden furze on his cheeks.

Maghrib had not known the boy long. They had found him living alone in a village, not far from this place. His parents were dead, and the boy had believed himself the only man left on earth. He had told Maghrib this story, and told him too, how grateful he was to the Travelers for finding him. "I would die for you, and these people," he had sworn an oath of fealty to Maghrib. "You have given me back my life."

Maghrib had never asked for such an oath from any of his men. He was the son of the desert. His Berber mother had seen a shooting star on the night of Maghrib's birth; such an omen was always a sign of destiny. It was natural that, like that star, he should be a Traveler, leading his people. He looked for nothing more from them than their love.

"What other way is there to cross the water?" he asked Phillip, noting that the boy had courage to come forward, unasked.

"Deep beneath the ground is a tunnel," said Phillip. "It lies under the sea, under the earth below the sea," he explained. "This tunnel is a passage from one land to the next. Your people can walk through it, Maghrib. We can drive our herds before us. The tunnel will lead us across to this green land beyond the arm of sea. The tunnel is the way."

Maghrib had barely begun to imagine such a thing, when Tadeo spoke sharply against the idea. "Drive our animals into a hole beneath the sea? This is madness, Maghrib. Don't listen to the boy. We are all that is left of humankind. Should we throw ourselves into a pit beneath the sea on the word of this child?"

The boy's eyes showed his anger, but he did not challenge Tadeo's words. "I know that in my

95

father's time, people used to cross in that place from one land to the other," he said calmly. "My father was a builder, and he often spoke of the day when this tunnel opened a link between the two coasts, as though a bridge had been laid beneath the ground."

Maghrib saw truth in the boy's eyes. Such a wonder was incredible to him—to lay a bridge beneath the sea! "Find this tunnel," he said to Phillip. "Show me the way. I will see it."

Tadeo Valdez rose from the circle around the campfire. His fury was unmistakable. "Would you listen to the wisdom of a boy, Maghrib? In this, you will find only a child's story, and bring danger to our people." Tadeo left them, his back held as stiffly as his anger.

Maghrib watched the man walk away. Tadeo was not that much older than the young Phillip; he was perhaps twenty-five. Was it possible that he was jealous of the boy? The thought stirred like the turbulent water before him. It was true Maghrib felt a fondness for the younger boy, for his youth and his courage. Phillip reminded Maghrib of himself at this boy's age. Could his feelings of affection for Phillip have caused such hurt and outrage in Tadeo?

"I didn't mean to—" Phillip started.

"No, you meant no harm," Maghrib quickly told him. "Come, tell me what you know about this tunnel."

"Better, Maghrib," said Phillip, "I will show you."

They saddled their horses and rode alone through the morning. A gray haze rose from the sea and followed them, riding like a companion on the water. It blocked the land beyond this channel, as though hiding it from their sight. Maghrib saw this, and felt a wonder, and a dread. Was Tadeo right? Would

96

the tunnel lead the Travelers into danger?

Maghrib rode beside Phillip, his dark thoughts as heavy as the fog.

It wasn't far. Phillip knew the way; this land had been his home. He led them along the coast, riding the broken cliff walls, and then down across the yielding shore of the beach, to the place of the wide house on the firmer sand . . . the entrance to the tunnel.

The building was massive. If all the Travelers stood against the front wall, arms held from their sides like crosses, with only their fingertips touching, they would not reach the end of it. Maghrib stared. Tadeo had been wrong. This was far more than a pit beneath the sea.

A paved rode led beneath the roof of this house. Maghrib and Phillip remained on horseback, and following the curve of the road, leading them into the structure. Inside the building, broken windows provided the strongest source of light. There were light fixtures in the ceiling, but nothing worked anymore. There hadn't been any electricity running for a long time.

"There are three tunnels," Phillip explained. "My father drew a picture of this place for me. Once, he rode on a train that passed through one of these, from France into England."

They had ridden too far into the concrete core for there to be anymore windows, or light. Maghrib felt the closeness of the place seal around him like the dark. He drew in the reins of his horse, unwilling to go further. "What lies beyond this dark?" It seemed to him that he could feel the beating of demon wings brushing against his face, and hear a whispered sigh.

"From here, cars were loaded onto wagons," said Phillip. "Each wagon held many cars or buses, and the wagons were pulled by either of the trains in the two rail tunnels."

"Two trains?" asked Maghrib. He was impressed with this fact.

"One going to England, and one coming from there," said Phillip. "All day the trains ran, and through the night. The tunnels were kept bright as midday, their great lamps burning even beneath the floor of the sea. My father said the tunnels ran deep under the ground, into the earth, below the ocean trench."

Maghrib urged his stallion back along the way they had come, until he was again in a place of light. Here, he felt calmer. Phillip joined him, and as they rode out into the sunlight, Maghrib asked the only question he needed to know.

"Can it be done again? Can our people find a way to cross through this tunnel? With torches, and with our flocks of sheep, camels, and cattle? Could the Travelers come through this passage, and come through to the other side?"

In the brightness of the morning, the boy who was no more than sixteen, answered solemnly. "It is so. It can be done, Maghrib. I have done it."

Twelve

Sidra lived within the hollow mountain and gained back her strength, cared for during the many days of her recovery by T. J. Parker, in the place called NORAD. Parker asked nothing of her, but brought her food, and kept her warm when the cold wind blew a breath of coming autumn from the land beyond the caves. For her, he found clothes, and wore them. He cut his hair, and shaved. For her, he once again became the man he used to be.

For Sidra, the first days alone with Parker were a time of healing, body and soul. Her spirit had been soul-sick when she'd fallen into Parker's care, grieving for the pain she had caused Seth by leaving, and grieving too for feeling so alone in the world. In the quiet comfort of these many-chambered caves, she had found solace for that hurt, and with Parker's attentive care, gained back the strength to go on with her life.

Words had come slowly to them both. Before she had been strong enough to speak, her eyes had kept him at a distance. He had sat across the room from her, bringing her food several times a day, helping her to eat, and then going back to the little stool against the wall. Each time she awoke, she would see him there, quietly keeping a vigil.

In time, she came to trust him. The truth was simple: if he had wanted to do her harm, he could have done so many times during the days she was so weak. He could have killed her, or frightened her, or left her to die . . . but he had done none of these things. He had saved her life.

Now, she was well again, strong enough to leave the caves if she chose to, but she stayed. She stayed because this place brought her a kind of peace. She stayed because she had no where else to go. She stayed because of Parker.

They lived on the food from the storage rooms in the deep cellars of NORAD. In these rooms had been stockpiled crate after crate of dried staples such as potatoes, rice, and noodles. She and Parker also enjoyed cans of vegetables, fruit, soup, and juice. The constant temperature of the cellars kept the dried food from perishing.

The days were a constant rhythm, one after the other, and slowly, she began to feel safe in them. She began to feel safe with Parker, too.

At night, they would sit in the well-lit computer room. The lights and sounds from the many machines shimmered and hummed like a field of colors with the drone of insects by a lake. She kept her silence like a medicine that eased and healed her. He stayed near, but didn't intrude into her thoughts.

As the days went by, she ventured more and more often to the world outside the caves, and Parker followed. He went everywhere she went. If she walked to the mountains, his were the echo of her steps. If she swam in the lake, he would sit on the grassy bank and wait for her to emerge from the water. "Go away!" she would shout at him, but he would stay. If she hunted for rabbit or deer, he would be behind her in the trees. Always, her breath was his breath, his eyes watched her, and she felt his presence near her, like an insistent shadow.

"Why won't you leave me alone?" she would rail

at him. Anger fueled in her, and her words were cold and cruel.

The day came when T. J. Parker put his life at risk for Sidra, when he was all there was that stood between her and death.

Sidra had dressed and moved silently that morning, leaving the caves while Parker was still asleep. It was pre-dawn dark, but she had followed the well-remembered trail that led into the forest. In her hand was the gun she'd taken from the store window so long ago. On the day she had taken it, a gun had given her courage to travel alone. That same gun now gave her courage to hunt in the still-dark of the morning. She felt its heavy weight in her hands, and moved deeper into the woods.

The woodland was mute and blind, like the unborn day. In the leafy canopy, above the black trunks of the trees—their bark like withered skin—waited the cougar. She was poised full length along one heavy branch, her sleek, well-muscled body stretching eight feet from head to tail.

The cougar's muscles tensed with the sound of something coming nearer to this splintered cavern of trees. A scent drifted into her flaring nostrils, and hunger clawed at her belly. She stood, four legs braced along the tree limb, her tail twitching in anticipation. Her predator eyes could see well through the veil of early morning dark. She could see the woman approach this stand of trees.

Along the tree limb, the cougar's body tensed, her head and forelegs crouched close to the rough bark, her back raised high, ready to spring. As she watched, a young rabbit hopped into sight beneath the tree. The cougar's sharp eyes took in the blur of movement, but she let the rabbit go. Her attention

101

was fixed on another purpose . . . and the hunted was coming near.

Tyler James Parker opened his eyes and listened to the sound of dull humming. It wasn't the noise of the computers which woke him. It was the absence of one now-familiar sound which stirred him into alertness. He couldn't hear Sidra breathing.

Eyes wide open, he waited. Nothing stirred. In a few minutes, when she didn't return from any of the other rooms, he called out, "Sidra." Only the hollow answer of the caves returned to him.

Parker's hands were shaking as he dragged at the pallet where Sidra had slept. His heart calmed when he saw that many of her things were still here, but her shoes and heavy jacket were gone. Would she have gone outside alone before dawn? For fresh air? For a walk?

Then, he saw that the gun was gone—and he knew.

He took nothing with him, only his courage, and ran barefoot into the woods.

Sidra moved on silent feet. Her steps were laid softly on the ground, moving her weight as an stalking animal does, toes taking the pressure first, then barely touching at the heals. She had been taught to hunt by her father, Josiah Gray Wolf. In the time she was with him, he had taught her how to survive in the wilderness, as if he had known she would be alone.

She thought of him now, the straightness of his back, the steady gaze in his eyes. He never looked away when he spoke to her. His eyes had said that she was important to him, that she was his first child. A part of her was Indian, like him. A part of her felt a belonging with this wilderness, and with hunting for her survival.

"Father," she whispered into the silence.

A shriek sounded above her head. Yellow eyes like lights in the dark. She raised the gun—just as the cougar jumped.

A heavy jolt of weight propelled her forward and drove her to the ground. Breath forced from her lungs, she struggled to her knees, gasping for air. Beside her, the cougar screamed again. In that sound, she could feel the claws that would rake her back, the teeth that would sink into her neck and crush her throat.

The gun was gone, knocked from her hands.

She heard the cougar's rough breathing, like air drawn through a boil of water. And something else—something struggling with the cat.

Sidra's hands beat at the ground, searching for the fallen gun. Where? *Where?* The first pale wash of dawn was rising from the earth. In its still milky light, she saw the handle of the gun, and reached for it.

"Sidra, run!"

She turned, and saw what had stood between her and death. Parker was bent over the cat. The cougar was on the ground before him, held by the weight of one knee like a thrown calf, it's neck pulled back and thrashing side to side. Its legs were slashing at the space between them. "Run!" he said again. "I can't hold her!"

Sidra did run. She scrambled the few feet to the mound of undergrowth, and snatched the gun from the scabrous thicket of leaves. Snatched the gun and moved back to the man and the cat . . . firing a bullet into the cougar's brain.

The wildcat's body thumped twice against the

ground, feet jutting forward in a stiff-legged dance. Its eyes didn't close, but the rage faded from them. A shudder stilled its final breath, and the great cat lay lifeless at their feet.

Parker stood up. His feet were bleeding.

"You came into the woods without shoes?" Sidra asked. With all that had happened, she marveled most at this.

"When I saw you were gone," he started to explain, then didn't finish.

"You thought I'd left you?" she asked. The thought passed through her mind. Was this how it had been for Seth, when he awoke and found her gone?

"The gun was gone," Parker said. "I knew you'd gone into the woods to hunt, and I was afraid for you. I didn't think," he stared at his bloody feet, ". . . I just ran."

His words wrapped around her like a blanket of warmth. Here was someone who cared about her more than his own safety, more than his own life. Here was someone who had stood between her and death. Here was a man she had lived with, but had not seen, until now.

"I will promise you something," she told him. "I will never leave you, Tyler James Parker, without first saying why. I will never go away in the dark of night, or in silence. You have my oath on this. From today, there is no need to watch my every move. I won't leave without telling you. Do you believe me?"

His gaze moved back and forth across her face, as if searching for the truth, and then he nodded.

"Good," said Sidra. "Good." She touched his hand, the fingers that had held the cougar's jaws from her throat. Now, those rough fingers closed around hers.

"You're a young woman. I've been alone a long while, and I'm over twice your age. I'm not the man for you," he said. "I know that."

She knew it, too, and yet, she was drawn to him. She wanted to heal the pain in his eyes, wanted to take the hurt from his voice. Physically, he was the strongest man she had ever known, but inside . . . he was wounded, and dying. If it was in her power, she wanted to bring this lost man, T. J. Parker, back to life.

"Until the day I tell you that I must leave, I want to stay with you," she said. She looked up, and faced him. "You understand what I mean?"

He didn't grab her to him, as she'd thought he might, but touched her slowly, his large hands moving with great care over her arms. "I won't hold you against your will," he said. "When you say it's time for you to leave this place, I won't fight you. You're free to go, whenever you choose."

Gently, he pulled her closer, the strength of his arms circling her back, and bringing them together. In that instant, she thought she heard a low, mournful cry. Her own? Or his? And then, it didn't matter. All that meant anything to Sidra was that she was no longer alone.

Thirteen

The Berber chieftain, Zechar al Maghrib, watched the face of his wife as he moved above her in the soft light of dawn. Rhissa's eyes were dark plains within which his soul existed. She held his spirit and his manhood, this woman whose gaze saw through him, who knew his love, and his fears.

She was his only wife, though not his only woman. Other women had known his touch. Other women had borne his children. But only to Rhissa had he given his love.

Her lips were slightly parted, her breathing shallow, as was his. She didn't cling to him, or dig her fingers into the flesh of his shoulders, as some of the women would. Her hands moved on his back, a gentle touch, binding him to her.

The God of his people, and of the desert, had led him to this woman. With her by his side, he had gathered a new people to him. Old Earth was gone. Its children were no more. He was the son of the new land. He was the son of the desert star.

At his birth, a shooting star had scorched across the heavens. His mother had told him the prophecy. He was the promised kingdom of that star. Through him, these people had been led to this place. Through him and this woman, his seed and his children's seed would renew the face of the earth.

Now he clung to the woman. He pressed at her body with a weight that was both love and need. All else vanished from his mind. In that one instant, as in the last seconds before birth and death, he was alone. He was the shooting star across the emptiness of the morning sky. Surging. Surging with a strength that was beyond his keeping. Closing to that second that was only himself, alone. He felt a measure of his spirit leave him, and he shuddered at its loss.

Rhissa wrapped him like a baby in her arms. Exhausted, Zechar laid his head on her breast. There he rested. In the comfort of his wife's arms, he gained back his strength.

Her gentle fingers stroked his hair and beard. "What is this I have heard about you going through the tunnel?" she asked him.

He didn't ask her how she knew. She was his wife. There were no secrets from her. Someone had told her, and now that she had asked him, it made no difference who had spoken first.

"Phillip says there is a way to travel through the tunnel to the land across the channel sea."

"The boy is young," said Rhissa. "Can he know so much? Do you believe him?"

Maghrib rose up on one elbow. His hand idly cupped his wife's breast. She was the permanent ground of his life, the home he brought with him. "Phillip is the age I was when I set out alone into the desert. He has courage."

"But does he have wisdom?" asked Rhissa. "What makes you believe you can trust all our lives to the words of one boy?"

"He says he has gone through the tunnel," said Maghrib. "He says he has been to the other land."

Rhissa sat up. Apparently not satisfied with this, she stood and moved restlessly around the tent. Her nakedness seemed not to disturb her. Maghrib watched the rounded weight of her breasts, watched the slow curves of her hips, and the tapering line of her legs.

"Have you decided to do this thing, my husband?"

He would not lie to her. "We will go into the tunnel. With our herds and flocks, we will cross to that land beyond the sea."

She dropped to her knees and knelt beside him. "And what if the earth caves in upon us? What if the sea sweeps into the tunnel and carries away our lives? Have we come so far, only to die in such a place?"

He laughed softly, and brushed his fingers across the smooth flesh beneath her chin. "We have not come here alone, Rhissa. The same God who watched over us in the desert watches over us here. We were led to this place, and to Phillip. I will not let the God of my youth stand waiting while I quake in fear. I would go, even into this dark passage beneath the waters of the earth, and I would take you, my children, and my people, with me."

"Are you afraid?" she asked him.

"No," he answered in truth.

Rhissa leaned closer, and kissed him. "To whatever land your God leads you, I go there as well."

They sat together in the tenderness of morning. They did not speak of the channel crossing again, but held each other until the full light of day. Only when her children called into the tent did Rhissa rise, dress, and go from him.

"You will tell the other women?" he asked.

"I will tell them," she said.

"Tomorrow," he said. "Tell them to put away their tents and the things of camp. We will ride into the tunnel with the morning."

"And let the eyes of Allah watch over us," she whispered, letting the tent flap fall closed behind her.

Moussa, a boy of four and Zechar's eldest son, rode on the saddle before his mother. The child was fair-haired, like his father, and his skin was so light that his mother could not see any taint of herself in this son who was the opening of her womb. It was as if Allah had made this child solely of Zechar, with nothing of its mother to color the boy. Moussa was Zechar's heir, and looked like him as much as father and son can look alike, with twenty or more years between them. The boy was Zechar, down to the way he held his head when riding—never looking to the side, at what he was passing, but always looking ahead, at what was before them.

Another child, a two-year-old girl, was tied into a carrying basket on Rhissa's back. This daughter, Itto, named for Zechar's mother, was dark as Rhissa herself, with the wide, dark eyes of the desert people, and shining black hair which curled over her brows and around her full cheeks. She held to Rhissa's head scarf, and fingered the bits of silver twisted into the cloth. Moussa was the son of Maghrib, the heir, but little Itto was the bright jewel of her mother's heart.

The tent poles lay in tied bundles across the camels' backs. The heavy skins of the tents were laid beneath the poles, to soften the weight of the burden. The quarrelsome beasts groaned, and goaded by a sharp jab, eased onto their bony knees, then rose one foreleg at a time, with the load swaying on their backs. Their young were tethered to the mothers' bridles with long ropes, and they bawled and tugged to be free.

All was noise and excitement. All was fervor to be away.

"The horses first," said Maghrib, declaring the way they would enter the tunnel, "then the camels, the herds of cattle, and the herds of sheep. Be of strong heart, my people. Where would God lead us, but to where we are meant to be? Take no fear into the tunnel with you. Leave it behind, as dust on the earth."

Brightly burning torches were handed to each rider, and to each family who would walk into the dark. Maghrib turned at the face of the tunnel, the stallion's hooves dancing in eagerness beneath him. "Do you trust me, my Travelers?"

A cry rose from the throng of people nearest the tunnel gate, and swelled as it followed the line back to the last child, and the last herdsman of the camp. "Maghrib! Maghrib!" they shouted, chanting his name like a litany of faith. "Maghrib, we are one!" the sound echoed against the hollow tunnel and came back to him.

"Away!" Zechar al Maghrib shouted. "We go!"

They took the center tunnel, the one without the heavy tracks for the trains. This center crossing had been built, Phillip said, as a safety passage between the two underground train tunnels. Doors led off from this center course, connecting it to the other two.

To Maghrib, it seemed as if the souls of the damned were trapped beyond the walls of the connecting tunnels. He rode into the open passageway, his eyes watching for the closed doors along the sides. If one were open . . .

The flame on the torch wavered, and he felt a change; the temperature was cooler here. The air smelled different, too. He saw an opening along the inside wall, a gaping mouth along the wall, waiting.

110

"It's open," said Maghrib. He held his horse's reins firmly, not allowing the animal to go another step into the passage. "Like a bared tomb. The dead of the ground can hear us walking through their graves. The door's *open*."

Phillip was at his side. "It's where the tracks met. That's all, Maghrib," the boy promised, "only the place of that crossing. Come, I will show you," he said, riding ahead of Maghrib. "I have been past this, many times. There is another one, further in, and then a long passage of sealed doors. Come," he called to Maghrib from a distance beyond the open portal. "The dead cannot hurt you."

Maghrib was shamed into courage by the boy's bravery. Slowly, he nudged his knees into the stallion's sides, and the animal moved with keen willingness into the dark. He was a living man, journeying through a nightmare of the grave. Above his head was a ceiling of cement rings, and then the chalk floor of the seabed. Above that was the weight of the water. How long, he wondered, hearing the sound of horses' hooves on the concrete rings, would the thickness of the ocean floor hold back the sea?

They moved slowly, the lambs bleating, and the cows lowing in the dark. He could hear the youngest children crying in fear, and the women try to hush them. He could hear the men praying. Maghrib felt breathless, small as the last tremble of life before death. He had come so far . . .

He was born in the first hour of morning. A streak of starlight crossed the sky at the time of his birth, and his mother named him Zechariah, son of the shooting star. The High Atlas mountains had been his boyhood home. He was of the Berber people, of whom only he and his mother remained.

His mother, Itto M'Hand, taught him the ways of

111

the Berber people. She fed him and kept him warm. She gave him life, and nurtured it until he was strong enough to go into the desert alone. Then, she sent him from her. She sent him into the Sahara.

In the vast emptiness of the Sahara, all was changed. There, he became like the Jazirat al Maghrib—the island of the west—and took on a portion of that name. There, he found the faith that would carry him through his life, and the belief in his own destiny. In the desert he found himself, and a wife, a new name, and the beginning of his journey.

His mother had died before he returned to the High Atlas mountains of Morocco. He buried her there, in the place of their people. Of her, he carried only a memory, and the words she had taught him. "Be strong, my son," she told him, "for you are the opening door."

He had not understood her meaning, but all his life he'd carried that sense with him, of following a pathway set out for him by an unseen God. He was the traveler, and those three hundred who had joined him called themselves his people.

In this cold, hidden rib of the earth, Zechar al Maghrib felt a change come over him. Entering the ground was a likeness of death. The open doorways to the two other tunnels were black eyes that saw into his soul. He, and all those with him, were walking through the dark seal of the underworld. They were passing through it, following him.

"You are the opening door," his mother had said, and now he understood her words. All that had gone before was over. He had become a nomad, a wanderer of the earth, and in the unseen track laid down for him by his God, he had found a nation, a people who were his own. Now, the time of wandering was coming to an end. He felt the sureness of this belief in the marrow of his bones.

Phillip slowed his horse and fell behind, letting Maghrib once again lead the way for those who called themselves the Travelers. Into the seam of darkness they rode: mothers and children, old and young, men and women of courage and of fear. Into the open rib of the earth. Beneath the heartbeat of the sea.

One of the old women began to sing a hymn. The sound of her voice trembled like the light of the torches. She sang one line, and then was silent. The open sky was too far away. This was buried ground. In the tomb, there is no song. Maghrib went on, hearing the sound of his blood and his heartbeat in his ears, the living music of this place. For a time that he had no way to count, they went on, the stallion moving forward to the urging of its master's knees, deeper into the dark.

The air was close and cold.

Tadeo Valdez rode far behind both Maghrib and Phillip. Maghrib had asked him to ride before the women and children, giving them assurance with his presence and his strength. If there was trouble, it would be to Tadeo that the youngest and most vulnerable turned. He was their protector. Maghrib's own wife and children rode in silent procession behind this man. He was the arm of Maghrib extended over the Travelers.

The stretch of tunnel separated them, hid them from each other's sight in the near dark, but they were a united people. As a whole nation, they were crossing through the dark valley, into a land of future and hope. They followed Maghrib not by the great torch of the sun, but by the light of their faith in him. It was a passage of more meaning than the simple movement of a people from one place to another. It was a passage of descending into the dark heart of the grave, into the fear of unending night. Maghrib led them like a star moving across the un- lit vault of the heavens. He had brought them here, and now he led them home.

In his thoughts, Maghrib remembered that all life begins in the dark, closed space: the seed of a flower germinating in the core of black earth, the quickening of a child growing in the comforting dark of its mother's womb, and the passage from the grave to rebirth, a regeneration of life out of the darkness of death. All life, from the creation of the world, began in the unending soul of the dark.

Even before he saw the first break of sunlight from the sealed walls of this tomb, Zechar al Maghrib felt a weight lift from his spirit. He had kept a constancy of faith with the people of the earth, and with the heart of his Berber mother. It was the remembered image of her face which lifted the darkness before him. They were her words which came to him now, seeing the end of the tun- nel.

"This child of my body will be like the spear of heaven, a star to shine across the earth. Be strong, my son. You are the opening door."

Feeling the strength of her spirit beside him, he led them forward, into the morning of light.

Fourteen

Jessica awoke from the night with one clear thought: *It's coming to an end; it's over.*

She tugged at the thick blanket, drawing it up to her chin. The chill of the message wouldn't go away. She hadn't dreamt it. The thought was simply there, as if waiting for her to awaken. *Coming to an end.*

And then what?

She had lived for twenty-three years within the security of this dome. She had witnessed the death of the outside world, and carried that loss within her. She had chosen life over giving up, and found love in a place where hope had died. In that love, she had been reborn.

Her children were of this sphere, this Eden. It was the only home they knew, the only life possible. But if this message was true — and she believed it was — then she would lose them. They would all lose. What had it all been for? Why had they been allowed to live, when Earth's abundance of humanity had died? Why had they been spared?

In her youth, Jessica hadn't claimed a belief in a personal, reasoning God. She hadn't accepted her Jewish heritage in that conventional way. Her parents had loved her enough to give her the freedom to form her own conclusions about such issues. And she had put it aside, planning in all good faith to decide later. When later came, her parents and nearly all the rest of mankind were gone.

Was it that personified, personal God who had spoken to her now? Not spoken in a voice, but in a sure and haunting thought? Was God still there for any of them? Did she believe?

She moved out of the bed, careful not to wake Quinn. It was almost dawn. She pulled a thin blanket over her shoulders, and stepped out into the corridor beyond their quarters. A strip of dim lights in the baseboards along the floor brightened the area enough to see her way. She wanted some time alone. And she wanted a place where she could look out onto the last stars of morning, and consider the future. Hurrying, as if the urgency of that waking thought was pursuing her, she walked to the observation deck.

The metal stairs were cold against her bare feet — cold as the questions in her mind. She sat at the console, pressed the panel to release the window shield, and watched as the familiar structure of the dome fell away, and she was staring through a sheet of clear, unobstructed glass, looking out at a silvered sky pierced with stars.

"In the beginning, the earth was without form and darkness covered the face of the abyss." She remembered the words from the Book of Genesis in her grandmother's Torah. Staring at the blanketing heavens, becoming a part of the healing dark, Jessica felt as if the world had been made new. A second beginning. Renewed creation. "And the Lord God planted a garden in Eden, and there he put man."

What was coming to an end? Life? The sphere? The earth?

She knew: the knowledge sprang from that same part of her that had known she would never see Cameron again after he left the dome. It was the

116

sphere that was dying, and with it, the people of this duplicated world.

"Oh, God," she prayed. "What is it you want me to do?"

Jessica stayed in that quiet room. She saw the heavens brighten with the dawn, and the seal of darkness lift from the face of the earth. In the grace of this new morning, she turned to all of her that was soul . . . and listened.

If they would be forced to leave the sphere, what could she do to save them?

Trinity Adair often thought of his step-brother, Cameron . . . and of Sidra. They had grown up together, the three of them—the first children born in Biosphere Seven. They were family, and more than that. At least to Trinity, Sidra was more.

He remembered the day he'd seen her swimming in the ocean. He'd watched in secret from the shore, wishing he could find a way to tell her how he felt, that he loved her. He could see it still, the glazed memory of that day, a silver radiance of sunlight on the water, Sidra floating with her hair fanned out behind her on the glass-like surface, her arms and legs and breasts, bare as the open sea.

He had almost spoken to her then, but Cameron had appeared, his swimming strokes cutting like quick blades across the still water. As Trinity watched, Sidra had come into Cameron's arms.

Now Trinity pulled back from that painful memory. Today was another life. Nothing was the same. Nothing could ever be the same again. Cameron had left the dome and taken Sidra with him. Maybe he hadn't asked her to go, but she had followed. Trinity didn't know who to blame. All that mattered was that they were gone, and he was still here.

117

Cameron had died four months after leaving Bio-sphere Seven. And Sidra? Sidra had found another life, away from the Outsiders. She had gone north. She had left him once again.

The girl beside Trinity stirred in her sleep. Cassi's thin body curled against him in the bed. Her mouth was soft, with pouting lips. Her hair lay in a smooth nest of dark wisps against her pale cheek. She woke, eyelids lifting like the wings of a blue-gray dove, and stared up at him.

"It's not morning yet," he told her. "Still dark." He bent close enough to kiss her lips. Her mouth moved against his, and the kiss became more than a greeting. Her arm slid around his neck, and pulled him closer still.

The dreams of the night were lost in the urgency of Cassi's body against his. She was real and with him. Sidra was a shadowed memory, and far away. In the silent embrace of Cassi's arms, Trinity forgot that other morning, the silvered light on the sea, the wealth of dark hair floating like a dream, fanned out on the glistening water.

In Montana's Cheyenne Mountain Complex, within the manmade caves of NORAD, Sidra Gray Wolf felt T.J. Parker turn toward her in the bed they shared. At fifty-five, he was the strongest man she'd ever known, stronger than Cameron had been, or Seth. The sinuous muscles of his arms, back, and legs, had been shaped by heavy farm work in his first thirty-two years. Living in this cave for the last twelve years hadn't changed that. His body was lean and set with strength. Often, she saw how he lifted heavy crates of supplies, or carried the body of a deer over his shoulders, or lifted her easily into his arms.

118

Yet, when he touched her, he was gentle. His hands were wide and long. They moved over her like soft polishing cloths. With him, she didn't feel consumed by immediate tides of heat and fire, as she had been with Cameron. And this wasn't the desperate yearnings of his needs, as it had been with Seth. With Parker, each time there was an act of love, it was his, for her.

Slowly, she felt a coldness in herself giving in to the insistent persuasion of Parker's hands, the warmth of his body against hers, and the awakening rise of her own pulse. He pulled her into this need with the patience of his love, the strength of his arms holding her, and the pleasures he gave and needed so much in return.

As if carried in the building currents of a river, she clung to Parker, letting herself feel whole and young again. So much had gone before to deaden her spirit: abandoning her family and leaving the dome, facing Cameron's death, riding away from Montana and Seth, and finally, learning to survive, alone. But here, with this man, she knew again that there was a need in her for love.

They were slow lovers, drawn to one another as much to heal each other's spirits, as to satisfy any physical desire. She kissed him, and knew that he was thinking of his wife. He crushed her to him, his mouth against hers, his fingers in her hair.

He kissed her, and she thought of no one. The dead were dead; the past was gone. "I love you," he cried out at the end. "I love you." She held him, knowing the words weren't for her. Shuddering in her arms, she let him weep. His grief was too hard to hold alone. He needed her embrace to comfort him, and in some way he didn't try to explain, her forgiveness.

And each time, when both of them lay side by

side and still, Sidra thought: I'm only here for now. One day, I'll leave. Someday soon, I'll go home.

It was her comfort, this thought. The feeling was like the chill of winter in the air. She knew the time was coming when she would separate from Parker, and travel back to the biosphere alone. Her mother was there, Daniel, her brothers and sisters — and Trinity.

The thought surprised her. She had grown up with Trinity. He had been a friend . . . and yet, not only a friend. She lay beside T. J. Parker and let herself dream, not of Cameron, or of Seth, or even of Parker, but of a young man with sea-blue eyes and sunstreaked hair. She let herself dream of Trinity Adair, and wondered: was he the reason she was going home?

The small tribe of the People reached the banks of a branch of the Missouri River in Kansas by mid-summer. The sky stretched overhead into a blue-white splendor, reaching as far as the eye could see. The area was green prairie, the seabed of an ancient inland ocean. Here, the earth was rich ground which would grow corn, wheat, and other crops to feed the increasing numbers of the People.

"We ought to stay here," said Crystal. "We could farm this land, and the cattle would keep us alive until the first crops."

They called the place of settlement the Lodge. The structure was a long log cabin, which they found still standing, as if waiting for their arrival. They caulked the open spaces between the logs with a plaster of mud and grass, and re-roofed it with the narrow timbers of birch trees and aspens. Like their forebears, they wove vines through the lengths of saplings on the roof, twisting the ropey sinews of the vines over and under each timber, and bracing the ends of the lacing with heavy planking along the sides of the house. Tight-fitting seams of thick sod were placed over the vine-and-timber framework of the roof, to insulate the building from the cold, and hold in the heat.

That summer, they planted a garden above the banks of the river, near enough to be seen from the doorway of the Lodge. Each man, woman, and child worked in the field, turning the soil with a plow they had found in an abandoned barn, pulling the weight of it with ropes tied beneath their arms. Planting. Watering the frail seedlings with bucket after bucket from the nearby river.

Stephen bullied them into working harder. He drove the women and children until they wept, but weeds were kept from the garden that summer, and when October came, the first crop of fall harvest burgeoned like a weight of life from the yielding earth.

In all of this, Brad remained silent. When the women came to him with bleeding hands from digging and hoeing and the stoop labor of pulling weeds, he turned away from their anger and their tears. When the children cried with hunger, and were given only a small share of food, he watched and said nothing. There would be little food for anyone that winter. He knew this, and knew that Stephen, with his bullying and his hard strength, might bring them through it.

Winter would be the test of their survival. Each week, the temperature fell lower. Soon there would be a freeze, and they would be forced to live on the harvest they had gathered until spring. If they could extend their rations with fresh-killed meat, and live through the blizzards and numbing cold of this first winter, they might live to see the abundance of spring crops.

But they must survive the winter. For that, Brad knew he must stand back and let Stephen have his way.

With his son, Andrew, Brad was kind. Often he gave the boy his share of food. At night, when they were alone and Andrew was a curled warmth sleeping against his father's chest, Brad would resolve to fight against Stephen. Andrew must never know such cruelty as Stephen forced upon the People. If it were Andrew who was the age of Tanner, or Shepherd, could he stand by and allow the child to be worked so hard, and kept hungry?

It's so we might live.

Only until spring. They would survive through winter—whatever it took. But after that, Brad resolved, he would stand up against Stephen. This man who had once been a shivering boy, afraid of everything, who had grown up to become a cold whip in his dealings with the People. Somehow, Stephen must be controlled, and soon.

Crystal didn't offer again to come at night to be with Brad, nor did any of the other women. He knew they resented him for not protecting them against Stephen. In the dark and spiritless nights before the breath of winter killed the land, Brad watched the glittering stars move like armies across the sky, and thought of other nights . . . other stars.

He thought of the Lady who had saved him from the river so long ago, who had carried him in her arms and given him back his life. He remembered his vision of the turning wheel of the heavens, with prophets, healers, men and women of courage supporting the shield of sky, and the voice of the Lady who told him, "You are a spoke of the wheel."

Had he done what she'd asked of him? Had he

122

brought the People to her?

Through the night, through all the long nights of winter, Brad looked into the sky and waited for a sign. He waited for the voice of the Lady to speak to him again.

Fifteen

Earth without man was a garden without a keeper. The living seas thrived with a resurgence of life: whales and dolphins, fish of every kind, shrimp, lobster, crabs, and mussels. The poisons created by man slowly filtered from the oceans of the world, and plankton bloomed on the face of the water, yielding its rich abundance to those at the top of the sea's food chain.

In the oceans' depths, toxins—from the air, from the rivers, from soil that leached into the water table below the porous land—all descended to the floor of the seas. The earth struggled back to a living, flourishing planet.

Where the hand of man had tamed the forests, wildness returned. Deer roamed unchecked. Black bear and grizzly were free to wander a wide range. Where civilization had forced itself on the land, the natural environment was restored. From the grasslands, forests, seacoasts, and deserts of earth, the world returned to an ancient order.

No one tore deep into the earth's crust for minerals or water. Green valleys were not filled with waste. No one polluted air, or water, or land. Man had thrived on the earth's abundance, and now the last of humankind was struggling to survive.

The earth would continue without people. It would go on, with its clean rivers and azure skies. It would go on with unpolluted oceans and uncut rain forests. It was itself a biosphere, a sphere of life.

From the humid jungles to the arid deserts, nature reclaimed her own. Tough vines forced their way through the wooden frames of houses. Grass grew in the cracks along the paved highways. Buildings fell, and were replaced by trees and plants. Mankind no longer held dominion over the earth. Like all the animals of the planet, mankind's existence depended upon the forces of rain, wind, sun, and the fertility of the land.

Once again, the face of God could be seen upon the planet—in green valleys, clean skies, and black nights on the endless seas. Life returned to the injured land, from a source that was far stronger than man. Earth, like a yeast that rises to its height, awoke from the slumber and the crush of humankind . . . and from the fertile womb of God, bloomed.

The land was born again.

Cassi Hunt hid behind the curve of the corridor and watched Trinity enter Anne Innes' room. The door closed behind him, and with this blocking of Trinity from her sight, Cassi's mind began to fill in the images she couldn't see. Were his arms around Anne? Was he touching her?

Words did not come to Cassi. She didn't speak. Never had. Instead, her thoughts were fixed as nails driven deep into her mind. It wasn't hate that was dredged to the surface of her consciousness—she wasn't social enough to have developed an understanding of hate. She had been labeled autistic, never really relating to people.

Her understanding was now, and had always been, the green world of the biosphere. She knew the plants in the way a mother knows her child. She knew the sea as her own life's blood. She understood the needs

125

of the sphere: to keep life going, to nurture a replication of the outer world. In her thoughts and feelings, Cassi was part of the sphere. She would have given anything to protect it . . . except Trinity.

Only in her passion for Trinity did she break through to a real link with human emotion.

Her thought was, when seeing the man she needed above all things walk into another woman's room: how could she rid this thorn from the sphere? Anne Innis was no more than that. To Cassi, it wasn't jealousy, or hate. It was survival. That moment, as the door closed, Cassi began planning Anne's death.

Trinity waited in the small rooms of Anne's quarters. The young woman had been trained in science by her mother, and had Cathe Innes' keen appreciation for knowledge. That was why Trinity was here, to witness something Anne had recently learned.

"This isn't just chemistry," said Anne, indicating the heavier of two white mice in a glass terrarium. "There's something else going on here. Look at the difference between the two. Do they look like they're from the same litter?"

"I have to admit, they don't," said Trinity, "but that doesn't prove that your gene modification is responsible for the change. They might have been born this way. It happens in nature, without any human interference. The smaller one might simply be a runt, or the larger one an aberration."

"He's an aberration, all right," said Anne. "He's my aberration. I caused this, and I can prove it."

She brought out a second terrarium, and another pair of white laboratory mice. The size difference was identical to the first set. "Now, what do you have to say?"

Trinity considered the possibilities of what she had done. Gene modification had just begun to be prac-

126

ticed before the CXT virus put a stop to such experiments. After the onset of the pandemic, the brilliant minds of science had turned as if with one consciousness toward saving the human race from this deadly assault. All else had been put aside, including gene modification. He had to admit, Anne's results were fascinating.

"It's remarkable," he said. "My God, Anne. Look what you've done. I'm impressed."

The worried look on her face broke into a wide smile. "It's all right, then? I mean, you don't think I shouldn't be doing this?"

He understood what she meant. Since the virus had been caused by an irresponsible genetic experiment of man, the view of the biosphere community for such risk-taking research had changed. The lesson of Biosphere Four had been a convincing one. Since then, research into gene alteration, like the example Anne had just shown, had been, if not banned, at least avoided. No one wanted to be responsible for a disaster that would take even one life from their world.

"Where is it leading?" Trinity asked, not ready to answer her question. The fact was, he wasn't sure what he thought. It was important, as far as he was concerned, for man not to give up the quest for knowledge. That trait distinguished them as human. On the other hand, if Anne was playing with nature, creating a cauldron of genetic soup, then he would be the first to demand that she put an end to the experiment.

"If I'm right, we might someday be able to identify the gene which carries the virus code. That would mean we could eliminate it in utero. Those children born with that corrected gene could leave the sphere. There are a lot of other practical purposes: preventing crippling diseases in infants, altering the genetic code for cancer and diabetes, insuring the best possi-

127

ble lives for the babies born in our world. Is that so wrong? I just want the chance to study the possibilities, Trin. We can't close our minds to it and pretend we haven't seen into the future. We're part of that knowledge, and we've paid a heavy price. I think we're meant to use it."

"Your argument's convincing," he admitted. "I feel as if we've been standing still in our approach to science, without any new knowledge, as if we've been afraid to act. Maybe it's time we started an aggressive program of study again. Who else knows about this?"

"Only you. I wanted to have my first results before I came forward with this information. They're so scared to try anything uncertain, Trin. I know they'll make me stop my research. That's why I came to you first. Jessica's too cautious."

He was quick to come to Jessica's defense. "Jessica and all those of the first generation brought us through the destruction of their world. You have to understand that. They saved us, Anne. Think what it must have been like for them."

She looked immediately contrite. "I know. I love Jessica, too. She's wonderful. And you're right, the courage of the first generation brought us through the unbelievable days of that terror. I can't imagine how it must have been: knowing that the people of their world were gone, everyone they loved. They were young and strong, and they fought to save us." Her voice deepened with emotion. "But we're the young ones, now. We need our own courage to break through the barrier of their fears."

Trinity heard truth and wisdom in her words. "We'll bring it up before the committee."

"The committee!" She threw up her hands, as if this was the most useless of ideas.

"It's all we can do." He was unyielding. No one in the biosphere had the right to risk the life of anyone in the colony without the full consent of the committee.

"They'll never approve my work," she argued. "They've been here all these years without seriously trying to find a way out. We have to try, Trin," she demanded. "I can't just give up like them."

"I'm on the committee," he reminded her, "and so is your mother. Rachel Nathan's on the committee, too. We're not against you."

"Rachel! She's Jessica's daughter," Anne cried.

It was obvious from Anne's expression that she realized immediately what she'd said, and the impact her careless words must have made on Trinity. He looked away from her stricken eyes.

"Oh, Trin—I'm sorry. I didn't mean it that way. Of course, you're Jessica's son, as much as any of them, but . . ."

"Don't worry about it." His voice sounded harder than he intended. The hurt was bleeding through. "We're one people, Anne, from the oldest to the youngest. We all count. And we have to have the approval of the committee."

She didn't acknowledge what he'd said. She was looking away, staring at the laboratory mice.

"Anne?"

"All right!" she shouted. And then in a softer, resigned voice, "All right. We'll tell them."

"Good."

He had been in her room less than an hour. When he left, he felt for the first time that there was real hope for the biosphere's future. . . .

Each member of Biosphere Seven, young and old, took their turn working in the granary. It was here that the harvest was stockpiled, and the seeds reserved for next season's planting. The wheat was ground in the stone mill at the far end of the storehouse, heaped into burlap sacks and tied with lengths of twine. The swollen bags were mounded against the wide back doors of the building, in a six-bag-thick, floor to ceiling wall of grain.

The storehouse air was chalky with grain dust, and hot. The narrow twin doors leading to the farm compound were always kept open for ventilation. Anne Innes was stooped near the back wall, filling the heavy grain sacks. Later, she would grind the late fall harvest of dried corn kernels into meal, and store the bags along the opposite wall. The granary was filled with a yeasty, fermenting smell, and the air was clouded with the choking rise of fibers from the disturbed mound of dried wheat.

Anne worked alone in the storehouse, humming a tune in rhythm to her bending labor. The soft cadence of her tune continued undisturbed by the furtive movements of the second person to enter the storeroom.

Cassi slipped quietly into the granary, three coarse rags soaked in turpentine clutched in her hand. She laid the bundle of rags against a mound of dried, bundled wheat. Then, with the silence known only to those who do not speak, Cassi scraped one of the crude matches she had made from the chemicals in her mother's lab. A narrow head of fire quickened to life.

She held the burning match to the corner of one rag until the turpentine-soaked fabric caught and flared, and then threw the other matches against the yellow tongue of flame. She was out of the storehouse before the first stack of wheat sheaves burst into a crackling blaze, pulling the granary doors shut behind her.

Sixteen

Anne's first warning was the smell, sharp and oily . . . and then the sound of a stack of fermenting grain igniting, and bursting into a hill of flame.

"No!" The single word choked from her throat. It was the first time in her life she had seen an open fire. Smoke and heat in a biosphere had nowhere to go. For an instant, she was mesmerized by the look of it. The bales of drying grass sizzled and sparked. The sounds of burning blistered into her mind, spattering and popping like heavy rain. Fascinating. Terrifying.

And then a roar burst from within the mound of grain, and an eruption of searing fire shot high into the rafters of the storeroom.

Anne screamed and ran for the doors, which were shut.

The knob turned easily in her hand, but the door wouldn't open. Something wrong. Something broken in the lock. She tried again, feeling heat building behind her, hearing bags of grain ignite. The doorknob twisted uselessly in her frantic grip. There was no way it could be locked, there was no lock . . . but it wouldn't open.

"Help!" she screamed. She pounded her fists on the solid wooden planes of the doors. Would anyone hear? The storeroom had been built with thick walls to keep the temperature cooler in the granary than in the farming biome. It was the only place in the bio-sphere unprotected by a sprinkler system. The danger of accidental soaking of their only food supply was too great.

"The room's on fire!" Anne yelled. "I can't get out. Open the door!"

Behind her, a barrel of milled wheat flour exploded from the intense heat. Pieces of the barrel hit her in the back, and the long dress she wore for warmth caught fire at the hem. Stunned, she stared at the lick of flame moving up the long skirt of her dress . . . stared until the fire touched her bare legs.

The pain was immediate and horrible. She tried to rip the dress off, but couldn't hold still long enough to unbutton the back. Her legs were *burning.*

She almost beat at the flame with her hands, anything to stop the fire from hurting her. Anything . . . then she stumbled into the stack of burlap bags. She snatched a handful off the shelf and slapped the empty bags against her burning dress. The touch of the rough bags against her seared legs was excruciating, but the flame was less. She screamed, and struck at the skirt of the dress again and again, until there was only the blackened edges, and her burned legs beneath.

The fire was too close to the door. She couldn't stand the heat any longer. *Oh, God,* thought Anne, realizing at last, *I'm going to burn to death in here.*

"Help me!" she cried again, and then ran to the opposite end of the storeroom.

Her back was against the wall of grain sacks, as far away as she could get from the unbearable heat. She stared at the growing fire, a live and terrible force, trapping her. It was hard to breathe. The air scalded her lungs, and black smoke was filling the room.

The fire would have her.

But not without a fight. Something in Anne Innes that was desperate to live fought against that thought, and she began pulling at the heavy grain sacks, trying to reach the doors behind them. The sacks were fifty pounds each, stacked floor to ceiling, six-sacks-thick, and tightly pressed against the rear wall of the storeroom.

She tugged at the ones closest to her, trying to pull them free from the others . . . trying to escape before the fire touched her skin again . . . but the bags were crushed together as a solid weight, and she couldn't move them.

She knew then she was going to die. And began shrieking.

Cassi heard the screams—just frightened at first, and then filled with mindless panic. She heard, and did nothing to help Anne. She had been the one who filed off the inside screws of the doorknob. She'd known that when the spindle clicked in, it couldn't open again. With the screws gone, there was nothing to turn the bolt. It was a way of locking a door that had no lock. She'd set the fire when Anne was in the room alone, and then pulled the door shut.

Now, Anne was dying—and that was good.

It would be over soon. The cries were weaker. Smoke curled out from beneath the doors. It seeped like a flood of black water over the farmland, and rose to become a veil of clouds against the top of the dome. In a few moments, the sunlight was shut out, and Cassi stood in the enfolding dark.

She was afraid now. The smoke scared her. It was thick and choking. Anne was still screaming. Why wouldn't she stop? Why wouldn't it end?

A cold fear started in Cassi—a certainty that she had done something wrong. Anne was going to live; everyone was going to know how the fire started, and the smoke was going to strangle them all.

"Fire!"

She couldn't see who had shouted. In this dark, she was blind as well as mute, but she could hear. Others were coming; she heard their shouts over the sounds of the fire.

"Why the hell aren't the sprinklers on?" Cassi knew that voice; it was Quinn's.

As if his words had made it happen, the sprinkler nozzles mounted in the glass dome, and along the walls of the sphere, sputtered into flowering jets of water spray, drenching everything—except the granary.

She saw Trinity then. He was standing with the others, his hair and face blackened with the wet soot of the smoke. New smoke billowed at his feet. There was no end to it. The water couldn't reach the fire in the storeroom.

"Oh, God," someone said. "It's all going up."

Trinity saw her. Their eyes met for a moment, and there was a question in his. Did he know? Could he read her guilt on her face? She'd done it for him. Didn't he understand? For him.

Jessica was at the doors, standing in the worst of the smoke and heat. She used her skirt to protect her hand, and was twisting at the doorknob. "It won't open," she yelled to the others. "Get a sledgehammer. Break it down. We've got to put out the fire!"

The first blow of the sledgehammer cracked off the doorknob. With the second impact, the twin doors burst open, and a wall of fire opened before them. Flames shot out like reaching hands. Their clothes were wet from the sprinkler jets; they took off their shirts, or their skirts, and beat at the fire.

It was going to be all right, Cassi felt the breath of hope whisper in her ear. They'd break down the doors and Quinn and the others would put out the fire. The smoke would go away, and no one would know how—

A terrible cry broke from behind the wall of

134

flames. A desperate voice, screaming.

"Someone's in there," said Quinn. He was standing closest to the flames.

The shriek came again, worse than the last. Unending. Unendurable.

"It's Anne!" Trinity shouted. "My God, it's Anne. She's trapped in there."

And then he looked back at Cassi. He knew; she could see the truth in his eyes. He would never understand, never forgive her for this. It couldn't be all right between them, now. Anne had ruined everything. Before anyone could stop him, he rushed into the granary through a narrow opening in the wall of fire.

"Trinity!" Jessica cried, and rushed forward, but Quinn held her back.

"Not that way. It's too hot. We'll try to reach them from the back doors. Half of you come with me," he shouted to the group fighting the flames.

Jessica stayed with those beating back the fire. Most of them were little more than children. They needed someone to direct their efforts, and watch out for their safety, too. "Wet these!" she told Bram, and handed him an armload of sheets someone had brought from the living quarters. "Lara, get shovels from the ag wing. We'll try to bury the flames."

Jessica had turned her attention for just a moment to those young people around her, and in that fleeting instant, Cassi rushed past her into that same narrow corridor within the wall of fire. She ran into the burning storehouse—to save Trinity.

Trinity felt the heat surround him, as if stepping into an oven that baked his breath away. His skin seemed to be cooking, searing the fire into his body. With every step into the room, he felt it more. "Anne!" he called. "Where are you?"

135

He couldn't see through the smoke. Only the red branches of fire showed through. He didn't need eyes for those; he could feel them twisting close to him, and kept moving.

"Anne!" he cried again.

If she were dead, he had come into this inferno for nothing. And even if she weren't, could either of them get out alive? The way he'd taken to come into the granary was gone. He couldn't see an opening through the flames.

He moved back from the worst of the fire. It was nearest the doors they had broken down. Farther back, at what he assumed was the center of the room, the air felt slightly cooler. He took a quick breath, feeling the heat scald his throat like a boiling hot drink. He took it in anyway, for it was air, and there was precious little in this room.

He couldn't find her. She was lost in here. They were both lost, he realized. Then, in the midst of the dark, a finger of light emerged. He saw it ahead of him, and went toward it. The fire pulled at him, drawing him nearer, but he kept moving out of its path.

The finger of light was a wedge, now. His eyelids were swelling shut, but he fought to keep them open. Fought to see. He heard a shout, and realized it was ahead of him. Someone was calling his name. He could hear the voice over the roaring in his ears. "Trinity!"

"Here! I'm here!" he shouted, and stumbled forward toward the sound. His foot caught under something, and he tripped—falling over the body of Anne Innes.

She moaned when he tried to lift her.

"Anne, come on. Stand up."

They were leaning on bags of milled flour. He tried to pull her into his arms, using the wall of bags behind him as a balance, when the wall shifted. He felt the bags give, and the wedge of light became an open column high above him. This was the back door, he realized. They had opened the back door and were pulling the bags away from the outside!

"Trinity!" Quinn's voice was unmistakable. "Climb up! We'll get you out."

He tried. If he'd been alone, he could have done it—climbed the bags of grain like when he was a boy—but with Anne in his arms, he couldn't gain any height. It was getting harder to breathe. Even here, the heat was unbearable.

"Anne's with me." It was all he could manage to say. His throat felt as if it had been sealed shut by the smoke and the heat. The air was gone.

"Get an axe!" Trinity heard Quinn's shout. What would he do—break down the walls of the store-room? It would take too long. They'd all tried, Trinity, Quinn, Jessica, but nothing was going to save them.

He was leaning heavily on the bags behind him, his strength gone. It felt as if he were sliding . . . as if the earth was shifting, and he was falling backwards . . .

Trinity's head slipped through an open space between the bags. Flour dust and smoke was so thick, he couldn't see—but there was a space. It was much lower than before. He felt the bags shift, and the wall moved again. They were coming for him. Quinn was cutting through the flour sacks with an axe.

"Climb over them!" Quinn shouted. "Come on, Trinity! Get out of there!"

Anne was still in his arms. With the last effort his body could give, he lifted her into the space above him. From the other side, someone pulled her through, and out.

He was losing consciousness, his thoughts flooding from him like blood from a wound. Lifting Anne to safety had cost him his life. He couldn't move to save himself. The black smoke filled his lungs and eyes like dark water, and he slipped beneath the smothering weight of it—dying.

Other arms lifted him to the breath of air above the wall of filled burlap sacks. Other hands gripped his arms and drew them above his head, pushing him toward the open space. Pushing him high enough for those on the outside to grab his wrists. Someone held him up. He was being dragged clear, out of the mouth of the fire. He couldn't see who held his wrists and was pulling him away from the flames . . . but he looked back into the inferno, and saw who had lifted him up.

"Cassi . . ." She had come into the fire to save him.

The heat of the bags burned his skin as they dragged him through the narrow opening. The fire, so close. He couldn't breathe. He couldn't—

Then he felt himself fall into arms that supported him, and pulled him away from the heat and the smoke. There was air. He felt it scrape into his throat and lungs. Air.

A horrible crash sounded in the biome. The granary roof collapsed, sealing all that was within it into the raging heart of the flames.

"Cassi!" Trinity shouted. Reaching for her . . . reaching, but felt himself slide irrevocably toward the dark, healing shield of unconsciousness.

Seventeen

Cassandra Hunt's body was found in the ashes of the fire in Biosphere Seven. Her boldness and courage had saved Trinity's life. It had not been enough to save her own.

The world of the sphere was changed after the fire. It was as if a shroud had enveloped them. Caustic smoke hung in the air, unable to escape the dome, or be filtered to the outside. They were a sealed structure, as incapable of circulating fresh air into their living space, as any habitat on Mars would have been. They couldn't simply open a window and let out the smoke and heat.

They had managed to put out the fire, but now were forced to live in the aftermath of the flames, breathing smoke-polluted air, and seeing their world through a dark, perpetual haze.

The youngest children were the ones most effected by the drastic change. Their lungs were less able to combat the effects of a perpetual cloud of ash particles in the air, or the stinging irritation to their eyes. Once healthy, these children began showing dramatic symptoms of asthma and other respiratory and skin allergies.

"We're going to lose some of them if we can't improve the quality of the air, and soon," said Cathe Innes. She and Jessica were the only women left from

139

the five of the original team. Like Jessica, Cathe had come to terms with this place. She had allowed herself to see the biosphere as her world.

"It's not only the children we're going to lose," she went on, "but everyone. Look at the leaves on the plants in the agwing. They're yellow and dying. We won't get a crop, Jess. We'll be lucky to harvest anything, after this. And it's not going to go away. Understand that."

"I do understand," Jessie came back at her. She was angry, furious at the circumstances with which they were faced. The biosphere had never been designed to contain a fire. Not only was there smoke and heat, but gases caused by burning plastic and other toxic materials. All of that had been left in the sphere, a deadly mixture for them to breathe.

"We have to do something," Cathe insisted. "We can't live like this." She spoke calmly, but emphasized her point. "The sphere won't sustain life. Not now. There isn't a choice anymore. We have to get out."

Jessica stared at the soot-blackened walls of glass. The words of the premonition she'd had were coming true. *It's coming to an end; it's over.*

"If we go outside, the virus will kill us."

"If we stay here," said Cathe, "we'll die, too."

"Oh, God," Jessica moaned softly into the palm of her hand. "What do we do?"

"We tried our best," Cathe told her, as if she had accepted the worst. "I think all of us knew something would happen . . . another tornado, an earthquake—hell, I used to have nightmares about rats chewing their way through the sealant between the panes of glass on the dome. I thought I'd wake up one day and find a hole in the wall big enough to stick my hand through. We never really believed it would last," she said, as if offering a kind of comfort.

"I'm not giving up," Jessica came back at her. "We

can't, Cathe." She gripped her friend's shoulders in her hands. "I'm depending on you. Don't let it go, Cathe. You were there from the first day with me. Remember when Maggie died? And Piper? Remember how we pulled together then? We have to try again. We'll find a way to—"

"Not this time, Jessie. You can't save us. It's over."

It's over. The words came back at her like haunting ghosts.

But she couldn't quit the way Cathe had. Something in Jessica's spirit remained unbroken. If it was true, if they were going to be driven out of the sphere, she would be fighting for a way to save them until the very last instant. She started away, moving purposefully from the farming biome.

"Wait a minute. What are you doing?" Cathe called after her.

"I'm going to talk to Paul Schefield in Biosphere Two. Maybe he has some ideas. And if he doesn't, I'm going to try everything else I can think of. We're not dying, Cathe. You hear me? We're not dying."

"I hear you," said Cathe. "I wish I believed it, but I hear you."

"Believe it!" Jessica shouted, and then hurried away. There was no time to waste.

Paul Schefield had given up on religion a long time ago. He had seen his teenage daughter leave the biosphere dome and die in the outside world. He had seen the end come to the way of life he loved. Life now was a struggle to survive, little more than that.

When the satellite monitor signaled a message, he picked up the phone with trepidation. What would he learn? These communications with Biosphere Seven, and the infrequent visits he received from the survivors living on the coast of Wales, were Schefield's only contacts with other people beyond the walls of this dome. In a way, these satellite contacts were like messages from an unseen angel, sacred and distant.

"I need your advice, Paul," Jessica told him. He could hear the strain in her voice.

"What's the problem?" They had always been there for each other, leaders in their communities, set apart from the others in a way that marked them as different. He understood that distinction. He had lived it. He heard the pain of it in Jessica's voice.

"We've had a fire." The words were said calmly, still in control.

"How bad?" He knew the dangers a fire could produce in an enclosed area. He'd lived with the fear of the same thing happening in Biosphere Two.

"Major," she said.

He knew what that meant.

"Any loss of life?" It was an automatic question. He was used to weighing factors. Determining action.

"Two of our people were hurt: Anne Innes, and Trinity. One young woman died, Cassandra Hunt."

He remembered the name. "Wasn't she the one who didn't speak?" He imagined the face of the woman in the fire, struck with terror, and voiceless.

"Cassi was autistic, we think," said Jessica. "She either couldn't, or wouldn't, speak. No one saw her enter the building, but it looked as if she deliberately went into the burning granary to save Trinity. She loved him. He would have died in the flames if he hadn't lifted him high enough for the others to pull him free. I think it took all her strength. She wasn't able to escape."

"How terrible," said Paul. His thoughts were racing ahead. It was a tragedy about the woman's death, but the fire was the real catastrophe. "How bad is the situation?"

"We're desperate, Paul. I'm supposed to find a way

142

out of this. Goddammit! I should know what to do. They're talking about leaving the dome."

"Don't let them do it." He was certain of only one thing. The virus was still active. His daughter had died proving that.

"How am I supposed to stop them? The children are sick, and the crops are spoiled. We're being forced out."

"Going outside means certain death; remember that." He couldn't offer her any comfort. There wasn't any. He could only give her truth.

"So we stay and wait for it?" she asked.

"You stay."

"Why?" The word was a plea. He felt the hurt in it reach inside him.

"Because it's the only choice you've got."

She was silent for a moment, and then said, "When the children start dying, I won't be able to stop them. They'll leave."

He knew that was true. "Until then, you fight like hell to keep them there. Do whatever it takes, but don't let them go outside. The old earth is gone. It's final out there. No hope."

"I know," she said softly, "Cameron . . ."

"I'll try to think of something," he offered. "Call me again in a couple of days. Together, maybe we can—"

"Paul," her voice stopped him, "I woke up one morning—several days before the fire—and I heard these words in my head say, 'It's over.' It felt like a warning. The fire didn't surprise me, really . . . as though I knew it was coming. I'm supposed to *do* something," she said, her voice adamant and strong.

The world was crumbling around him. Paul Schefield knew Jessica wanted to cling to some belief. She needed him to say that he agreed with her, that maybe it was a sign of God, or hope, or something. But he couldn't believe in God, not anymore. God

143

had let mankind die. God had let Paul's daughter die, too.

"Don't wait for miracles," he told her. "Act upon the conviction that you're the only chance you've got."

"It's a miracle we're still alive," she said, and disconnected the line.

Still holding the receiver in his hand, he had to wonder if that was true. They were alive. But was it a miracle, or a curse?

The sky outside the biosphere was brilliantly swirled with red. If he were a superstitious man, he would have said it looked like an omen of something coming. But he'd given up such fantasies long ago. The strange sky probably meant a storm. He watched for another moment, then put down the phone, and walked to the wall, laying his palms against the cool panes of glass.

Beyond the dome was an earth Paul didn't belong to anymore. The immense size of it frightened him. He thought of Jessica, and the others of Biosphere Seven. Would they find a way to filter the air? Or would they be driven from the Garden like Adam and Eve, into the country of an uncertain world, where death waited at their doorstep like a hungry animal.

In the night, Jessica sat alone before the computer console. Her journal was the one thing she had kept for herself. Her entries in it were the only written record of their lives, an account of how they had held back the destruction.

In the silent room, she wrote of all they had accomplished in these nearly twenty-five years. If any of them lived, or if someone should find this journal later, she wanted them to know and understand the people of this biosphere.

She wrote: We came here for the good of mankind. We wanted to help the earth, to learn how to live in harmony with plants and animals.

What will the future world say of us? That we were careless with how we used the planet? That we risked too much, and lost? Or will they say that we were fools, unable to see the bounty at our feet?

Now, when I know it is coming to an end, I wonder if we did the right thing in bringing new lives into this plight. They had no part in our failures, or our faults. They were innocent, and yet they will die beside us, these blameless children. We brought them into being, but cannot save them, anymore than we can save ourselves. What right did we have?

I ask myself the same question over and over. At night, when sleep will not come to me and I am alone with thoughts that tear at my soul, I ask: Oh, God, how can I save them?

Jessica saved the file and turned the computer off. She stared at the blank screen, as if hoping for an answer to appear. None did. *I have to make it happen,* she thought. *Somehow, I have to find a way.*

Eighteen

The land beyond the tunnel was green and welcoming. Zechar al Maghrib rode at the head of his people. The great throng of them grew, as more and more of the Travelers emerged from the dark mouth of the tunnel. Men and women openly wept to have come safely through the channel beneath the floor of the sea. Children clung to their mothers, and the mothers held their infants above them saying, "This is your home."

Like the others, Maghrib was moved to tears by the sight of the new land. The remains of a city was set amid the rolling green hills and beside the wide waterway. A broad avenue of trees graced the sides of the paved highway along the main road. The air was fresh and fragrant with a cool breeze that smelled of rich grass meadows, oak and alder trees, and the salt breath of the sea.

It was as though a change had come to all of them. They had wandered across the many faces of the earth, gathering a people to themselves from the lonely survivors of scattered cities, and from the deserts, forests, and plainslands of their world. They had become a nation, the Travelers, and now they had found a final pasture for their herds and their families. They had come through the dark tunnel, and found a home.

Maghrib, on horseback, was surrounded by his followers. Their joyous cries and jubilant shouts enveloped him. "Maghrib!" they sang into the cold morning. "Maghrib! Maghrib!"

He laughed, hearing their voices lift with happiness. A yoke of fear had fallen away from them, and he was happy, too. The land was a green dream, a blessing they had been led to by the hand of a caring God.

"Here we will stay," he told them. "Here we will begin again the world we have lost. We are home, my people. Like the trees of this land, we will grow and set down roots. From this place, we will travel no more."

He reined the stallion hard around in a tight circle, black hooves dancing on the stony pavement, then urged him forward through the surging crowd. The throng parted, making a narrow break in the cheering circle, and through this passageway Maghrib rode, until he was once again at the head of the multitude.

From here, he led them. They carried their children, and drove their herds away from the grave markers of the city, and into the pleasant countryside, where streams of clear water refreshed them. The cattle, sheep, camels, and horses were nourished by the grasses of the valley. That night, they set their tents beneath the skies of England.

Rhissa came into her husband's tent. Their two children slept in Rhissa's shelter. This other dwelling was for Maghrib alone, and any woman he wished to invite into his arms. This night he wanted only Rhissa beside him.

A small fire illuminated the interior of the tent, and by its soft glow he watched as she drew back the camel-skin flap, and stepped into the burnished light thrown by the low flames. She wore only a simple white caftan. He could see the shape of her legs

147

through it, and the rise of her breasts beneath the thin cloth.

"You are beautiful," he said, rising from the mat he rested upon, and tracing the dark line of hair at her temple. It gleamed like black-polished water, soft and falling from his hand, the weight of it a thread connecting them.

She bent and closed the tent flap, then came into his arms. With gentle, familiar motions, they were together. Each knew the other's needs. Each touch, a caress. Each whispered sigh, the voice of love. They lay on their sides, his chest pressing against her back, his hand over her breast, and her legs locked between his.

With other women, Zechar's need for sex was a drive that spilled recklessly from him. The passion was a short fuse, lingering only long enough for the act to be complete. He had known many women, and had sons and daughters by some, but he had only known love for one woman, and she was beside him now.

In this tent, they were alone. In this tent, they were the only man and woman on earth, as they had once believed they truly were in the desert. He was not Maghrib, the leader of the Travelers, but only Zechar, her husband. With unhurried tenderness, the awakened longings of love lifted into a need that could not be held back. At last, he crushed her to him, his arm tight across her chest, his face buried in the warmth of her neck.

"You keep me alive," he said, his lips brushing her shoulder.

"Alive?" She turned in his arms, facing him.

"Knowing that I'm real," he explained, "not Maghrib the leader, but only Zechar the man."

The fire had burned low. They were silhouettes within an amber shade. His lips found her mouth, kissing the softness there, lingering at the fullness

148

along the curving bow of her smile.

"Will we settle here?" she asked, as if they had been talking of nothing else.

"Could you be happy in this place?" He wanted to know her feelings. It was important to him that this woman, with whom he had shared so much, be content. "Could this land be your home?"

She didn't answer quickly. It was as though she needed to linger on the thought. She moved away and sat apart from him, covering herself before she spoke. The glow from the fire brushed sweeps of light like paint strokes over her skin. Once again, he thought how beautiful she was.

"This country of green hills and so many rivers is strange to a Berber woman born to the desert."

He wondered what she meant by these words. Did this place seem so different to her? "We have known other green lands since our days on the desert. Are you so troubled here?"

"No, not troubled," she was quick to tell him. "The other countries . . ." words seemed to fail her for a moment, and then she tried again, "we were traveling through. This land will be home. I feel as if I've found the God of another place, one who belongs to other people, and now I want to call him mine."

Her words struck Zechar with a force he had not expected. She was a simple woman, but her thoughts were like his, born of the stark and beautiful desert.

"Do you understand my fear?" she asked, her dark eyes wide with worry.

"I know you pray in secret to Allah," he told her. "I have seen you."

She looked away, but he touched her cheek and turned her back to face him. "Surely, this God you pray to is maker of all places and creator of all mankind. Remember, we were led here, Rhissa."

"By you," she claimed too quickly.

"No," he corrected her, "by the will of the Unseen

149

One. We were brought through the channel beneath the earth. Buried. Did you feel nothing of death there?"

She nodded. "It was like a tomb. I felt the candle of my life quake in me, as if it might burn out and leave me in that dark."

"It did for many," he said. "Human life has ended for most of the world. The cries of man pleaded with their God, but they were shown only the face of the tunnel, the face of the grave."

Rhissa clung to him at these words. "Don't speak of it," she said. "Their voices are like whispers in my head. I carry them with me like an unborn child."

He took her back into his arms. "No longer will you hear them," he promised. "We have become that unborn child, going through the dark passageway between life and death, and delivered into a place of green valleys and sweet water. Can you believe this, my Rhissa? We were brought here by the hand of your God. This land has been given to us, and we are born into it as surely as any child is born of its mother. The God of this place is our God. You need have no fear."

She looked unsure.

"There are sacred places in the world," he explained. "The desert is one. This land is another. We belong here."

"I belong with you," she told him. "I know only that. If you are sure, that is enough."

He would have liked it better if his words could have taken the look of worry from her eyes, but he let the matter go, like water running between the fingers of his hand. The thoughts were too hard to hold onto, too hard to explain. He was certain. The feeling was as strongly set in his mind as his need to leave the Sahara had been. Was Rhissa right? Was it enough that *he* was sure?

She lay down beside him again, and a feeling of

peace soothed his concerns through the night. All was well. He held the world in his arms; she was all that truly mattered to him. He was a father who loved his children. He was a leader of his people, and he cared for them. But to the man, Zechar al Maghrib, this woman lying close in his arms was everything that made his life worth living.

"You are my world," he whispered. He brought his kiss to the warm curve at the base of her neck, breathed in the familiar scent of her hair and her skin, and slept.

The Travelers crossed the low hills of this welcoming land. The herds grazed in the rich meadows, and the people fished in the cold rivers. They followed the ancient pathways to the fields where cattle roamed wild, and avoided the abandoned cities with their hard roads and empty houses. The cities were warehouses of the dead. In the open country, the land had returned to nature. There, they felt welcome.

In this slow wandering across the new land, the Travelers became familiar with Britain's gentle, sloping dales and flat farmlands. They walked the earth of this country as if it were the first time anyone had seen it. They were learning its size and shape, the bounty it offered in fields, forests, and meadows. It was a sheltered haven, set apart from those stretches of earth which were the lands they had passed through on the way here.

For many weeks, the Travelers roamed the countryside, camping at the foot of the many slanting knolls and mounds which dotted the open grasslands. Windbreaks of small woods had slowly reclaimed tiny forests in spots where stone fences once marked productive farmsteads. Nature had reasserted its right to the land, and there were many places where the evidence of human settlement was roughly overgrown with shrubs, thick hedges, and a rich scattering of wild grasses once so carefully weeded from the gardens of man.

Monuments marked ancient places along the way. Zechar and his son, five-year-old Moussa, wandered out into a field where a wide ditch encircled an oval meadow, grown with standing stones.

"What are they?" asked the boy, showing only interest and not fear.

"They are markers left by the first people of this place," Zechar told him. "It says that they lived here, that they were of this valley." He lifted Moussa onto his shoulders so that the child was nearly as tall as the stones.

"Was that long ago, Father?"

Zechar didn't know the history of this place, or of these people. He only knew that humans had set the stones into the ground, and that they had wanted a remembrance of something here. He felt the sureness of that belief. "This was a holy place," he said to his son.

"Could we put up a stone, too? Could it say that we live here now?"

Moussa asked for so little. Zechar hated to deny him anything, but on this he could not give in to the boy. "Never disturb any holy place," he told him. "This was a prayer between the Unseen One and man," he explained. "No one has the right to change it."

They left the long avenue of stones, crossed the ditch, and followed the road down to where the Travelers were camped in leather tents. These were not the last stone circles they would find on the moorlands and on the flat plains of farmland across Britain. The land was seeded with them. Like the houses in the abandoned cities these stones were a graveyard, too. Only the prayers of those long dead, those who

152

had set the stones in their places, were older.

To Zechar, and to the others of his camp, it seemed as if this island in the midst of the world was theirs alone . . . until they crossed the waters of the river, and found another band of survivors.

Nineteen

Zechar and the Travelers found the cluster of British survivors living in a narrow valley, two days ride beyond the Severn River. They were twenty-four in number: eight men, six women, and ten children.

They lived in houses beside a great farm. Their herds of sheep, cattle, and other wildlife were penned into stone-fenced fields, or kept in barnyards. There were chickens and geese, goats and pigs. Dogs barked at Zechar and his people when they approached, not feral packs, but tamed working dogs guarding their masters.

Tadeo Valdez, riding beside Zechar, had drawn his weapon, ready to kill the first fiercely barking dog, a white Irish wolfhound, when a tall man stepped out from among the band of survivors and called the hound to him.

"Culluch! Come back!"

The dog turned and trotted obediently to his master's side.

Tadeo kept the long-bladed hunting knife in his hand, ready to throw if needed. He was a good marksman. If he had thrown the knife, in the next breath the dog would have been lying dead at the feet of their horses.

"Put your weapons away," said the Briton. "These dogs are no danger to you. They're tame, understand? Pets. Do you know the word?"

Zechar said nothing, but watched Tadeo. The Spaniard didn't put his knife away, but waited for Zechar to tell him what to do.

"One man has a stave in his hand," warned Phillip, who rode at Zechar's other side.

"Sheathe your blade," Maghrib told Tadeo at last, "but stay ready." He would not willingly spill blood here, not even the dog's. Berbers believed that shedding a dog's blood, like the murder of an innocent man, was a sin that stayed with the slayer for the rest of his life. He would not deliberately bring this taint onto any of his people, or himself.

"Who are you?" the tall man who had called back the wolfhound asked. He directed his question to Zechar, noting the deference paid to him by the others.

"I am called Maghrib," Zechar told him, "and my people are the Travelers."

"There are so many of you," the man seemed amazed. "How did so many live? We are only twenty-four, in all this country. Only twenty-four."

The man might have pretended to be a greater force, for his own protection. The admission struck Maghrib as honest, and so he gave honesty back to the stranger. "We are from many countries, gathered into a single band over a long time. Like you, we were small groups of survivors once."

The man stepped out from the crowd, bolder now. "Why are you here?"

"To live in this land," said Zechar. "We have been brought here by our God."

"Brought? How did you come to this island?" the man asked. "By boats?"

Phillip made a motion as though to warn Maghrib against telling these people the secret of the way they had crossed the sea, but Zechar needed no warning. "We found our way," he said, "by the will of the Unseen One."

"And where will you stop?"

"Here," answered Zechar, swinging his leg over the saddle and stepping down from his stallion. "We stop here."

The man who had stood before the twenty-four Britons was called Arthur Penn. He was the leader of the small band, if there could be said to be a leader among them. They were more of a family than a nation, a group which had clung to each other for survival.

Unlike the other seven men of the camp, the one called Arthur seemed unafraid of Zechar, or the Travelers. He stood the largest of the Britons, with hair and beard the color of autumn wheat. His skin was earth-toned too, not the white clay paleness of the others, but more the tint of a freshly turned field. His cheeks were ruddy, burned brown by the sun, and his eyebrows thick and shaggy. The great wolfhound, Culluch, was always beside him.

Two days were spent settling the people of Zechar's camp and finding pasture for the herds of cattle, sheep, horses, and camels, shepherded by the Travelers. They had become a mighty tribe of people and livestock, and spread out, they covered a wide stretch of land.

"Our Britons are fearful that you will take everything from us."

"And you? Are you fearful of us, too?" asked Zechar.

This man, Arthur, was different than the other farmers. He was never called their leader, but he was there whenever they needed someone to speak for them. He had put his life between the Britons and the new people many times since the Travelers rode into this valley. In each instance, his was an action where there had been no time to think. His protective gestures seemed instinctive.

156

Zechar noticed that Arthur didn't answer the question.

"You outnumber us," said Arthur, "and your herds graze the land our sheep and cattle must have to survive the winter."

"Your people need not live apart from us," Zechar told him. "We offer you a place among the Travelers." It was the same offer he had made to every group of people, or single person, they had met along the way. "We are a nation of many countries," he explained, "but we are one people."

The man called Arthur smiled. "You are a wealth on the land," he said, "far more than your herds of cattle and sheep."

"Then you will join us and become a part of our nation?"

"No," Arthur told him. "We are Britons."

This need for separateness surprised Zechar. "We are a people of many nations, within the Travelers. We speak many languages, have worshiped the many faces of God in different religions, and have come from countries so far apart in nature that we had little understanding of one another. And yet, we have blended into one people. Would it be so hard for the men, women, and children of this valley to do the same?"

The smile left Arthur's face. "We are an island people who have known many invaders to find their way to our shores, and though they have stayed, and became part of us for a time, we have never become anything else. We are now, and will always be, Britons."

Zechar kept his silence. This was more than a faith of words. This was a faith of true belief and strength. He admired the man, and out of respect, let the matter fall away from them like the dropping rain. Soon, he knew he would be forced to stand up to Arthur Penn for the rights of the Travelers, and for possession of the valley, but for now, he simply enjoyed the man's company.

"What name do you call the white-faced sheep that graze on these—"

His question was interrupted by a shout from young Phillip Boussard. On horseback, the boy raced across the grassy hill calling, "Maghrib, come quickly!"

"What is it?" Zechar yelled back.

"Your wife—Maghrib, you must hurry!"

Zechar had spurred his horse before the boy's last words were spoken. The stallion's hooves tore at the soft turf of the hillside, as horse and rider thundered over the grass. Fear rode with Maghrib, a terror that his sword and strength could not conquer. If something had happened to Rhissa . . . He couldn't lose her. He whipped the stallion faster, and crouched low over its strong neck. His one thought sounded in his mind like the labored breath of the beast . . . *Rhissa, Rhis-sa, Rhis-sa.*

Zechar was at the camp, but couldn't see her. He was dimly aware of Arthur Penn and Phillip's horses riding behind him. He reined the stallion to a skidding halt and turned back to Phillip. "Where is she?"

"In the barley field," Phillip shouted. "There!"

Zechar spurred the horse again, drawing the reins hard toward the lower meadow, and the stallion galloped in the direction of the field. The heath was divided spears of high barley grass, with the heads of grain waving at the top in golden wisps. At first, he couldn't find her, and then he saw where she had fallen. Her body was almost hidden by the tall grass.

"Rhissa!" Zechar cried. He jerked the reins so hard the stallion almost threw him, and leaped to the ground.

"She's barely breathing," a woman said. She was one of the Britons. "She just dropped in the field. I was with her, and there was nothing wrong. She tried

158

to tell me, but it was as if she couldn't catch her breath. Her face swelled, and then . . . oh, God, I think she's stopped breathing."

Zechar lifted his wife into his arms. Her face was swollen, as the British woman had said. Rhissa's lips and eyelids were puffed and distorted. He held her, clutching at her shoulders, not knowing what to do.

Arthur and Phillip rode into the field. They were both down from their horses and rushed to Maghrib's side in a moment. The air was still with dread. Only the drone of the honey bees hovering over the barley tassels in the field, broke the quiet.

Maghrib was frantic, calling to Rhissa over and over, and shouting to everyone near him, "What did this? What made her fall?"

"Put her down," said Arthur. He was withdrawing something from the waistband beneath his shirt.

"What?" Maghrib was confused, afraid.

"Put her down," Arthur said again. "Quickly! She's dying."

Maghrib obeyed this insistent voice. He was shaking, unable to control the very real terror that Rhissa was dying, and there was nothing he could do to save her.

He laid her down in the grass, and as he did so, Arthur's raised fist came down hard against Rhissa's thigh. To his amazement, Maghrib saw that the man had stabbed her with something.

"What have you done?" Maghrib yelled, grabbing Arthur's wrist.

"It's a hypodermic needle. She's in shock. She's been stung by a bee. I've given her an antihistamine from the syringe. It will help her to breathe."

Maghrib didn't lessen his grip on the man's wrist. A twisting movement of his hand would snap the bone. Arthur didn't try to pull away.

"There wasn't time to explain what I was doing. It may already be too late."

159

As Arthur spoke, Rhissa began to stir. She took one deep breath, as if she had been smothering and was suddenly freed. Her gray coloring began to improve, pinking more with each following breath.

"Let me take the needle out of her leg," Arthur persuaded Zechar gently. "I don't want it to break off in the muscle."

Zechar released him. He had almost forgotten the hold he had on the man. Zechar was staring at his wife, watching her breathe, watching life return to her. In a few minutes, the swelling receded from Rhissa's eyelids, and he could see into her soul.

"Rhissa. What did this?"

She tried, but couldn't speak.

"It was probably a bee sting," said Arthur. He had his hand on Rhissa's wrist, as if listening with his fingers for the life that beat there. "She was allergic to it, and her body went into shock. She would have died without the antihistamine. I think it worked. She's better."

Maghrib now stared at this man. The others stared at him, too. What Arthur Penn had done was bring someone back from death.

"Zechar," Rhissa's voice was low. "A bee," she struggled to tell him. She glanced toward Arthur, and nodded. "A bee sting."

There were many questions Zechar needed to ask, but for now, he only held his wife in his arms and rejoiced as life returned to her.

"Carry her out of here," said Arthur. He was back on his horse. "Take her to the tent, and let her rest. She'll be all right."

Zechar lifted his wife onto his horse, and led the stallion back to camp. What had happened was an experience he would never forget. He had seen a man bring his wife back from the unwaking dream of death. And he knew by the amazement on the faces of the Britons around him, that Arthur Penn had revealed a secret about himself this day, one that the others had not known. What kind of man was he? And how long had he kept this secret from them?

Maghrib wasn't sure, but he sensed that Arthur had put himself in danger by this act. If he had kept this secret from his own people for so long, why had he been willing to allow the truth to be seen now? What would happen to him, now that they knew?

Penn was much more than the simple farmer he appeared to be. He was a man with secrets. And, thought Zechar, *he is a man of mystery, and power.*

Rhissa could speak clearly, now. Maghrib walked beside her, grateful for what he still had, and what he had been given. He knew without doubt that any favor Arthur Penn might ever ask of him, he would do. He owed the man a debt of blood. Somehow, he would find a way to repay it.

Twenty

In Kansas, in the settlement the People called the Lodge, Brad McGhee prayed for a sign to be given to him from the supernatural being he called the Lady. He had not asked as Prophet, but as Brad McGhee, the man he had been long ago. With his young son as his only solace, Brad felt the loneliness of this place. The first cold frost of winter had killed the remainder of the plants in the field. The People would have no other harvest until spring.

He had asked for a sign of what he should do. His conscience made him believe that he hadn't done enough to lead the People to a kind of union with the Lady. She had been the one to save his life, to carry him in the strength of her arms from the riverbed where he lay dying. He had been blind and lost with fever. She had claimed him as one of her own, and restored his life.

But she had taken his life, too. His years as Prophet had kept him set apart from the others, made him different. He had been lonely in a way that none of them would ever understand, for he had drawn away, and not been one of them. He couldn't be one of the People, and be the Prophet who would guide them, too. Still, he had served her. For years, he had denied himself a normal human life, and been instead the spokesman for the Lady. She had claimed him and he had never sought to change that — until Andrew was conceived.

Brad rose from his bed, careful not to wake Andrew in the small cot near him. The morning was cold. The icy hand of winter was in the air. Brad bent, pushed a few branches into the low embers of the fire, and waited while they caught and started to burn steadily. Then he leaned two split pieces of kindling over the flames of the branches. In moments, the fire was warming the bedroom they shared.

Staring into the fire, Brad remembered the dream he'd had during the night. He had woken from it, anxious and desperate. It had taken several minutes to calm his fears, and to assure himself that nothing was wrong. The dream had been that intense. Even upon waking, it had seemed so real. Something terrible had happened. He didn't know what, but he understood that he needed to help in some way. If he didn't, what he loved most in the world would be taken from him. That was why he had added wood to the fire, warming the cold room, believing his fear was for Andrew.

But now, staring into the low flames, he remembered something else about the dream. In a fleeting vision, he recalled another fire, from somewhere in the locked memory of the night. There had been smoke. He remembered the smell of it. He had tried to see through the gray cloud, but ash hung in the air like a curtain. Behind the veil of smoke, danger waited.

Andrew stirred and woke. The boy's dark hair and eyes were like his mother's. His face was round and babyish with full cheeks and a sweet smile. This son, granted to him like a blessing from a merciful God, had given Brad the courage to leave with Stephen and the colony, and lead the People north.

"Daddy, up." The boy stretched his arms to Brad.

163

He lifted the child from the tangle of warm covers. Brad noticed how much Andrew had grown. He was heavier now, and had started walking. He could say several words, and make himself understood for anything he wanted by gestures. The boy was a funny little mouse, soft and warm-hearted. To Brad, this child was all he had of real life. Everything else, his role as Prophet, his part in leading the People, seemed as if it didn't belong to him.

His need to be Prophet was fading, and maybe that was why he had asked for a sign. He was afraid he was losing that part of himself which had served the Lady, afraid that he should try to hold it to him.

"We'll have some breakfast, Andrew," Brad said, and after dressing Andrew in warm clothes, carried him downstairs to the community kitchen for a meal. It was another day, and time for dreams to be put away with the dark veil of the night.

Put away, Brad thought, *but not forgotten.*

In Cheyenne Mountain, Colorado, within the manmade complex called NORAD, Sidra woke from a dream of summer. She had been floating in the water of the biosphere ocean, drifting effortlessly on her back across the flat water. Above her was the familiar triangular pattern in the glass dome, joined and meeting like a community of stars, or people. The sun was streaming through the glass, and she squinted her eyes to watch the patterns move in the bright glare. The sensation was one of flying, soaring like a bird to the concave summit, and moving among the triangle masses, clear as the sky above her.

The dream had been as gentle as the smooth water, but quickly changed. She felt a dizzy, spiraling rush just below the glass, as the dome ceiling cracked and opened. Heavy segments of triangular panes fell around her, splashing into the blistering sea. As the glass fell, she soared upward, through the broken dome and into the freedom of sky above the sphere.

It was a dream, Sidra thought. Nothing more. And yet, fully awake within the cave of Cheyenne Mountain, in this protected place that kept her safe, she felt a loss of the sense of freedom she had known so briefly in the dream.

Leaving the biosphere had been a release into that world of freedom. She had shared the few sweet days of it with Cameron. Leaving the camp of the Outsiders with Seth, Willow, and Jonathan, had been running away. And here, in this cavern beneath the mountain, she had returned to the cage. This was no more than that, a cage that sheltered and sustained her. Real life was somewhere else. Real life was waiting until she had the courage to find it. The only thing she was sure of was that it was outside this place.

The weight of that thought pressed on her mind. It held her like the dome of glass above the biosphere held the zone of life. She was as much a prisoner here as she had been inside the sphere. It was time to leave, she knew. She had healed in body and spirit. Like a bird with a broken wing, she had been caged and cared for. Now it was time for her to soar free.

Where will I go? Where do I want to be?

The answer was immediate and sure.

She rose and began to pack the few belongings she would need for her journey. She was the eldest child of Josiah Gray Wolf. Like him, she had gone out into the world, found others, and now would come back to her People. She was going home.

Freedom meant choices. She would go back to the family and friends she'd known. Like her father, she would live Outside, in the camp beyond the sphere.

This was a world beyond the keeping of the biosphere, but beside their love. She would return to the desert. She would go alone.

Her decision to go without Parker was based on more than the fact that he had left the colony of Outsiders so long ago. It was more than the reality that he had lived for so long apart from them. He would travel with her, she knew, if she asked him. But she wouldn't ask.

Just as the glass had fallen around her in the dream, so her relationship with Parker had cracked and fallen into pieces for them. She had known it always, that it would be this way, and had told him. They had been together for a time of healing for both of them. He had saved her life, and being with her had given Parker back his sanity, his life. They had each given hope and future to the other. No, she wouldn't bring him with her.

Sidra had seen a face in the dream. She had thought of Trinity often, more and more in recent days. She had dreamed of returning home . . . to the one face she wanted to see more than any other — Trinity Adair.

She wouldn't bring T. J. Parker with her to the camp of the Outsiders. She was going home to the desert, to the People, and in some way she didn't fully understand, to Trinity.

Willow Gray Wolf's body was awkward in the last heavy months of pregnancy. She stood just inside the open doors of the barn, bending over a bin of grain for the horses. The first snows of winter had fallen in the valley beside Mirror Lake, but it would be spring before the child was born. Her back already ached with the strain of carrying this unfamiliar weight. Three more months. She stood and leaned backward,

166

trying to ease the ache from her muscles.

The child within her stretched, too. She felt it moving, a swimming turtle in a human sea. Her hand came to rest over the place where the baby's foot or knee pressed its shape against her belly. She closed her eyes and let her senses drift only to that spot where she and her child touched and met.

A rush of feeling engulfed her. For that moment, she *was* the child. She knew the reaches of its internal world as clearly as she knew her own. She felt and heard the beating of her own heart, as the baby felt and heard it. She felt the warmth and darkness of the womb, *her own womb,* and the mind of the child learning the first lessons of its life, here, in this closed and isolated world.

It was wonderful. Wonderful!

A movement jerked at the side of Willow's vision. There was a swift blur, and then a sudden rush of motion knocked her off balance and almost to the ground. For an instant she couldn't breathe. Then she smelled the strong odor of the animal crouching near her.

It was a feral dog, half shepherd and half wolf, with a massive head and gray-white eyes. Willow's first thought was that the dog was starving, and had come into the barn to kill one of the yearling calves kept in the stalls through the winter. Instead, the dog had found her. The black lips of its long muzzle were curled back into a warning snarl. A low, throaty growl rumbled from behind the white points of its exposed teeth.

Thinking only to scare the animal away, Willow moved closer, waving her arms and threatening the crouching dog in a loud voice, "Go on! Get out of here! Get!"

The gaze of the wolf-dog's eyes stayed locked with hers. Watching. Waiting.

Willow took another step forward, pushing past the animal's instinctive fear of her, coming too close, invading its range of safety—and in panic, the wolf-dog lunged.

The attack knocked her to her knees. Willow twisted away, hitting the wolf-dog's muzzle with her forearm. He didn't cower away like another wild dog might have done, but came at her again. In that instant, she knew. This dog wouldn't simply savage her arms or legs. Like a wolf, it would go for her throat or belly. It would try to kill.

Her child. It would tear the child from her.

Only now did she hear other dogs. How many more, she couldn't guess, but there were quick darting movements circling her. This was a pack of feral dogs, survivors because of their size and aggressiveness. As a pack, they would bite and tear at her, distracting attention from the lead animal, who waited for his chance to close his jaw on her throat, or tear open her belly.

Now genuinely afraid, Willow touched her head to the barn floor and laced her fingers over the back of her neck. She pulled her body into as tight a wedge as possible, trying to protect her baby for as long as she could. "Jonathan!" she screamed. "Jonathan!"

One of the dogs bit into Willow's ankle, gripping and shaking her leg with the rough side-to-side motion of its head. Pain shot through her as she felt the teeth scrape against bone. She tried to kick free of this agony. Another dog bit her back, its jaw clamping onto her buckskin dress, unable to bite through, but pinching the tender skin beneath.

"Jonathan!"

The dog at her ankle could not be kicked loose. It hung on, gnawing and worrying the badly bleeding foot. She tried to pull her leg free, kicking hard, then felt the bone in her foot snap. It broke with the

168

sound of a cracking branch. An agony of unrelieved pain split through the bone and up her leg. The shock of it stayed behind the closed lids of her eyes, brilliant, excruciating.

She would have to turn over. The pain was too great. It would force her to twist and beat at the torment, exposing her throat — exposing her belly. Some part of Willow's spirit retreated inward, trying not to know this pain, not to feel it. She had been prepared for childbirth, for whatever she would need to endure then, but this piercing hurt had come without warning. The dog shook her broken foot savagely, and all that was human in Willow needed to turn over and reach for the dog, to fight back with hands squeezing around its throat. *All that was human.*

But another nature existed in Willow, that part which had guided her to safety after the tornado, that which had given her knowledge of how to save Sagamore's life, and that which had told her the future for herself and those she loved. That beyond-human nature remained whole and undefiled by the dogs' attack. It lifted what was Spirit Woman above the pain and fear, and from above her own body, she was a witness to what happened.

She saw Jonathan run into the barn, the stark lines of his face reflecting the horror of what was before him. "Willow!" he shouted. It was a cold day of winter. He had been chopping wood. In his hand was a long-handled axe. He swung the blade end of it at the pack of dogs, scattering them to the corners of the barn.

From above, Willow could see herself lying in a pool of blood, one leg dragged straight from the huddled body and twisted. She felt nothing. From here, she saw that Jonathan stood between the growling dogs and the barn door. She felt and understood the panic of the trapped animals; it beat like wings at

169

her spirit. Their terror pulsed as a living thing, and she knew that because of their fear, they would act.

She wanted to shout to Jonathan. *Move!* She wanted to cry out that the dogs would run from the barn if allowed to escape. They were afraid, and their fear would turn to aggression. They would attack him because he had given them no choice. From this place of witness, she could see, and knew, all that would happen. She wanted to warn Jonathan, but she couldn't. The watcher could not speak.

Spirit Woman remained in this protective place, like an unseen cloud hovering above those below her. She saw the lead dog leap at Jonathan. The others of the pack moved as one joined motion, following the wolf-dog's attack.

Surrounded, Jonathan beat at them with the axe, swinging the wide blade in a killing arc. The wooden handle struck one dog squarely on the head. It dropped lifeless to the floor. The lead dog's teeth sank into Jonathan's shoulder, the dog's weight forcing Jonathan to his knees . . . exposing his throat to the pack.

From the floor of the barn, Willow screamed her husband's name. She knew. The child in her knew. Her spirit hovering above them knew. Defending his wife and child, fighting off the pack of feral dogs to save their lives, Jonathan would lose his own. On this day, in this hour, he would die.

He struck at the dogs before him, killing another, wounding a third. Two more raced at him with bared teeth and savage growls. The wolf-dog hung onto Jonathan's shoulder, pulling him forward, trying to drag him low enough that the others could finish the kill, but Jonathan struck at the lead dog. He swung the axe and cut a deep gash in the wolf-dog's side. The axe hit bone, and stuck. Blood spurted from the wound, and from Jonathan's shoulder.

The dog, finally letting go of Jonathan's shoulder, tried to bite at the axe imbedded in its side. Man and dog slid together to the straw-covered barn floor. The two other dogs were on Jonathan now, excited by the blood. He held his hands before his face, and they bit his arms and sides.

Drawn back from the safety of that place of witness, by her husband's need, back into the pain of herself, Willow tried to stand, fell, then crawled to Jonathan's side. With all her strength, she pulled the axe free from the animal. The wolf-dog whined, but didn't move. She swung at the two dogs that were savaging Jonathan, but missed. Both ran from the barn, escaping.

Willow's foot was badly broken. A splinter of bone stuck out of the skin just above her ankle. She couldn't put any weight on her right leg. Even to drag herself the few steps across the barn had been an unbelievable agony.

"Kill it!" Jonathan cried to her. His shoulder was spurting blood. She knew from the look of the wound that the dog had taken her husband's life. All her medicines wouldn't be enough to save him. He had lost too much blood.

She raised the axe. On her knees, she lifted the heavy axe and meant to split the skull of the wolf-dog . . . but something stayed her hand. A look of awareness was in the dog's steady gaze, as if it knew that she would take its life, even as it had taken Jonathan's. The dog knew, and waited, unable to escape its final moment.

"I'm going to get help," Willow told Jonathan. "You saved my life," she said, "my life, and our child's. I will never forget that . . . or you."

Willow lowered the wedged head of the axe to the ground, braced her hand on the smooth end of the wooden shaft, and stood, putting all her weight on her left leg. Using the axe as a crutch, she hobbled from the barn, through the snow, and into the house.

By the time Willow's brother, Yuma, raced from the house by the lake, Jonathan Katelo was dead. The wolf-dog had disappeared, dragging itself from the barn and into the cover of trees and snow, where, despite a thorough search by the four young men of the house, it was never seen again.

Twenty-one

For Seth Katelo, the long trek west had been a hardship and a time of learning about himself. He had discovered that he could be alone, afraid, but not stopped by his fear. Fear was a common thing, as much a part of him as breathing. It made him careful, watchful for any sign of trouble. He was stronger because of his fear. He had learned to use it, and learned how not to let it control him.

Traveling had become a familiar way of life. In what seemed like a long time ago to him now, he had ridden south to the biosphere with Jonathan, and had thought that if he and his brother were parted somehow and he were left alone, he would die of that terror. Being alone. But he hadn't died. Instead, he had found a new beginning. He had traveled north again to the house by Mirror Lake, and to his family.

Now, endless days of riding across the land seemed to be what his life had become. He'd seen so much in the time since he'd left Montana. He'd seen a wide sweep of a world that seemed to have been waiting for something. He was one man, alone—and this was the world that was left to him.

Often, in the night, he thought of Sidra. He looked at the blind eye of heaven and remembered the meaning of her name—inheritor of the stars. Where was she now? Was she happy? Was she alone? The thoughts were kind wounds, those that slowly bled away the pain of losing her, giving him time to heal from within. And he was healing. He felt stronger, depending only upon himself for survival. He knew a satisfaction that came with this freedom.

The days of travel had often been rough and sun boiled, but now the weather had turned cold. Winter held the life of the land, and Seth's life, also. Like the earth, he would live or die by the forces of nature. If the land died, the animals that lived on it would die as well. If that happened, there would be nothing to sustain man.

Winter, he discovered, was milder in the west. He had journeyed south and west, crossing through a mountain pass, beyond an arid desert, and into a western rain forest. From there he had traveled south, through another kind of forest. Trees stood like giants in that place, and Seth knew a solitude there that he had never felt before. He had never known a church, but in that cathedral of living spires, he felt a communion with God, if there was one, or with nature if there wasn't. *Or maybe, the two were one.*

The thought came to him in that place of high trees and broken sky. In its simplicity, this belief became the seed of Seth's religion. The power of this unnamed faith carried him through the many weeks of travel to come, when he was alone and hungry, and when he felt overwhelmed with fear. Like the earth itself, he turned to that God and nature who renewed and supported life.

He left the forest, and rode for many days across an open grassland that was rich with game. In an impulsive act not learned from anyone, Seth built a small fire as an offering to this God he now called upon by name. On the fire, he placed small bundles of sweet dry grass, precious grain from the leather pouch carried in his saddlebags, and a portion of the deer meat which allowed him to continue in this wilderness.

174

The scented smoke rose to the wide, dark mouth of heaven, where Seth hoped God would see the fire, breathe in the fragrance, and look down upon him with compassion. Beside the fire, he dug a narrow pit in the earth. There, he planted the seeds of grain, in an offering to the life force that was in and of the land. The two were the same force, he knew, in the land and above. The two were one, and he was an equal part of both.

The offerings had been small gestures, but after he'd made them he felt less alone. The sky no longer threatened. It seemed to watch over him. The earth held his footsteps and supported his life. He spoke to the ground, trees, and sky, as though all were living beings, like himself.

"It's turning colder," he said. "Won't be much longer before the first snowfall. You trees will stay warm enough with your feet tucked into a blanket of ground. Can't say the same for me. I'll need a shelter, plenty of wood for fires, and something to live on until spring."

Each day, he rode west, sure that the snows of winter would stop him soon, but the snow didn't fall. A deep cold swept across the land. The grass whitened and withered. Leaves fell from all but the evergreens, and the evidence of game thinned in the valleys — but it didn't snow.

With nothing to stop him, Seth kept moving onward in his journey. He rode west toward the setting sun. Each night of winter, he thought, *Tomorrow it will snow, and I'll be forced to remain here.* But each morning there was no snow, and he went on. Day followed day. Week followed week. Nights bundled into months.

And then, one perfect morning, he was there. The salt he had smelled all that day was there before him. An ocean of blue-green water, unimaginably wider than any lake he had ever seen. Unlike the glassy stillness of a lake, the ocean moved with a rhythm of its own, rising to frothy peaks in the sea, then crashing onto the sandy shore and moving out again.

The sound drew Seth closer, the waves a heartbeat of sound — the living breath of the sea. He stood before the greatness of it, stunned and filled with awe at its majesty. Here was the Pacific of which his mother had spoken. For this he had left everything and journeyed alone from his home beside Mirror Lake. He dropped to his knees in the shallow surf, letting the water wash over his legs, and spoke to the water like a welcome friend.

"I've come so far to get here. Today, seeing you, my journey has ended. This will be my home."

There were many shelters along the beach for Seth to choose from, houses that had once been living places for man. In one, he found a ready supply of stored driftwood, more than enough to build the small fires which would keep him warm through the end of winter. In another he found the woman.

She was as tall as he, slim-waisted, but with a strength that was evident in arms and legs, and the straight line of her back. Her hair was long and dark, falling like a shining weight from the high forehead and along the sculpted borders of her high cheekbones. She was young, not yet twenty, with a gentle face, gray-green eyes, and a brightness burning in her cheeks like twin offerings of fire.

Her name was Rebecca. If she'd ever had a family name, she had forgotten it long ago. Here she didn't need one. She had been alone since the age of a little child. She couldn't tell him what had happened to her family, or remember them. They had simply gone, and she had been left alone to live.

To Seth, Rebecca was his family as soon as he saw her. It was as if she had been put there at the end of his journey to be the new life he had traveled so far to find. They asked few questions of each other. The

176

past didn't matter. They had both learned to live with being alone, and yet they had found each other. It was enough for Seth that Rebecca was there when he awoke. He fell asleep each night listening to the slow, steady rhythm of her breathing beside him.

He remembered that once it had been like this for his father and mother. They had been all there was for each other, until children made their two lives many. It became his hope that one day he and Rebecca would know children of their own, and that these lives would be as full of happiness and peace as the lives of his family beside Mirror Lake.

When he thought of Sidra now, he wished her well, for he was free of his need of her at last. Willow had promised that something was waiting for him. She'd been right. A woman named Rebecca had been waiting. He had found a better understanding of himself, that he could be strong alone. A place of beauty and peace had been set apart as if especially for him — a blue-green ocean called Pacific.

Winter in the flat plains of Kansas bore down upon Brad. Like the others, he felt the heaviness of the endless days of cold. It was as if a chill breath had blown the spark of life from the land. The earth was barren. The seeds in the ground waited. The hungry animals in their dens waited. With one mind and one heart, the People waited, too.

Tempers were short in the Lodge. Stephen drove them to work harder than they felt was necessary, and could be cruel in his words and actions. Two days ago, Brad had seen him strike one of the children, six-year-old Dillon. The boy had forgotten to do some task Stephen had required of him, and the man's temper had found an easy target in the fear of a child. He'd struck the boy hard on the cheek. For

177

that, Brad had pushed Stephen to the ground.

"You won't touch any of them again, Stephen," he'd warned, meaning the implied threat. "I've allowed you to bully them until now, but we've had enough. Remember, you're one of us, not above us, and it's time you understood it. Never lay a hand on any of them—"

"Or what?" Stephen mocked him. "What will you do, *Prophet?*" The name was spoken as a taunt. Stephen glared at him in undisguised anger. "What would you do to protect the People? Would you kill me? Would you do anything except pray to your God? Your Lady? Ask them!" Stephen shouted. "Ask them who they trust with their lives. Me, who forces them to work? Or you, with your endless prayers?"

Brad glanced at the faces of those gathered. They stared at the floor, and no one would lift their gaze to meet his eyes. It was clear that much of what Stephen had said was true. He had allowed Stephen's tyranny for too long. No one trusted Brad to protect them anymore. They had lost their faith in him, and what he represented.

"They may fear me," Stephen taunted him, rising to his feet, "but they despise you. You're weak, and they know it."

The hard truth of Stephen's words struck Brad like a felling blow. He knew that Stephen would say anything to hurt him, but there was a truth to his bitter words that couldn't be denied. In many ways, he had been weak. He had allowed Stephen to become a tyrant, and they had all suffered as a result of this.

"You're right about me," he admitted to the cowering boy, grown up to become the bullying man before him today. "In many ways, I haven't been strong enough for the People. I let you drive and frighten them, because I believed our situation was desperate."

He made eye contact with Stephen, and in that message, there was no mistake. "We're here now, and they're safe. That dangerous journey is behind us. Understand me," he warned Stephen, moving a step closer, "I won't let you hurt any of them again. If you try, I'll stop you, with whatever that takes."

Stephen's eyes glared hatred at him. "I'm the leader here," Stephen said angrily, "and everyone knows it!"

"Remember what I've told you," Brad warned him, then turned to walk away.

"I'm not afraid of you!" shouted Stephen. "I'm not afraid of anything!"

But Brad was afraid—afraid that the day was coming quickly when he would have to choose between protecting the People, and keeping his vow of peace, prophet, and spokesman for the Lady who was his God.

Each day, Brad felt farther and farther removed from the feelings and duties of a prophet. His heart had turned away from the voice of the spirit, and back to the needs of a man. He thought of the women and children of this place, his own son among them. He thought of Jessica. More and more, as the long winter days turned into sleepless nights, he thought of the woman who had been his wife so long ago.

In bed, he closed his eyes and remembered. They had been young. The world had been a place of future and hope. They were in love, and eager for the life that awaited them together. He remembered his wedding night, when he'd held Jessica in his arms and promised he would never leave her. Promises broken, and promises kept. He had left the camp of the Outsiders, but in his heart, Brad had never left her. He carried the image of her with him, always.

A dream of love surrounded him, and within it he

saw Jessica's face. She was behind the glass wall, beyond his touch. Her eyes were pleading with him in words he couldn't understand. *Jessie.*

The truth was, he was alive again, as if he had come back from the dead. His years of serving the People as their prophet were over. Something in him had changed. He had returned to the man he had been when Jessica was his wife, and now he was simply Brad McGhee.

The dream reached out for Brad: in Jessie's pleading eyes, in her arms stretched forth and trying to touch him, in the words he couldn't understand. All that he wanted was to go to her—man, husband, father. All that he was tried to reach through the glass to this woman who was his past, and future.

A darkening swirl pressed between them. It filled the glass like a thick cloud, and he knew that he was losing her. Her face was hidden, and the shadow tore her from him as surely as death. Then he saw the flames.

Brad awoke knowing that what he'd witnessed was not a simple dream. It was a vision, certain and intended for him. He had prayed for a sign, and at last, one had been given to him. He had no doubt that what he'd just seen would happen, or had already happened. *Jessica in a fire.*

His body was cold and shivering in sweat, a reaction to his fear for her. *Had she died?* No, he calmed himself. If Jessica had died, somehow he would know.

She needed him. The dream had been a warning, a cry across the wilderness. He had felt her terror and the call of her voice. He had to go to her.

How could he leave the others? It was winter, and the People were struggling with their own hard battle for survival. Stephen was a threat to all of them.

Strangely, it was Stephen who forced the decision. As if playing a role decreed by fate, this bullying man brought everything to a head. Man asks, Brad understood, and God answers—although not always in the way man expects.

The answer to Brad's prayers came on a day of reckoning between himself and Stephen Wyse. There was no choice, and after what followed, there was no other way but the path that would lead Brad and his son back to Jessica and the biosphere.

Twenty-two

Shepherd Hallinger, Walker Gray Wolf, and Tanner were the oldest boys living in the Lodge. Because of their closeness in age and their shared hardships, the three had become loyal friends.

Tanner, the eldest at fourteen, was still the newcomer to the People. After the rough start he'd made with everyone, and having been left behind by the group on the journey to Kansas, Tanner had never again tried to reclaim his control over the younger children around him, or of anyone else. Instead, he worked hard, said little, and stayed out of Stephen's way as much as possible.

Walker Gray Wolf was looked upon by many as his father's replacement. He was tall as his father had been, and shared the darker Indian coloring that set him apart from the others. The way he thought set him apart, too, for he was not like his father in his attitude concerning the People. He had always been one of them, and never hoped to become a leader, like Sagamore. He wanted nothing more than to hunt and fish, to grow a crop in its season, and to play pranks on his friends.

In judging these three boys as future rivals for his control of the People, Stephen Wyse wrongly singled out Walker as his main competition. Walker was Sagamore's son, and it seemed most likely to Stephen that this young man would be the one to try to wrest his position from him. Stephen wasn't about to let that happen. He didn't need to hurry; there was no rush. He took his time and carefully planned a way to rid himself of Walker Gray Wolf. It would be a hunting accident. No one could hold him to blame after the young man was dead.

What Stephen failed to notice was that the youngest of the three boys, Shepherd Hallinger, was the only genuine challenge to his control. Singled out by Sagamore for his training, Shepherd was the boy who had found his way back across the desert alone to save Sagamore's life. He had listened to the stories told beside a lonely campsite when Sagamore had taken him out alone and taught him to hunt and track. The lessons learned from these stories were far more than how to bring down a pronghorn antelope, or break a horse, or follow animal tracks washed out by rain. The lessons had taught Shepherd how to become a man the People would turn to one day as their next leader.

Sagamore had known and told Shepherd long ago. It was the first time Sagamore had spoken directly to him, not simply answering a question. He had said, "You are the first of the young men of our camp."

"I'm not the oldest," Shepherd told him, thrilled to have heard himself called a man.

"There are others who are older," Sagamore agreed, "but you are the first."

"The first?" Shepherd had wanted to understand. He had wanted the words to mean what he'd hoped they meant: that Sagamore thought him special, that this wise one noticed him as being apart from the rest of the boys of camp, that he saw him as becoming a man like himself.

"You are the novice now, listening and learning, but one day the novice will be called upon to lead the People."

This was much more than any dream Shepherd had

ever imagined for himself. His hope had been to learn the ways of a hunter, the ways of a man. What Sagamore said frightened him. He hadn't known what a novice was, but he'd known what it meant to be the leader of the People, like Sagamore, and had never thought to be such a one.

Now Sagamore was gone. Shepherd couldn't go to him and ask the many questions which filled his mind. *How would they live until spring?* The thought of starvation was with him, and he feared for the People. Many were too young to hunt or provide for themselves. The winter was harder in Kansas, the snows deeper and the wind blew against them like crystal knives. Already, some of the children were sick. He wasn't sure what to expect from this new land. What would keep them alive if the snows became too high and stopped them from hunting?

What should they do about Stephen?

The man was too hard on the weakest of the People. Stephen had grown in his own eyes since Sagamore's death, since the day they left the camp of the Outsiders. He had become something cruel and fearful. It was known that Stephen had a gun, and the bullets for it. Where he came by such a thing Shepherd didn't know, but he was sure that if angry enough, the day would come when Stephen would use this weapon—not as a hunter of game, but in an act of violence upon one of the People.

And finally, if Sagamore were here, Shepherd would ask him the other great question that troubled his heart and mind. *What does a man do for a woman to make her notice him?*

What he wanted was for Kara to notice him. She was beautiful, and gentle, and loving. Her blindness kept her from seeing the look in his eyes when he watched her. For that, he was grateful. He found himself watching her so often. How would he explain how he felt to her, if she could see the longing in his face? If she saw, she would know. He felt the same way about her that Tanner did. He loved her.

Sagamore would have known the answers to these questions, but Sagamore was dead. Shepherd had no one to turn to for guidance but himself. The questions remained like mountains in his path. Always, he was thinking and worrying a way around them. He was thinking of what Sagamore would do if he were with them on that morning Stephen called Tanner, Walker, and Shepherd to him, before the eyes of the People.

"These three boys will soon be called men among us," said Stephen.

Shepherd was embarrassed by Stephen's words, as if some visible change had come over him and the other two, a change that everyone could see. Stephen's announcement would make it clear, even to Kara, that there was a difference about him now. Her recognition of that difference was something he desperately wanted, yet didn't want. It was a secret joy and torment, and he hated Stephen for calling the attention of the People to something so private and personal.

"We are a gathering," said Stephen, "a tribe of mankind like those from many places in our forgotten world. Like those young tribesmen of old," said Stephen, "these boys need to be given the chance to prove themselves, to leave their boyhood behind and be recognized forever after as men."

"What is this, a test?" whispered Walker. "He's crazy. I don't trust him."

Stephen turned and stared at all three boys. If he'd heard Walker's reckless words, he didn't let his feelings show. His face was cold with anger, but there was nothing in his tone of voice to mark a change when he said, "I'm leading them on a special hunt."

185

There was nothing obvious to be seen, no smoldering rage or exploding fury.

Shepherd stared into the cold wells of Stephen's eyes. What he felt returned in that gaze was Stephen Wyse's fear. He knew the man's unending terror, felt it like a pull at his own courage. Stephen was afraid of *them*.

A man who's that afraid is dangerous, Shepherd thought. He didn't want to go on the hunt. He fingered the bear claw on the leather cord around his neck. It had been Sagamore's gift to him, a totem to protect him from harm. With Sagamore gone, would the totem still have power? Would it protect him now?

Where's Prophet? Shepherd wondered. *Why isn't he stopping this?* He looked for the man, but Prophet was not among those in the gathered crowd. It was clear that Stephen had waited until Prophet was away from the Lodge to call for this trial of manhood. Again, Shepherd wished he could think of a way to avoid going anywhere with this man. Stephen was behaving like a cornered animal. Even a rabbit will strike out when its terror becomes too great for it to bear. From what Shepherd could see in Stephen's eyes, the man's terror was already over the edge of sanity.

"This is stupid. Let's refuse to go," he said to Walker and Tanner.

Tanner stared at him, an unspoken question standing like a space between them. "I'm going."

"Me too," said Walker. "If Mr. Wyse-ass wants a show, I think we ought to give it to him."

Shepherd saw that Stephen had overheard the remark. There was a slight twitch of Stephen's eyebrow in Walker's direction.

"Shut up!" Shepherd warned his friend. "He's listening."

"Who cares if he listens?" Walker was grinning, boasting to prove his bravery before them. "I'll say it louder if you want."

"No," said Shepherd. "Don't." Walker was his friend, but he was too much of a risk-taker. Walker liked to be dared, liked to push things to the end, and sometimes over the edge. It was a trait that made him exciting to many people. Adventurous. Only this time Shepherd understood where Walker's reckless brand of courage was leading them. It wasn't to adventure, but into danger, and maybe death.

"Are you ready?" Stephen asked. He spoke in a voice loud enough for all the People to hear. It was a challenge.

Walker strode over to stand beside Stephen. Tanner followed close behind. Shepherd waited a single heartbeat . . . two . . . and then he made the decision, and walked slowly to where his friends now stood.

"Good!" called Stephen. "Mothers, childhood friends, all of you," he called to the crowd, "say goodbye to these young ones. They leave this day as boys; what comes back to you will be men," his voice was high and loud. "The future leaders of this camp!"

A hesitant cheer lifted from those families gathered before him. Merry Logan looked uncertainly at her son. It was clear that she'd had no warning, and had been as unprepared for this event as Shepherd now felt. He smiled at his mother, hoping to ease her worry. The smile she gave back to him was cautious, and guarded. It was obvious that she was afraid, too.

"I need Shepherd to stay home with me," she told those around her, never looking directly at Stephen, as if she couldn't bring herself to stand up to him. "I need help with the baby, and Shepherd's too young for this. I need him here." Her voice broke with these

187

final words, and she looked pleadingly at the other women and children of the camp.

No one spoke up in her support.

"Mothers always see their sons as children," said Stephen, laughing off her concerns. "You've depended upon him too much to help you with the baby," he added, tipping Merry's face up to stare at her. "It will be good for both of you to have a break. I won't have any mothers leaning so heavily on their sons that they cripple them. We need men in this camp, and men we will have."

They left immediately, trailing after Stephen as he made a great show of leaving camp. A few called words of encouragement to them as they passed. Dillon cried, "Bring me a bearskin, Tanner."

Shepherd slowed his steps as he passed near Kara. She was at the back of the crowd that had parted to make a path for them. As he came near, Shepherd reached out an arm and hugged her to him. The crowd laughed at his boldness, and then cheered, covering the sound of the words he whispered into Kara's ear. More than anything, he hadn't wanted Stephen to hear.

"When Prophet comes back to camp, tell him to come after us," Shepherd whispered hurriedly to Kara. "Stephen's planning something. I think he wants to kill us. Do you understand?" he asked her quickly.

She nodded. The smile had gone off her lips.

"No one else," he warned. He couldn't see into Kara's eyes. They were like closed doors hiding her thoughts from him. Her face was a serious mask, not revealing the worry his words must have cost her.

He took a step away, intending to follow Tanner, but then as much of a surprise to himself as to anyone, turned back, and to the delight of the people

188

gathered around them, leaned close to Kara and kissed her on the lips.

Shepherd had to run to catch up with Walker and Tanner. Stephen was far ahead, leading the way to the hunt he had planned. The sky was the color of dirty ice, and a cold wind sang in Shepherd's ear. It sang of winter, and snows that had fallen a thousand years before. It sang with a voice from the lonely grave. It sang of the dark, unending sleep. It sang of death.

Twenty-three

When Brad returned home, the Lodge was in an uproar over the hunt. Strident voices sharp with tension came at each other like clashing storms in the night.

"We shouldn't have let them go," said Merry. "They're too young, and it's winter. Why does he want them to hunt in the dead of winter? We have enough meat for now. Why did he do this?"

"Stop complaining!" said Crystal. "You're always whining about something, and I'm sick of listening to it. Stephen took them for a hunt as a special favor. He's trying to do something nice for your son, for all three of those boys, and all you can do is complain about it. Why don't you stop feeling sorry for yourself? Do something useful for a change. Make your son some new clothes. Have you looked at what he's wearing lately? Do you ever look at him? The boy's in rags. Think about that instead of trying to scare yourself over nothing. They're with Stephen, after all. They'll be perfectly all right."

Everyone knew that Crystal had been sleeping with Stephen in recent weeks. The two were an odd pairing, especially since everyone thought Crystal hated Stephen for threatening to leave her behind when her baby became sick during the journey to Kansas. Brad had thought Crystal would never forgive Stephen for that, but she had surprised him. It was Brad she hadn't forgiven. She had turned to him for help, and he had failed her. After that, she had turned more and more to Stephen. Now, apparently, she felt that all of them should trust Stephen.

Brad wasn't so sure. He didn't like the way this sounded. Why hadn't Stephen told him about the hunt? He could have waited until Brad got back to camp. The fact that he didn't wait said that he hadn't wanted to be stopped.

"What do you think?" Merry asked Brad. "Are the boys all right with Stephen? Are they safe?"

He didn't know how to answer her. As far as he was concerned, no one was safe with Stephen Wyse. The man had become a danger to them all. He didn't want to worry Merry, or the others. It might be that he was making too much of this. Stephen had done impulsive things before. It was possible that this was nothing more than that. Possible . . .

"Prophet," said Kara, "I want to tell you something."

The girl he'd found cowering in a dark attic had now become a graceful young woman. She pulled at his hand urgently.

"It'll have to wait, Kara. I have to find out what Stephen's been up to while I've been gone." He gently pulled his arm away.

"That's what I need to tell you," said Kara. "Come on." She pulled at his wrist insistently, and after a second thought, he willingly went with her.

"Are we alone?" she asked, when the noise of the camp was a hushed sound.

"We're alone. What is it, Kara?"

She started to say something, her lips moved, but for a long uncomfortable moment, no sound came forth. When it did, it was a choking sob. The eyes that saw nothing brimmed over with tears, and she cried as if in pain, as if she couldn't catch her breath.

"What is it?" Brad put his arm around her back. He could feel the thin points of her shoulder blades against his muscles. She was small, and shaking in fear. "Take a deep breath," he said gently. When she'd done it, he added, "Now, tell me. What's wrong?"

"Shepherd told me something, right before he left with Stephen."

Brad didn't like the way this was beginning to sound. "Go on."

"He said not to tell anyone else," she cried.

"Tell anyone else what?" Brad pressed her, knowing it was hard for her to say the words, knowing she was hurting with fear. "Help me, Kara. I can't do anything for them until you tell me what Shepherd said to you."

She knotted her hands together, knuckles working in knobs of living flesh. "He said to tell you to come after them. You have to hurry. Prophet, he said he thinks Stephen wants to kill them."

Brad felt the chill of the day deepen. It was dark in his soul, dark and trembling. The boy was right, he was sure of it. This was what Stephen intended. This was why he had waited until Brad was gone so he couldn't be stopped. Stephen's insane fear of anyone daring to threaten his power had driven him to this action. He would take three boys on a hunt, thought Brad, but the quarry would be the boys themselves. Was he crazy enough to kill all of them? Or would he try to make it seem like an accident, killing only one?

Which one would it be? The thought horrified Brad. He was trying to decide who would die. "Come on," he said to Kara, taking her by the arm and leading her back to the Lodge.

"Can you stop Stephen?" Her tears were dried and gone. She was calm again. No one would be able to tell she'd been crying. A quiet acceptance had seemed to come to her.

"I'm going to try," Brad promised. "You wait for us here," he said, putting her hand on the stair railing of the house.

"Don't let Stephen hurt them. If you hurry —"

"I'm leaving now," he told her.

"What about Andrew?"

"He's been with Emily since earlier today. She'll be willing to watch him a little longer for me, I'm sure. Whatever happens, Kara," he added, "you did your best."

He left her standing at the bottom of the steps. It was an image he would carry with him on the hunt: the still grace of this sightless young woman, waiting with faith and hope for her dream of peace to become truth.

Stephen led Walker, Tanner, and Shepherd to a cave far away from camp. He knew the cave; it was one he'd found while exploring weeks ago.

"This will protect us from the worst of the cold," he called back to the three boys. He'd run them hard for the last two miles, and they were straggling, forced to keep up with his relentless pace. "Gather some wood before you climb up to the cave, he shouted, as they stood gasping, trying to catch their breath. "We'll build a fire to keep warm, and then we're going to talk."

He saw their heads lift at that. They didn't like it, but they'd do things his way. That was the point of being here. He would control what happened, and when. He stood at the face of the cave and stared down at them. *They think they are so smart.* He remembered what it felt like, being a teenager. He'd been a teenager when the old world died. Everyone had left him — his mother, his father, everyone who'd promised to love him and keep him safe.

193

After they died, he'd had to become his own protector. There wasn't anyone else to look out for him. He'd had to grow up fast. And he'd been alone, not like these three. Even Tanner hadn't really been alone. He'd had the adults of his group with him for awhile, and then . . . at least Tanner had the other children. No one among the People knew what it was like to have been a young boy left alone in the world. How afraid he'd been. How afraid he was, even still.

These boys wanted everything Stephen had. He knew they thought they could become leader, each one of them. That wasn't going to happen. He watched them climb up the steep slope to the cave, stacks of dry kindling in their arms. And he thought, *It'll just be an accident. No one will ever know.*

Tanner came into the cave first. He was carrying the largest armload of wood, and he was the tallest of the three boys. Walker was nearly as tall, and bent over with the weight of the kindling he brought. Shepherd was the youngest and the smallest of them. He carried little firewood in his arms, but his eyes had a watchful stare, as if he was waiting for something to happen. *Did he suspect?*

"Drop the kindling near the back," said Stephen. "It'll stay dry there, even if it snows. Looks like we've got enough to get us through tonight." He gave the three a friendly grin.

Walker grinned back at him; the boy had an easy smile. A fool. Tanner looked away, glancing at the floor of the cave. The kid knew enough to be afraid of him; that was good. Stephen's glance moved to Shepherd. The boy was staring at him. There was something in his eyes Stephen didn't like. It wasn't fear. He'd have used that against the boy. No, it was something else, pushing back when Stephen pushed.

He felt a little thump in his heart. Why was the kid staring at him like that? Maybe he'd got it wrong.

194

Maybe this was the one he should kill. You couldn't tell with little snakes. They grew up, some of them mean as vipers. It was always best to stomp 'em early, he'd learned; then you didn't get fanged by sixteen-foot rattlers.

Shepherd felt a heat inside him that was not from the fire. It was an uneasiness, working and working through him, his whole body ready for something to happen.

"You looking at something, boy?"

"I'm watching the fire behind you," Shepherd said, and pointed to the dancing images on the cave wall.

"Come on over here," Stephen told him, and made room beside himself. "Now you won't need to be looking through me, will you?"

"I thought you said we were going to hunt," Walker complained. His long legs were stretched casually close to the ring of firewood.

He's not like his father, thought Shepherd. Walker wasn't bad, but he would never be the man Sagamore had been. There was nothing of greatness in him. Sagamore and Walker were of the same blood, but far different in spirit. Walker was simple and fun. He looked for ways to enjoy living. Walker's brother, Tad, was more like their father. Shepherd could see a plainness in this youngest of Sagamore's children. It was a quality that reminded him of the man himself. Maybe Tad would become like—

"What are you watching?" Stephen asked, his voice low and menacing.

Shepherd realized he was talking to him.

"I told you to quit that staring, didn't I? You got something to look at? Tell us what it is, boy." With his finger, he poked Shepherd hard in the ribs.

Tanner was on his feet. "Leave him alone. Don't

195

you touch him." Tanner wasn't looking at the floor anymore. He was glaring hate at Stephen, and there was nothing to disguise it.

The heat Shepherd had been feeling in him was boiling now. He could feel it shudder through him, trembling in every muscle, getting ready.

"I don't allow any rudeness in my camp," said Stephen, getting up and taking a step toward Tanner.

"I was just daydreaming." Shepherd was on his feet and hoping to prevent what he knew would happen, what he felt was coming.

"Let's go hunting," said Walker. "Isn't that what we came here for?"

Shepherd watched the easy moves as Walker stood up from his place by the fire. "It's cramped in this cave. We're all getting on each other's nerves. If we're gonna hunt, let's do it."

There was a moment when Shepherd wasn't sure what would happen next. Stephen seemed to be wavering, as if deciding what he wanted most. *He's crazy,* Shepherd thought. Not for the first time that day, he wished Prophet was there, anything to put a barrier between Stephen and them. Because Stephen was going to kill them if somebody didn't stop him. Stephen was going to get rid of anyone who might challenge him.

Would it be now?

"Walker's right. It's too crowded in this cave," said Stephen, a smile returning to his lips. "You boys are ready for a little trouble. Let's go hunting."

They moved down the face of the canyon, into the ravines where snow was piled deep as standing bodies. Their legs sank into the softness, and the cold made Shepherd's hands and feet numb. He thought of Sagamore constantly. What would his teacher do? How would he save them? Thinking of Sagamore made Shepherd feel as if the man was with

196

him, a spirit guide on his journey. He fingered the bear claw at his neck, and kept going.

Stephen stayed far ahead of them, way out in front, leading them deeper into the canyon. A copse of pine and scrub oak lay ahead. It was dark within this woodland, the pale winter sun sliced by the arching limbs of the trees, and the bough-laced canopy of green above them.

In the sudden dark of the woods, Stephen disappeared.

Walker had been following close behind Stephen. When Walker stopped, Tanner and Shepherd quickly caught up to him.

"What's going on?" asked Tanner. His breathing was labored, for they had been moving fast and hard through the snow.

Walker looked confused. "I don't know where he is. I lost him."

"Lost what?" asked Tanner. He was looking around the dark woodland, his eyes wary and darting glances at Shepherd, the sky, and the nearest tree trunks. He looked nervous.

"I was right behind him. I don't know how he could have moved so fast without me seeing him," Walker went on, his eyes wide and confused, "but . . . Stephen's gone."

"Great!" said Tanner, outraged. "The man's crazy. First, he brings us hunting in the middle of winter, snow up to our asses, leads us out to the back of hell, then loses us in some stupid woods. A goddamn idiot!" he swore under his breath, just loud enough for Shepherd to hear.

"Stephen!" Walker called.

"No, don't!" Shepherd stopped him. "You're telling everything in these woods that we're here. I'm not so sure we want them all to know."

Walker did a kind of half-spin, twisting around as

if he'd heard a bear suddenly breathing down his neck. "Shit," he muttered. "I hadn't thought of that."

"Yeah, well, think of it," said Shepherd. He was looking around, too. He wasn't expecting to see a bear, or any other predatory animal, except the kind that walked on two legs and carried a gun. For the first time since they'd started the trip, he felt he knew what Stephen was planning to do. The thought chilled him colder than the snow.

"You two head back to the cave, and stay together," he warned Tanner and Walker.

Tanner shot him a glance of annoyed astonishment. "Where do you think you're going? We've lost one member of this hunting party. I don't figure we ought to lose another. You're staying with us."

"Can't do it," said Shepherd, and darted past the older boy, moving into the cover of the trees. He rushed a few feet ahead, zig-zagging between the trees, scrambled over an outcropping of rock, then disappeared from sight as easily as Stephen had before.

Tanner and Walker searched the area for several minutes. They followed the footprints in the snow until they were lost on the rock face.

"What's going on here?" asked Walker. His voice sounded nervous and scared.

"We're playing some kind of game," said Tanner, anger seething in every word, "and I don't like the rules."

Another minute passed in total silence.

"You think we should wait for him?" asked Walker.

Tanner didn't answer immediately, but finally he said, "No, he wanted to be alone so bad—let him do it. Come on," he told Walker, and started off across the snowpack.

"Wait a minute!" yelled Walker. "Where the heck are we going?"

"Back to the cave." Tanner was already far ahead, and not slowing down to talk.

"Okay, okay," said Walker, slogging fast through the deep snow to catch up. "Wait for me!"

Shepherd scrambled down from the tree as soon as Walker was out of sight. He had to hurry. From the tree top, he had seen the fresh track of Stephen's footsteps leading away from the woods. Stephen had used the trees, too. It was the only way he could have disappeared without leaving footprints. Neither Tanner or Walker had looked above them. They had focused on what was out in front, and they would continue to do so, never looking for what was above their heads or behind them.

That's where the danger would come from.

Shepherd ran as fast as he could through the thick snow, not worrying about leaving tracks now. He had to get there before it happened . . . before Stephen killed them.

As he ran, he felt the other tracker close beside him. The spirit of Josiah Gray Wolf, the Sagamore, was with him. Shepherd was the hunter trained by Gray Wolf himself. The boy's mind was filled with the lessons taught by the wise one, the leader of the Outsiders and the People. Now, he thought of all that he had learned from this man, this true father of his spirit. And with the memories as close beside him as his skin, he hurried like fast flowing water over the smooth coat of snow.

199

Twenty-four

Stephen felt the wind blow its chill breath against his bare neck. His head was bent forward in a strained stance, baring the naked patch of skin between his head and shoulders. The ice wind seemed to cut right through his body there, but he stood his ground and never moved from the spot.

He was on the edge of an overhanging rock formation, high above the splintered ravine. The muscles in his shoulders ached from the labor of holding this cramped position for so long. *Those boys were taking their sweet time getting here.* As the thought came to him, Stephen's neck muscles seized up, throbbing miserably. For a minute, he stood up straight and brushed his hand under his shirt collar, rubbing at the hurt.

The sky was pearled with silver-white clouds, a flat sheen that reflected the dull radiance of the snow. It made him dizzy to stare at that sky. He might fall back and tumble into the canyon, if he looked too long . . . he might fall screaming into that sky.

He hunched back down to where he ought to be, kneeling, knees pressing the weight of his body against the hard rock. From here, he could see the whole length of the canyon. They would have to cross through the ravine below him in order to get back to the cave before nightfall.

If they weren't lost. The thought enraged him. These were the three who wanted to take his place someday, and they couldn't follow their own trail of footsteps through the snow. If they were that stupid, they deserved to freeze to death. He'd be doing the People a favor to get rid of them.

But that wouldn't look so good, he knew. Not all three at once. It would look as though maybe it was his fault. Everybody would blame him. No, he couldn't have that. So he waited in the cold, the river of wind sweeping across his bare neck. He waited for these three boys to cross below him . . . to where one of them would die.

The pistol Stephen held in his hands was the one he had brought with him from New York, years ago. He had been about the age of these three, back then. He held the Browning 9mm flat between the palms of his hands. The handle had rough wooden grips, and the gun metal was a dull blue gray, with a hint of movement in the way the colors came alive as he turned it, like rippling water.

This gun had saved him back then, when he was young, alone, and scared. He still felt alone, always, and he was still scared, but the gun had made a difference. It had given him power, and he wasn't a kid anymore. Those three boys were the young ones now.

The sound of a dry twig snapping underfoot caught his attention. They were there, just below him. In another moment they would be coming out of the sheltering woodland and into the exposed ravine. He crouched low, pulled back the slide to cock the pistol, and felt the first of thirteen cartridges enter the magazine. He took aim for the spot, just ahead of where he'd heard the twig snap, and waited. In his mind, he could hear the rhythm of a clock counting off the seconds, *tick, tick, tick*.

He'd say he thought it was a bear, or a deer. He'd say it had been a terrible accident. How could he have known they'd be there? The waiting was a teasing torment. Which boy would emerge from the trees first? Which one would die?

And then he saw him, stepping out into the dim sunlight, the eldest of the three. Tanner, taller than the others, moving on long legs that carried him swiftly toward his death. The hunter's eyes followed each movement of the prey, and his finger slowly squeezed back on the trigger.

"Stephen!"

When Stephen Wyse heard the shout and spun around, it wasn't as the man of thirty-seven, but as the scared fifteen-year-old street kid, afraid for his life. They were coming for him . . . they were coming! . . . and they wore the face of death.

The ruined shot discharged from the nose of the pistol, missing its target and impacting wildly into the snowbank behind where Shepherd Hallinger was standing, only a few feet away from Stephen.

"No!" cried Stephen, raising his arm to shield his head, but it was too late.

The rock Shepherd had thrown to deflect the pistol's aim hit Stephen a hard, glancing blow along the side of his head. The man stumbled back, arms flailing for balance, but there was nothing to grab onto. His feet skidded out from under him as he staggered backward off the rounded bluff of the precipice. He fell, and the fired bullets sounded as his final screams.

Brad saw it all. He stood on another promontory of the cliff face, overlooking the ravine. He'd been too far away to stop Stephen, but close enough to see what had happened. If Shepherd hadn't been there, if he hadn't had the courage to throw the rock and shout Stephen's name, Tanner would be dead, and maybe Walker, too. The boy had saved two lives, even at the cost of one man's death. Shepherd hadn't killed Stephen. It was Stephen Wyse himself who had forced this day to happen.

The thought which came to Brad was quick, and clean, and sure. *A man can't change his fate.* He might postpone it, but the day would come. Male or female, the day would come, and what was always meant to be, would happen.

Brad ran across the stone ridge, rushing to where the young man stood alone and gazing into the deep face of the canyon.

Long ago, in confidence, Sagamore had told Brad that he had seen Shepherd as the future leader of the People, seen it as a vision in his mind. Now, on this acknowledged day of fate, Brad believed he had witnessed the vision of Sagamore's dream, and seen the hopeful future of the People standing in the courageous spirit of a twelve-year-old boy.

Stephen's death brought a marked change to the People. It was as if a pall of gloom had lifted from them. Winter became not the harbinger of their existence passing away, but the cold, clean beginning of a new time for them, a new life that was building in this place. His death bought them a freedom they had lost.

With Stephen gone, there was no set leader among them. Brad turned away from this role, choosing instead to work simply as one of the People. When decisions needed to be made for the welfare of the whole, they were made as a community, and not by the choice of any individual.

It was right, Brad believed, for now. He knew a

time of change would come to them. He had seen into the future, a glimpse of their world to be, and he knew that a day would come when it would be right for one man to stand out among them. He knew that this man would be Shepherd, and that he would lead them to a greatness they had not dreamed possible.

So much was to happen to their world. This tribe, this community . . . they would be the core of that change. It would be through them that the future of mankind would reclaim its birthright, through their children, and the descendants of these few. As Prophet, Brad had seen a world that was a resacrilizing of the earth, with man and nature in accord. Humankind would once again become the caretakers of the ground which gave them life. The world had been washed clean of all that had corrupted its life force. Earth was once again returned to the original, simple garden, and man would one day see himself as part of that garden, in all its complexity.

Of all this, Brad was sure. He was comforted by the sense of a new beginning. A breath of spirit moved across the face of the land and the People, blessing them with a resurgence of origin and source, the wellhead of waters, blessing them with a hope of restored life.

And yet, even with all of this to comfort him, he was not content. In daylight, he witnessed nature returning its bounty to the land. The regenerative power surrounded him. But at night, he dreamed of Biosphere Seven, and of Jessica. He was witness to a different world, then. That world was dying, and Jessie was dying with it.

Brad remained with the People for as long as he could. With the women and the oldest children, he gathered enough firewood to see them through the final days of winter. With Tanner, Walker, and Shepherd, he hunted for game, enough to sustain the families until the first spring harvest. He bent his back to the labor of building a storehouse, an outside oven, and another barn for the livestock the People had gathered to their fold. In all this he labored, knowing he would leave.

The dreams pulled at him. It was as if a voice was calling, and he knew the sound of that voice. She lived in him, and in the torment of his dreams. *For how much longer?* The question stole into his mind and left him wanting. He needed to find the answer, even as he needed air to breathe.

And so, he said goodbye to the People.

"How will you survive?" asked Merry Logan, "The ground is still frozen. We may have another blizzard. Wait until spring," she pleaded.

He couldn't wait another day. A certainty had come to him that Jessica's life, and the lives of the others with her in the dome, would not last beyond winter. She needed him desperately, and the need was now. A blizzard could not stay him from her.

"Must you take the child?" asked Crystal. "Leave him with us." Brad knew she had always cared for Andrew. It was Crystal's milk that had fed the child as an infant, and her protective maternal feelings caused her to urge Brad to leave the boy with her, in the safety of the People.

"I don't know if I will ever return to this place," Brad told her honestly. "My son wasn't given to me so that I might leave him with others. I am his security, and he is my continuance."

He spoke to all of them, the People of this land, this restored promise of God. One by one, he said goodbye to them. One by one, he cut them from his heart. He left only Shepherd until the last. To this one, he must leave something more.

They had walked together away from the settlement. The timbers of the Lodge could be seen from the hill on which they stood. "Will you come back to us?" Shepherd asked him.

Brad knew the truth, and gave it now. "No."

The boy's face showed the grief this answer had caused him. "It doesn't seem right. You brought us here. And now you're leaving, even before the first harvest. You belong here, Prophet."

Brad shook his head. "When I was Prophet, I belonged with the People. Not now."

"Have you changed so much? Have you stopped caring about us?"

"I care," he tried to explain his feelings to the boy, "but part of me has already gone from here. My thoughts are with those in the biosphere."

"Your heart is there, too," said Shepherd.

Brad didn't deny it.

The boy seemed lost in thought, and then he said, "I always believed Sagamore would be with us."

"He is," said Brad. "You know that; you feel it, just as I do. He's with the People through you."

Shepherd stared at him. "I feel that sometimes, but —"

"You feel it because it's true," Brad insisted. "Learn to trust those feelings. We're all more than flesh and blood. There's spirit working in us, as much a part of our being as our need for food, or air. I believe Sagamore's spirit is part of you," he told Shepherd, putting his hands on the boy's shoulders. "After you will come another, and after that one, another still. It doesn't end," Brad told him.

Shepherd's eyes were wide with awe. "Sagamore once said that I would be —"

"The leader?" Brad brought the word to them.

206

He looked into the young man's eyes. "And so you will," he promised. "One day, that fulfillment will come to you, just as mine comes now to me."

Shepherd was silent, as if feeling the understanding of what had been said. At last, he nodded. "Then you must go," he said.

"Yes," Brad told him, and together they started back down the hill.

It was as though a scepter had been transferred, one to the other. A shield of strength had been given, placed in a boy's hands, and a right of future. The sun hallowed the living earth, and the promise of spring brought a blessing to all that lay beneath the sheltering dome of sky.

Twenty-five

A chill wind blew across the length of Britain, coursing down its valleys and its plains. The source of this wind was the freezing waters of the cold North Sea. The wind had traveled over ocean waves, with no land to stop its gathering strength. Now, shuddering in its massive might, the icy wind spent itself against this green island, and like the cries of a demon, it broke its torment on the land.

The Travelers huddled in their tents. Many of them had known the wind storms of their native lands, hot desert zephyrs which could skin a camel from the unending drive of battering sand, but they had not experienced the life-sapping cold of a winter gale on an island off the north Atlantic. They had never known such bone-aching cold. In misery, they waited for the wind to cease.

In Zechar al Maghrib's tent, Arthur Penn sat close to the small sunken pit of fire at the center of the enclosure, and explained to the Berber chieftain how it was he had known how to save Rhissa's life.

"I had just become a doctor, in the days before the virus," Penn said. "I worked here, in Britain. I was young, determined to make a success of my life and the education that had cost my parents so dearly. My career had just begun, working with a research lab and studying the effects of bone marrow transfer in cell modification."

Maghrib looked at him blankly. "I know nothing of this," he admitted. "My life has not been a study of books," he said, "but of man."

Penn smiled. "At that, you have done far better than I."

Maghrib saw a sadness in the Briton's eyes. It was there in every word he spoke, and every sigh. "You are, as you say, a doctor. You have saved my wife and I am grateful. Why would you keep this gift of healing a secret from the others? Why would you hide what might have helped them?"

Penn turned away from Maghrib's steady gaze. "I was afraid."

"Afraid?" The man had not seemed a coward when he'd rushed into the crowd gathered around Rhissa and stabbed her with the needle point of the syringe. He had not seemed a coward when he'd risked exposure of his secret by this act. "If it was fear that kept you silent," said Maghrib, "why did you act now, and not before?"

A slow smile, painful to watch, tore like a rending seam across Penn's mouth. "I have lost so much of what I was," he said. "I could not call myself a doctor now. But that allergy to bee venom is something I share in common with Rhissa. If I'm stung, I have thirty seconds to live unless I have an injection. I live with that fear, and have kept the serum with me, always. It was with me the day that Rhissa was stung." He shook his head at the play of fate. "How could I stand and let her die, when I had the power to prevent it?"

Maghrib saw that the man's act had cost him much. He waited, staring into the yellow face of the fire, and let Penn tell the story as it came

209

slowly from the hidden boundary of his soul. The wind shook the tent, but inside, a warmth of friendship was building like the welling heat of the fire.

"Before the virus," Penn recounted the strange turn in the course of his life, "medicine was a sacred thing. Doctors were looked upon as healers, protectors, and saviors whom people turned to when stricken. I *saved* lives with these hands," he twisted back to face Maghrib, his hands raised before him like icons.

Maghrib touched the man's fingers with his own. Penn's outstretched arms dropped back to his lap.

"Tell me of the days after the virus," Maghrib began to pull upon the thread of truth from this one. "Tell me of the days when the world was dying, and you could do nothing."

Penn shot him a wary glance, then his eyes filled with tears. The man wept as he spoke, never stopping for the tears that coursed the rough hollow of his cheeks, as if unaware of their presence.

"When the people began to die," said Arthur Penn, "we tried everything. We worked each day until we dropped into exhaustion on the chairs of the lab, and slept a few hours. When we rose, we drove ourselves again." He shook his head, remembering. "The search was for a way to change the viral code through blood cells, or bone marrow, or genetic modification."

Maghrib listened attentively, unsure of what all the details meant, but understanding that Penn had been desperate to find a way to save the people of his world. And he had failed. His world had died, but for a few survivors like himself. Was that why he had stopped being a healer?

"At first, the blood work showed some chance

of success. We put all our efforts into it, hoping, praying, but we found that all our experiments only held the virus back a few weeks. When it surfaced again, it showed its deadly force in an even more virulent strain, and our patients died."

"You were young to have known such human suffering," said Maghrib. "Such a thing scars a man."

There were no tears on Penn's face now. "Have you ever seen anyone die of the virus?" he asked. His voice was hard and bitter.

"I was born after the old world ended," said Maghrib.

"Then you cannot know what it was like, or the scars it left." His gaze was steady, and met Maghrib's as an equal.

Zechar nodded. "I was wrong to guess your feelings. In the last days, what happened?"

Once again, he saw Penn seem to retreat into himself. The man was hidden, still. "Death happened." Penn wrapped his arms tightly around his knees and rocked before the fire. "By the time we were sure the blood transfusions wouldn't work, we'd started on bone marrow transplants. Our research in that area seemed to offer great promise, but it was too late. Around us, the heartbeat of the world had stopped. We lost them . . . too many to care for, too many to heal. And then," Penn spoke slowly, "our own team began to die. We never finished our work. No one was left. The doctors, as well as their patients, were dead. All dead."

Maghrib felt the man's genuine pain, but the questions were still there. He needed answers. "Surely, doctors were needed even more, after. You might have helped the people who remained."

"Helped them?" Penn glared at him. "You don't

understand. After, when the old world was gone, who do you think the survivors blamed for the disaster which took everything from them?"

Maghrib didn't speak.

"The scientists in their laboratories. The doctors! We were the ones who caused this horror to happen. They hated us, and rightly so. We had betrayed their trust. We were the ones who'd started the experiments, the ones who'd risked their lives. In revenge for that, they murdered every doctor and scientist they could lay their hands on."

Now Maghrib understood. Penn had kept the fact that he was a doctor secret in order to protect himself. He'd been afraid to let them know the truth. "Your fear that they would find out your secret must have been great, all these years."

The pain he saw in Penn's eyes was the man's only response.

"And yet, you came forward to save my wife. You must have thought about it, before—"

"Only for an instant. She was desperate, couldn't breathe. She would have died if I hadn't helped her. I knew that. The man who'd been in hiding for so many years hesitated," he admitted, "but only for a single moment. She needed me. I never really had a choice."

Maghrib felt a swelling of emotion catch in his throat and chest. A bond had been forged between him and this man, one he would not allow to be broken.

"If they take my life for this," said Penn, "then so be it. I'm not sorry. There was nothing else I could have done."

"No one among my people will harm you," promised Maghrib.

Penn's glance was unsure, doubtful. "The Britons may feel differently."

"If any man, woman, or child in this camp brings you harm," said Maghrib, "that one will die. That is my oath to you. Tomorrow I will tell them. From that day, you need never again hide what you are."

Penn shook his head. "It's too late," he argued. "We can never go back, never become what we once were. I must leave this place."

"The old Earth is gone," said Maghrib. "We are a people of a new world, and we need a healer. The Unseen One has brought us to you for a reason. Only the One Above knows that true purpose, but our people are in need of your knowledge of healing, Arthur Penn. For them, I ask you to remain among us. Teach us what you know," he said, "and be our healer."

Penn was silent for so long, Maghrib thought he hadn't heard. Then at last he lifted his head, glancing up from the firelight into which he'd been staring. "There is a syrup we could make for cough, if the people would gather enough of the herbs that I tell them."

"They will do all that you ask," promised Maghrib.

Penn's expression changed. He seemed to grow more confident. "And there's a powder I could make from tree bark; it's good for bringing down a fever."

"Then you will stay?"

Penn stood. The shuddering light from the fire dressed his skin in heated color. "If they allow me to live among them, and to heal their suffering . . . then, I'll stay."

Maghrib stood, too. The two men clasped hands. An oath had been sworn, a promise given. Outside, the winds of winter broke over this island of the cold North Sea. The warmth of spring was far away, but in this Berber tent, beside the heat of a fire, a seed of hope and future had been planted, and had begun to grow.

To Maghrib, the words he had spoken echoed in his mind. *The Unseen One has brought you to us for a purpose.* He was sure that this was true. What that purpose was to be, only God alone could tell.

It was said among the Travelers that the day the man called Arthur brought the light of his knowledge to their world, that day the earth began once again to recognize the human race as one of its own.

Arthur Penn had kept a secret far more valuable to the world than his learned wisdom as a doctor. He brought information about a place that neither Maghrib, nor any of the Travelers, had known existed. He told them about a magical place, hidden on an island, a glass city where the people were shielded from the virus. He told them about Biosphere Two.

Penn had not only known of the existence of the biosphere off the coast of Wales, but had planned to conduct valuable research at the site. That was before the virus changed everything. His research team was gone, and he had never thought about traveling to Biosphere Two alone. Later, Penn hadn't wanted to draw attention to the sphere's existence. He didn't know if any of the scientists still lived, but for their safety, he had stayed away. He had seen how scientists were treated by survivors. Now, he admitted to Maghrib that it was possible that some of these scientists had lived.

To Maghrib, the images Penn's words evoked

were mystical and compelling. He saw, in the vision of his mind, the clear walls of the city by the sea. He imagined a world of green forest and summer, a fantasy captured within walls of glass, and laid against an outer boundary of white frost and winter cold. To Maghrib and the others, it was as if Arthur Penn had told them of a place called Paradise.

"We will go there," said Maghrib, speaking for the whole community.

"It may have been destroyed," warned Arthur. "So many scientists were killed. You must understand," he turned to face the gathered crowd, "it may be gone. Why risk so many lives? Wouldn't it be better," he asked them, "to send a small party to go and search for the sphere, leaving all others here through winter, where they have warmth and food? Surely, the children should remain in this valley."

Maghrib looked out among the people. He saw anxious faces, excited by the revealed images of Penn's secret world. From what Maghrib could see, all of the Travelers wanted to see for themselves this land of constant summer. He understood their desire to witness it, for he felt the same way himself.

It was a difficult decision, one which battled in his mind like living armies, but in the end he was swayed to Penn's argument. "Four men will journey to the sea cliffs of Wales, and the island of the biosphere," he announced to the assembled community. I will go," he told them, "and Arthur Penn. We will take with us Tadeo Valdez, and Phillip Boussard. All others will remain here through the winter, and wait until our return."

A loud protest rose from the crowd, as evenly as bread rising in an oven. They had heard the same words as Maghrib; they had dreamed the vision, too. All of them wanted to take part in the journey.

"We have a right!" shouted one man.

"You keep the wonders for yourself!" said another.

Penn stepped forward, as if to reproach them, but Maghrib placed a hand on his shoulder and drew the man back. It was Maghrib's voice alone which addressed the angry crowd.

"We will not go as a nation to find this land. Instead, we will go as nomads, like those seekers of truth from the stories of our beginnings. It is too dangerous for all of us to leave. To make such a journey in deep winter would mean the death of some. I must think of the young and the weak among us."

"Let them stay behind!" a broad-shouldered man spoke up. Many of those standing near him nodded their agreement.

"And who among you will stay and care for them?" asked Maghrib. "Will we abandon our oldest and youngest, and those too ill to make this journey? Will we leave the cattle and the sheep in these valleys? The camels, and horses, too? Will we cast aside everything which claims us as a people?" he demanded, his voice growing loud.

The murmur of voices dropped into pulsing silence. The people stared at him. In their eyes he saw regret, and longing.

It was the broad-shouldered man who answered Maghrib's challenge. "When you return to your people, Maghrib, the Travelers will be here, in this peaceful valley, waiting for you. We are a nation, as you have reminded us, and you are our leader. May a merciful God watch over us all."

The voices in the crowd lifted, and the expressions on the faces of the people turned from regret, to hope. "Maghrib!" a woman called out, the name sounding high and clean. "Maghrib!" Others joined the chant until a thundering of wild cheers elevated like a risen host to the watchful heavens. "Maghrib! Maghrib! Maghrib!"

In the heart of the Berber child who had grown into this man, another voice whispered. It was the soft, lyrical voice of his mother, Itto M'Hand, and the prophesy she had foretold at his birth. He heard it again, now, as though she were beside him still.

"This child of my body will be like the spear of heaven, a star to shine across the earth."

He had been named Zechariah, son of the shooting star. For his mother, and for all her people of the Gued'oula tribe of North Africa who had lived and died in one land, Zechar raised his arm high above his head and cried out, "We are the firstborn of this new world, and the earth is our inheritance!"

Twenty-six

With Sidra gone, T. J. Parker felt a loneliness begin to devour him like cold devours a lake with ice. It happened slowly, a paralysis that had worsened every day since she left. He had become healthier when she was with him. His mind was clear, and he understood things. He hadn't spoken to his dead wife and children, not in all the time Sidra was here, and now he feared that he would lose his fragile hold on sanity, that he would slip back into becoming the animal who had lived alone in this cave.

She hadn't been in love with him, he reminded himself. The truth was, he hadn't been in love with her either, but he had loved being near her. He had loved the companionship, and the bond of trust they'd shared. She had never lied to him, never told him she would stay . . . and he had known she would leave, but it was harder than he'd imagined, being alone again.

A real fear struck him, and shuddering at the thought, he prayed he wouldn't go back to stark madness by summer.

With Sidra, he had been healed of the hurt that weighed on him like a stone. With her gentleness and caring, he had found escape from the loneliness which tore at him. He had found hope. Now that hope was gone.

She hadn't said goodbye. Had she been afraid to

risk it? Had she feared he would have stopped her? *Would he?* He didn't know.

The weather was warm enough to work outside the shelter of the cave. His body ached with the need for something to do, hard work to tire him, tasks to keep him busy. The cave had been too easy for him, providing too much. He had food, warmth, and shelter. There was nothing that demanded his attention, not field nor foe. Nothing needed him, and he needed nothing that was outside the walls of NORAD.

Or did he?

Parker walked a few feet from the entrance, down the slope of hill to where the stream carried snow runoff like a vein of life along the foot of Cheyenne Mountain, and to the ravines below. He watched its passage, remembering how it had been when he first came here.

He hadn't been alone, back then. He had carried the memories of his wife and children with him, never releasing them from his mind and heart, never letting them go. Never able to let them go. He had come away from the colony of survivors outside Biosphere Seven, so that he could live only in those memories. He couldn't bear to lose them. For them he had fled.

Until Sidra came to him, he had remained in the world of his own mind. He had held onto the guilt and pain of his wife's death, his childrens' deaths, because it made him feel their presence with him still. Hurt was better than nothingness.

Until Sidra, he hadn't been alone.

The emptiness Parker felt now, with Sidra gone, stood like a weight on his soul. He couldn't go back to this. He lifted his gaze and looked at the trees, at the forest surrounding him. New leaf buds were forming at the tips of their branches. Even in the winter, there is life. It seeds itself from within, and when ready, the plant will grow.

He felt the seed of that force of life budding within him. He had survived past his winter. He had known what it was to be a soul alone, and now he sought a communion with life. More than anything, he wanted never to be alone again.

He knew then that he would leave Cheyenne Mountain.

Sidra had ridden south, back to the biosphere. He knew she had left him, as well as this place. He wouldn't follow her. In the time she was with him, she had given Parker a freedom from the demons of his own mind. She had healed him and he would ask nothing more of her. Like finally releasing the memories of his wife and children, he would let Sidra go.

A bird cried, and he turned toward the sound. Beyond this mountain pass was a glacial valley, spreading north to the rich plains and fertile range lands of Wyoming and Montana. Sidra had said there were people in Montana, at a place called Mirror Lake.

It would be a hard crossing. The snow would still be a deep cover over the ground. Such a journey would be an exhausting labor for both mind and body. And yet, some newly-born need in T. J. Parker cried out for the awakening strength this arduous pilgrimage would demand of him.

For the first time in many years he knew he wasn't running away from life. Like the bird whose cry had beckoned him north, he was looking toward the future. The weight in his heart lifted as he saw hope build on the dream of tomorrow.

He stared at the sky above him, and wondered what the sky was like over Montana. Sidra had said there was a colony of people at Mirror Lake, her sister, her brothers. He thought of them now. If he left right away, he could be there by spring.

* * *

Brad followed the trail the People had made when they'd come north to Kansas after the flood. He brought two horses, a white mare carrying their provisions, and the brown stallion he rode. The child was bundled into a fur-lined pack fitted close against his back. He had to stop often to feed the boy, and to release him from the restrictive bonds, so that Andrew's legs could kick freely and his arms wouldn't grow numb from lack of movement.

Brad had feared a new snowfall might trap them, but the days had been warm, one building on another until he had seen the first new leaf of spring in a valley below the ridge line. The woods had opened into a wide meadow that glistened wetly with the promise of green spears of grass. He had ridden into the sunshine, and the day had been washed clean of shadows.

At night they slept in the open. Brad curled the child against him, the heat of their bodies touching and warming each other beneath the weight of the buffalo hide blanket. A blazing fire drove away the worst of the cold, but never the fear in Brad's mind, for it was dreams of a fire in the biosphere which haunted his sleep.

Andrew woke in the night and cried. Brad was his comfort, and in a way, the child comforted him, too. They were returning home, to dreams that had happened, or would be fulfilled.

"Do you remember your mother, Andrew?" He spoke to the child with calming words, and the boy listened with eyes open wide. "She loves you very much, I know that. We're going back home to see her, you and I."

The moon rose slowly in the sky as Brad talked to his son about Jessica. "I remember the days before she went into the biosphere. We had just been

221

married a few weeks and no one knew about it except us. It was our secret, a bond between us. Now, we have you."

Andrew's eyes closed and his low, even breathing said he was asleep. Brad went on talking, as if the boy was still listening. Remembering the days. Remembering the love that had held him captive for almost thirty years. He gazed at the pale image of the rising moon, and he told his sleeping child about the woman he had once loved. Still loved. He told his son about Jessica.

Then, closing his eyes like the boy, Brad slept and dreamed of another time, when he was young and fearless, and the earth was an open treasure. He dreamed of holding Jessica in his arms.

The banks of the river had disappeared beneath the rush of water swelling at their sides. Sidra's horse pawed the soft mound of earth beneath it, showing a fear of the gushing torrent.

"It's all right." Sidra leaned forward and stroked the mare's neck. "We're not going to try it. Not today, anyhow."

She made a rough camp beside the river, under the shelter of a cluster of aspen trees. New rainfall started that night, and a wind that blew the stinging droplets into her face like needles. She pulled the blanket over her head, shivered in the wet cold, and felt a miserable pity for the worse conditions of her horse. The whole night she lay awake and listened to the river rise and slap against the muddy slope.

Dawn brought a daylight that was ashen. The rain had worsened, and was now a full-fledged storm. Lightning cracked low in the sky, and a tree on a hill near her burst into sudden flame. Being exposed to the open rain meant she couldn't build a fire, or find food, or sleep. She felt trapped like a bird or small desperate animal, waiting for the storm to end.

Toward dawn of the second day, a silence woke her. She had fallen into an exhausted sleep and listened now to an eerie quiet that seemed to throb like the blood in her veins. She felt it, rather than heard, for there was no sound at all. It reminded her of something . . . a memory of stillness that broke into —

And then she did remember: Sagamore and Elizabeth, a wall of water flooding the camp, carrying away a child, carrying away their lives. Sidra scrambled to her feet, ran slipping in the mud to where the mare stood trembling, tethered to the tree. The loose bridle had pulled into a tight twist of leather, and Sidra's cold fingers had to work hard to set it free. The mare shied at Sidra's touch. The warm brown eyes were wide with terror. It stumbled and slipped on the wet ground.

"C'mon," she said, pulling at the bridle, urging the frightened animal up the hill, away from the river, "we've got to get out of here."

The mare whinnied and struggled, her hind legs skidding out from under her.

"Get up!" Sidra cried. "It's going to —"

Her words were drowned out by the roar of thousands of tons of water coming at them like a striking snake. She saw the head of the thing, silvered in the morning brightness, crushing everything in sight.

The mare was up again, moving without Sidra's urging, climbing the hill ridge, away from the terror, away from the sound. And Sidra ran, too. The earth shuddered beneath her, and she ran. Clawing at the sodden ground for purchase, pleading with her eyes to the hilltop and the sky, she ran from the wake of certain death below.

The hillside pulled beneath her, crumbling into

the rage of water at its base, breaking free and sliding in liquid bodies to the river. She felt it give beneath her, moving like a child to the urging of its mother, moving to the greater force.

"No!" she screamed, and dug her fingers into the exposed roots of the tree above her. She felt the earth collapse and fall into the heaving torrent, the splash from it striking her dangling legs like wet fire.

"God!" she screamed. "God!" Her hands were wet, barely able to cling to the slippery roots of the tree.

There was no one to save her, and nothing but her own courage, her own panic, to drive her on. She felt the tough roots begin to tear, and with a strength she didn't know she had, she pulled herself up and grasped one arm around the wide trunk. It was enough to hold her from falling while she swung the other arm up and around. Then her hands and fingers climbed the broken webbing of bark, her body shinnying up the sturdy trunk until her legs were tightly wrapped around it.

She clasped her arms around this support. The chasm thundered beneath her, the power of the water lessening as the height of the flash flood passed beyond the jagged point of ground where she clung to the tree. She heard the might of it diminish, but couldn't look down. Her gaze was still fixed on the hilltop above her, and the pale sheet of sky.

As if in an image from a dream, she saw the mare. It stepped into the shield of light and stood at the crest of the hill. That image was the catalyst which drove her beyond her own courage, for she had nothing left. Because of the mare, Sidra risked climbing onto the limbs of the tree, risked dropping to the muddy earth above it, and on her knees, scrabbled up the ridge bank to the top of the hill.

Only then did she look down at the sea of destruction below her. The earthen bank where she had waited out the storm for two days, where she had fallen into exhausted sleep, was gone. In its place was a crater wrought by the pounding force of the incredible cataclysm.

The river felt too close to her, even from this height. She didn't want to look at it, didn't want to think of what might have happened if her fingers had slipped from the muddied tree roots. Unable to stop the terrible shaking, Sidra grasped the horse's bridle in one hand, laid her arm over its neck, and crossed over the crown of the hill to a grassy plain beyond.

From there, a wide path led along the base of the foothills, twining in and out of the tree line until it broke upon another opening a mile or more down river, another crossing point. Here the watercourse was low, a few feet deep at the most. Sidra had to blindfold the mare to lead her into the icy stream. The riverbed was strewn with boulders and tree branches. In a low place, Sidra saw the floating carcass of a small deer. *That might have been me,* she thought, and moved on.

When the river was at her back, she gave it one parting glance over her shoulder, and said as much to herself as to it, "I'll never come this way again." She knew it was true. The flood had almost claimed her life, but she had survived. She would go on.

Riding the mare, she followed the range of foothills into a tree-shrouded valley. There, in an abandoned cabin and small barn, she and the horse took shelter for the night.

Twenty-seven

The children would die. Forced to breathe the polluted air of Biosphere Seven, many already showed symptoms of serious illness. Two of the younger children had developed profound cases of asthma. There was little Jessica, or anyone, could do to help them. The drugs needed to combat asthma were not a part of their emergency supplies. Even if they had been, the constant exposure to the smoke-heavy air would impair the effectiveness of any drug. They needed to leave the dome.

Quinn entered the living quarters he shared with Jessica. He'd been gone most of the morning. So much needed to be done every day in order for them to continue to survive, and few were well enough to work. He returned now with a message. "Cathe says two of her children, Dalton and Maria, are too sick to get up this morning. She'll stay in their quarters today and care for them."

"Damn!" Jessica reacted as if she'd been lashed, and cried to heaven. "What do you want from us?"

The news was a double hardship. As a community, they needed Cathe's help in maintaining the essentials of subsistence in the dome. Cathe was the expert in hydroponics, tissue culture, and all other forms of alternative plant cultivation. The

226

vegetation within each of the biomes was as much at risk as the people. If too many of the plants died, the toxic gases would not be absorbed by the plants and would quickly build to a lethal level. Without the food the plants provided, the animals and people would starve, and the struggle would be over for all of them.

Quinn touched his hand to her back. "C'mon," he tried to soothe her tension, "bring it down a little, babe. The kids may be a lot better by tomorrow, and Cathe will be back working with us again."

Jessica shot him a baleful glance.

"All right, maybe she won't," he admitted. "Hell, I don't know how we're going to get through this any better than you do. Maybe we're *not* going to get through it. Christ, is that what you want to hear? Doom and failure?"

"No." She was angry, but not at him.

She'd been on the computer link-up that morning to Paul Schefield at the Biosphere Two station in Wales. Neither she nor Paul had been able to think of a way out of Biosphere Seven's crisis. Paul had been sympathetic, but Jessica needed feasible ideas, not pity. She was frustrated, tired, and discouraged. Because of that, she'd taken those feelings out on Quinn.

"I'm sorry," she offered. "I can't stand to wait for what I know is going to happen. They're going to start dying one by one, Quinn. The children first, and then some of us older ones."

His eyebrows lifted skeptically at that. "Us older ones?"

"You know what I mean." She ignored the little boy look on his face. "You and I, Cathe and Daniel, and Griff, we're all past fifty. Some of us will be the next fatalities."

"I don't buy it," said Quinn. "It's not the way I'm gonna end. My brother always promised me I'd die in a cat house."

"Will you get serious!" she yelled at him.

"Can't do it," he said, all seriousness now, "not the way you mean."

"Why the hell not?"

"Because you're writing us off, Jessie. I'm not ready to do that, not by a long shot."

She was angry at his unwillingness to look at what the situation was. "You don't want to see how desperate things are."

"I see!" he shouted back. "I see what we've got, if that's what you mean. I'm looking for what we can do about it. I'm going to go on looking, too. The last thing I'll be doing before these eyes close a final time and you plant me in the ground to fertilize your precious crops, is looking for a way out of here."

A smile forced its way across her lips at the ludicrous image. "I don't think you need to worry about—"

"Just don't put me under the squash vines," he went on emphatically. "I hate squash."

"Quinn," Jessica held one hand upright between them like a wedge, "if I promise not to plant you in the vegetable garden, will you stop this?" She was laughing. The tightness in her chest had eased, and she was smiling at his nonsense.

"I'll agree if you'll give me a kiss," he pushed his advantage even further, and pulled her against him.

"I've got to save them," she said, and her eyes were suddenly brimming with tears. The emotion was there, raw as a fresh wound.

"We will," he promised. With a gentleness she loved, and an eagerness that never dimmed, he kissed her. "I'm here to help you," he said, "remember?"

She nodded, kissed him back, and whispered, "Thank God."

Trinity had come upon something exciting. It was an obscure reference in a medical text, its contents made available through computer file data Trinity had recently broken into from the central storage banks of the former director of the Biosphere Project, Jordan Exeter.

The Texas multi-millionaire had died nearly twenty-four years before, trying to force his way into Biosphere Seven when the results of his secret experiments had reached an emergency level and threatened all human life. He had almost made it inside the dome.

Trinity knew the details of that day from the stories that Quinn told. Exeter had used an undisclosed override code to block the computer's locking system. He'd made it to the steel doors of the desert biome and in another instant would have breached the security of the closed sphere, but in that moment, a woman named Piper Robinson—one of the ten original team members of Biosphere Seven—had run with the exposed wires of live electrical cables into the sea, and Quinn had touched those same wires to the steel doors of the desert biome. Both Exeter and Piper Robinson had died, but the biosphere had been saved.

Now, a generation later, Trinity had found a way to unlock the safeguarded computer files of Jordan Exeter. Releasing the security hold involved using a system of code words related to Exeter's life. The final restricted directory name for the files was Kyle, a trace to Exeter's past, the name of his father.

Through these documents, Trinity had discovered the undisclosed data on tests which had been conducted in the isolated laboratories of Siberia's Biosphere Four. A scientist named Mikhail Kapov, and others of his team, had been amassing analysis of the effects of gene modification on blood and tissue samples. The research had been intensive, with the primary focus on blood and bone marrow exchange.

Trinity stared at the computer monitor in awe. What he was looking at was the blueprint for the virus that had eventually developed in Biosphere Four, mutated, and caused the destruction of mankind.

"Oh, God." He breathed the words like a prayer.

He wasn't a doctor, but the experiment had been put into layman's terms for Exeter. After studying the reports, Trinity believed he understood a large part of the process by which the Siberian team had produced tissue duplication with identical properties of gene modification. The procedure was simple enough for him to comprehend, if not completely grasp, and it seemed as though it should work. But he knew it had a fatal flaw. That error had created the virus, and the worst human annihilation on earth.

He studied the documents Kapov and the other scientists had presented to Exeter. They spoke of culturing cells of mammalian tissue, duplicating specialized functions, the serum in which the cultures must be grown, and the time needed for cell division. He looked at the essentials of the growing medium: sodium, glucose, specific amino acids and water. His thoughts were racing ahead of the words on the screen. All were readily available within the biosphere.

Trinity felt a connection to the dream of this

230

document, to the men who had died bringing this dream to a shattering realization. His heart beat with such force, it seemed to lift his body and hold him in a separate level, apart from the computer room, the biosphere, and even the earth. For that one instant, he was a world alone, alive, and absolute.

I could do it. The thought was a birth as real as any child of man. *I could make it happen.*

It was a heady courage . . . the first step of an infant, walking on the moon, seeing the footprint of nature in a cell, and changing it.

Trinity printed the secret documents, afraid that they might somehow be lost in the internal workings of the computer. Still trembling from what he had discovered, he took the printed files to his room, sealed and tightly taped them into a plastic plant specimen bag, then stuck them in an unused clay pot. He covered the sealed documents with a transplanted orchid and a dry layer of tree bark.

That night, he lay in quickening stillness beside the plant, and imagined how in the morning he would tell Jessica about what he'd found.

"What are you saying?" Cathe Innes's voice vibrated with anger. "That you want to try to duplicate what Biosphere Four did? Are you crazy? They killed everyone with that *experiment*. Everyone!" Cathe had stormed into Trinity's room, outrage in her voice, eyes, and manner.

"Calm down, Cathe," said Jessica, who had come into the room after her, "we're just talking about it, that's all. Nobody's going to do anything that could endanger the colony."

"Endanger!" Cathe contended sharply. "He'll kill us."

Trinity backed away from this unexpected reaction. He had imagined that his mother would be amazed and thrilled by his discovery. Instead, Jessica had broken their confidence and discussed the matter with Quinn, and with Cathe. Now, all of them were there to accuse him.

"We don't think you've thought this through," Quinn said to him. His voice was rational and calm. "I know it's tempting, finding the data that the Siberian team worked with, but—"

"I can't believe you're even considering the possibility of producing the same experiment," Cathe ranted.

"It wouldn't be the same experiment," Trinity tried to make her understand. "I wouldn't take it that far. It would involve new trial research, using their findings, but exploring alternative combinations. They failed because—"

She cut him off. "They failed because they were wrong. They risked too much, and their mistake cost the lives of nearly every man, woman, and child in the world. Did you really think we'd let you do that here?"

Trinity turned on Jessica. Hurt colored his words. It made him react like a boy. "Why did you have to tell her? It was only meant to be between us. Why couldn't you just trust me? You would have trusted Cameron!"

"That's about enough!" Quinn stepped between them. "I know you're angry, but I'm not going to stand here and let you say those things to your mother." Anger was apparent in his eyes.

Trinity felt alone. "She's not my mother, though, is she?" Everyone important in his life had abandoned or betrayed him. His birth mother, Maggie, the man who had been his natural father, Mike York, Cameron, Sidra, and now even Jessica.

Quinn reached out to grab him, but Jessica moved in the way and laid a restraining hand on Quinn's arm. "We had to ask Cathe; she's our expert on cell culture. We had to know if what you're considering would be too dangerous. There's the welfare of all these people to consider, Trin. It wasn't an act of disloyalty to you. I'm their leader," she told him, "and I had to be sure. Please understand."

Her eyes were pleading with him, and he almost gave in to her. He loved Jessica, no matter what he'd said earlier. She had been the only real mother he'd ever known, and he was ashamed of his outburst. She deserved better than that from him. He did understand what she was saying. He knew she had to protect the others, but . . .

"The only thing he needs to understand," said Cathe, fury still evident in the tone of her voice, "is that whatever idea he had for this experiment is over. We've taken care of that. Tell him."

"Taken care of it?" Trinity had been distracted by Cathe, but now he glanced back at Jessica. "What does she mean?"

"It wasn't what we wanted, Trin," Jessica began, "but—"

"We deleted the file," Cathe declared bluntly.

"You what?" He couldn't believe it. *Deleted the file!*

"We weren't taking any chances," Cathe told him. "It's gone."

They had done it without telling him. All the information from the Siberian project . . . lost. The incredible amount of research that had gone into the documents, the success or failure of each trial, all of it erased from the computer's memory bank. It was inconceivable. How could they have made that decision and acted on it immediately?

233

What about group decisions? Community approval?

"Do you realize what you've done!" he shouted at them. He felt as if the balance was gone from his life, as if he needed to hang onto something. "What you discarded in an irrational instant was probably the most important document of the entire human race. You threw away our chance at survival!"

"No," Cathe argued. "What we did was guarantee that you, or someone else, won't eliminate what little hope of future we still have. I'll be damned if we'll let this kind of self-annihilation happen to us twice," she swore, "not in my lifetime."

"Trinity," Jessica tried to reach out to him, but he pulled back.

"I don't need to hear it," he said, his voice sounding flat and distant. "From now on, I don't need anything from any of you."

He walked out of the room, leaving them standing there. He was sure about very little, but about one thing he was positive: he was different from them, and he was alone. The truth was, maybe he always had been.

He heard Jessica call his name, but he walked away and didn't answer. The only thing important to him now was that the printed copy of those documents had been saved, and was well hidden within the planter of orchids in his room.

Twenty-eight

The four horsemen of the journey, Zechar al Maghrib, Phillip Boussard, Tadeo Valdez, and Arthur Penn, rode side by side across the low hills and snow-covered vales of Britain. The land was like an indulgent mother, offering roads that were neither steep nor dangerous.

"The country of this island is a soulful place," said Maghrib.

"But not the weather," said Valdez. "It's freezing cold, and the wind is bitter."

"I've never known such a wind," agreed Phillip, pulling the corner of a woolen scarf closer around his neck. "It wants to stop your blood."

"It's a northeast wind," Arthur told them. "Britain has always lain in the path of that wind, and in the path of the raiders who came from the northern coasts. It is her history, and her triumph. A northeast wind has brought us more than cold, in its time. It brought us Celts and Goths, Norsemen and Saxons."

Maghrib didn't recognize the names of these tribes of men, but he thought he understood what Arthur meant. "You were a nation whose beginnings were a joining of many peoples, a blending of the journeys of that wind."

Arthur nodded. "Yes, many. We knew the Romans, too. They built the roads and laws of this land. All were our teachers. All became a part of what we were. Now everything is lost."

Maghrib carried the vivid image of the people from many lands and cultures finding this place, settling here among the low hills and gently sloping meadows. He thought of the Travelers, the survivors he had gathered to this new nation of man. They were one community, but a mix of many races and cultures.

"Nothing is truly lost," said Maghrib. "In us are the many nations of the world. What was taken from here, from this place, has been given back. We are the lost ones, returned."

The four men continued riding. No one spoke, but Arthur glanced across at Maghrib, and the unshed tears in Arthur Penn's eyes spoke for him.

Scattered across the level plains of this island were the markings of a long history of mankind. In lonely meadows stood tall stones, some in standing circles, and some in tomb-like cairns.

"Madre de Dios!" Tadeo held his hand before his eyes when he saw the stones. He spurred his horse and rode quickly beyond the area. It was as if he feared that the rock might live.

Maghrib felt no such fear. He came down from his mount and walked for a time among the tall stones. This place was sacred ground, and the markers were signs that the spirit of the Unseen One had moved the heart of man to create such shrines to their beliefs.

"Come away, Maghrib!" shouted Tadeo from a safe distance beyond the meadow.

"I am learning," Maghrib called back to him. He stood at the center of the stone circle and closed his eyes. Was it possible that he felt something, or was that only in his mind?

"Maghrib! Maghrib!" Valdez continued to cry out, until at last Maghrib opened his eyes again, smiled, and waved at the frightened man. He walked away from the center of the circle, unharmed, but feeling as if he'd lost something.

Maghrib was beyond the surround of stones when a sound, or a play of drifting shadows, made him turn and look back. There, at the center of the sacred ground, stood Arthur Penn. His face was tilted upward toward the sky. There was nothing different about the light or the sounds, and yet something had changed. As Maghrib watched, held by the vision, his breath, and the sun, and the whole sky, waited. The clouds pulled back, and a wash of sunlight descended over the Briton.

Maghrib felt and saw the moment of change, when the man he had known as Arthur Penn became something more. It was a *choosing,* and a healing issuing from the stones. The ground seemed as if it were alive, holy, and powerful. A shudder ran through Maghrib. He knew that what he had seen was real. A choice had been made. An offering accepted.

As quickly as the moment came, the dark clouds rushed together with equal speed, and sealed away the vault of sky behind a solid gray mass. Only then did Arthur leave his place at the center of the circle.

"He was touched by God," whispered Phillip Boussard, standing at Maghrib's side.

"You saw it, too?" asked Maghrib, turning to glance at the young man.

Phillip nodded. "That light . . . I will never forget."

None of them spoke any more about what they had seen that day. Like a silent pact between them, they kept to themselves whatever feelings the witnessing of that moment had stirred.

Tadeo rode apart from the others for a time. By late afternoon, he had gained back enough courage to ride abreast of them again, but always with someone spaced between himself and Arthur. He would not look at the open fields if they passed other standing stones, and the land had many. It was as if he, more than any of them, believed in the power of what he had felt in that place of the circle, and feared it.

That night, when they camped within the shelter of an abandoned church, it was Tadeo who stared into the fire and told each of them their part in this journey.

"You are the walls of our house, Maghrib. Our people, the house, stand together by your strength alone. I am a hawk soaring around it, sometimes swooping down into the space, but flying away again when I grow too close. Phillip is the pure light which sees into the window of the house, and brings an offering of warmth and goodness." He stopped and continued to stare into the fire.

Maghrib was captivated by the story. "And Arthur?"

Tadeo stood, breaking from the firelight's apparent hold on him. His eyes, when he turned and faced Maghrib, were serious and troubled. "Arthur is the earth the house stands upon. He is the very ground," said Tadeo. "He is this land."

The light from the campfire died out long before Maghrib could free those words from his mind. He was the walls of the nation, its strength, and Arthur was the earth their house was built upon.

In the hour before the dark flowed into the bright river of morning, Zechar al Maghrib knew

238

that he had been led to this place by the guiding hand of the Unseen One. While the others slept, he left the shelter and stepped outside into the cold. The air was icy with the memory of snow. It stung his eyes and skin, stung even the breath he drew into his lungs. The cold was terrible, and yet he stayed.

He waited, knowing it would come.

In the still instant just before dawn, a shooting star streaked across the heavens. This was what he had waited for, the promise of his God. Such a star had been a sign at his birth, and he knew the meaning. It was the mark of a new leader. Accepting this new light as Arthur's omen, Maghrib stepped back into the warmth of the shelter, laid down near the others huddled around the fire, and at last closed his eyes and slept.

For many days, they traveled. When it was too cold, they waited through the worst of the winter storms in the stone churches across Britain. Within these ruins, Maghrib felt a kinship with the people of this island. He was more convinced than ever; it was a soulful land. Everywhere was evidence of the people's need for the spirit. In the standing stones, in the rock cairns, and in the churches whose spires reached into the heavens. These were a people who had sought out their God. This land bore a memory of their pilgrimage to the Unseen One, of their longing to reach the spirit.

It was a place where Maghrib at last felt he belonged.

The hardest part of their journey lay before them. After days of severe weather, a break in the storm allowed the four riders to cross the Severn river and journey into Wales.

The earth here was not the rolling hills and gentle plains the countryside had been before crossing the Severn. Here, the land bore a rougher beauty. There were high pinnacles, and broken crags. The earth sank into deep recesses before them, and crumbling sea cliffs held back the cold swells of the Atlantic.

Maghrib was surprised that men had lived in this place.

"It will never be an easy home," Arthur said, "but the land is sown with the blood and bones of its people. They drew a strength from what the ground demanded of them. They were rugged, like the land. Like the sea cliffs," he pointed into the distance, "they were buffeted, but stood."

"We have come to the end of it," said Maghrib, standing on a high promontory overlooking the ocean below them.

"Not yet," said Arthur. "There is a smaller island. That is where the biosphere will be found. We must cross the sea to find it."

They left their horses to graze on the high grass plains overlooking the western sea, and in a steep descent to the sandy shore, walked to a line of abandoned boats still tethered to the quay. Some were little more than kindling, but two were small skin boats, which Arthur called *curraghs,* and seemed sturdy enough to carry them over the powerful waves.

Tadeo was reluctant to step into the boats. "The waves will swallow us," he warned.

Maghrib understood the uneasiness; he felt it too. Many other times, Tadeo had proved himself to be a man unafraid of any danger, and yet he was careful and wary of all the powers of nature.

"We have come too far to stop now," said Maghrib, and stepped boldly into the first curragh. "Sit with me," he called to his friend. "The waves will carry us together."

Tadeo hung back only an instant, his glance taking in the high, breaking waves. Arthur and Phillip settled in the second boat, and before the next wave could crest again, Tadeo ran into the surf and stepped into the small vessel beside Maghrib.

"If you are to die in this sea," he yelled over the sound of the waves to Maghrib, "I go with you."

Arthur led the way, showing them how to use the small oars of the skin boats to force a freedom from the shore. In both curraghs, the four men lent their arms and backs to the labor, and pulled at the straining oars until the constancy of the waves had lessened, and Arthur shouted for them to stop. In this place Arthur was the leader, for he knew both the land and the sea better than Maghrib. It was Arthur who had told them of the biosphere on tiny Bardsey Island, and Arthur who brought them to it now.

They drifted for a few minutes, watching as the face of the sea flattened and lifted before them. Maghrib's breath was labored from the hard effort of rowing. Like the others, he slumped, letting his arms and shoulders cave inward. In the time they waited, while Arthur watched for a sighting on the horizon, Maghrib drew in breath after breath of clean salt air, and rested.

"There, to the west!" cried Arthur. He pointed toward a distant spot, where the gray swells of the Atlantic still hid the jot of land. "Row for that point!" he shouted to them.

With a deep sigh, Maghrib once again picked up the oars. The curraghs bobbed at the top of the waves. The two men in each boat worked furiously to steer them toward the point of land Arthur had seen. Maghrib heard himself groan with the effort,

241

but he kept on. The sea was constant. The waves fought against them, and if they stopped even for a moment, a space of water quickly grew between the curraghs. It was possible that they might lose sight of each other in the sea. Knowing this, he worked to keep up with the other boat, and they remained within view of one another.

Slowly, the dark smear above the waves in the distance became the shape of an island. As they rowed, the shape grew wider, until at last Maghrib could see the stretch of sandy beach along its shore. When they neared the beach, they put the oars inside the curraghs and let the breakers carry the skin boats onto the sand.

The strand caught them, and the boats were held in place against the urgent sea. The four men clambered out and dragged the water-heavy curraghs higher onto the sun-draped beach. The air was warmer here, but they shivered in their wet clothes. Both the clothing the men wore and the skin boats were soaked.

"I thought we would die in that water," declared Tadeo. His color was poor, and his legs buckled beneath him. He sat down hard on the wet sand. "I would as willingly stay on this island always, as to test that sea again."

"We all felt that same fear," said Maghrib, "but our journey here was safe and without harm to any." He sat on the sand beside Tadeo, hoping to calm the man by his presence.

"We'll rest until we gain back our strength," said Maghrib. "Later, if he can remember the way after so many years, Arthur will lead us to the place called Biosphere Two."

Unlike Tadeo, Maghrib had been positive he would make it to this island. His vision of the shooting star, and what he had witnessed in the circle of standing stones, convinced him. Coming here had not been their will alone. Another force was at work. He was sure; they had been brought here for a reason.

Twenty-nine

The afternoon sun was a slanting light by the time Maghrib, Arthur, Phillip, and Tadeo had walked the distance of three miles to the center of Bardsey Island. The isolated cleat of land was a refuge for sea birds. The island was a source of fresh water and nesting sites. At the center, away from the salt spray of the ocean, was an area of lush vegetation. They passed tall trees whose leaves remained green, even at the end of winter. There were plants with blooming flowers, and the air was warmer, as if heated from beneath the land.

"A tropical ocean current passes the island," explained Arthur. "This place has always been an Eden of sorts."

Maghrib understood the idea of Eden. He had heard about it from survivors who still carried the old religions in their minds. Eden was a place of beginning, a sheltering, a protected garden within the world. He agreed with Arthur. This island felt like that.

"We're near the site now," Arthur told them. "When we get there, when the biosphere's visible, we must go forward very carefully."

Tadeo, who seemed suspicious of every sound, asked, "Why so carefully? Isn't it they who need to be careful of us?"

Maghrib heard the sadness in Arthur's voice when he answered. "Yes. They have good reason to fear us. We carry the virus, and we're human. The biospheres were blamed after the deaths began. It's likely that they set up some protection for themselves."

"What do you mean?" pressed Tadeo. "Some kind of traps?"

"I don't know," said Arthur. "It may be that they had protective devices in place before the virus, to guard against animals damaging the dome."

"Electricity? Is that what you're saying?" asked Phillip. "But how?"

"I don't like this." Tadeo didn't wait for the answer. "I don't like it at all." His glance moved over the shrubs and trees, scowling.

The hesitation in the men was obvious. "We'd better hurry if we want to get there before dark," said Maghrib. "It would be better to see it in the light."

Even Tadeo seemed to see the reason in this, and they moved forward again, breaking a trail into the garden center of the island.

"What is that?" asked Phillip, after a time.

Maghrib had noticed it too, a sweet-smelling, strong fragrance in the air. It made him think of fields of flowers, and the tangled roots beneath plants.

"We're almost there," said Arthur. "Look."

Maghrib followed the direction of Arthur's hand, and cresting above the treetops was a cut of glass that glowed with a red-orange crown of the setting sun.

"Sweet Mother," muttered Phillip. The boy's hand quickly rose to his forehead and chest, making a sign of crossing himself.

"Why do you do that?" Maghrib asked. He had never seen such an act, and was curious.

"For luck," said Phillip. His eyes were scared.

"We'll go in one at a time," said Arthur. "That way, if there's a problem . . ." He didn't finish the sentence.

"I'll go first," said Maghrib. He was drawn to this place, in spite of all that was fearful about it.

"I know them," said Arthur. "It might be better if I'm the first one they see."

Maghrib considered it, but decided against the plan. "No," he said. "You are the only doctor we have. You hold that knowledge within you. Now that I have led them to this land, your life is more important to the people than mine."

Both Phillip and Tadeo offered to go first, but Maghrib shook his head. He had led them across the desert and beneath an ocean; he would lead them now.

"Wait for my call," he said, then moved into the darkening spaces between the line of trees.

He didn't think about traps or the ending of his life. Instead, he thought about a woman past her youth who sent her only son away from her into the desert to find his place among the peoples of the earth. He had never seen her again, his mother. It was the courage of this woman, Itto M'Hand, that sustained him then, and now.

He walked amid the arched column of trees, his eyes and mind taking in the first full glimpse of the sphere. When he stopped, it was because the beauty of this place stopped his breath. Staring at the walls of glass, he waited for his heart to slow before he could go on.

It was unreal, a building with crimson veins of sunlight running through the triangles of glass, making the structure seem alive. It was larger than the many buildings he had seen, standing alone at the center of this island, as if the land had waited for it and had known of its existence long ago

. . . even as this plain of earth first rose from the waves.

The corona of sunset was dropping like a curtain down the face of the sphere. Maghrib knew there wasn't much time. The pressure of his blood hummed in his ears as he stepped out from the concealment of the trees and crossed the open meadow between the grove and this crystal cavern. Halfway there, he stopped again.

A man from within the biosphere was staring back at him.

"Come no closer!" the man behind the glass wall called to him. The voice was louder than a living man could speak, and seemed to come from above and all around Maghrib.

He felt uncovered, standing in the open meadow. Easily seen. The last burning shield of sunset was melting into liquid color on the glass. Dark would follow. In that dark, he could find his way into hiding again. His fear tempted him, but they had come here for a purpose.

"Who are you?" asked the man within the sphere.

"Zechar al Maghrib."

"An Arab?"

"A Berber," Maghrib corrected him, "born in the High Atlas mountains of Morocco. I am the son of Itto M'Hand." He had told too much, he knew, but the man had asked him and the words flowed from Maghrib with no stopping.

"Good God, a Berber! How the hell did you get here?"

Maghrib took this as an invitation to tell his story, and started forward again.

"Stop!" the man in the glass ordered. "What do you want with us?"

For the first time, Maghrib noticed there were others behind the clear walls of the dome. He saw one woman, then another. Two men stood beside the first, and a child. They didn't speak, but on their faces he saw a message, and it was fear. These great ones, in a world of glass, they were afraid of him.

His own fear left him at that moment. He spoke to them as he would have spoken to any other band of survivors he found along his journey. These people were survivors like him, and he spoke to them now as the leader of the Travelers.

"I have crossed mountains, and deserts, and plains of empty lands to come to this island," he said, ". . . to come to you. I have seen what is left of the world outside your glass walls, and I bring the knowledge of that world to you."

"Why?" The question came from the man who had first spoken. Others joined him now, many. "Why would you help us?"

"Not for myself," said Maghrib honestly. He hadn't known of the existence of these people until the Briton had told him. None of this was his will. "Some greater force has brought me out of the desert, gathering a nation from a silenced earth, bringing them through a tunnel dark as death beneath the sea, to be reborn in a new earth. It was the Unseen One who had led us here, to a healer called Arthur, and finally to this island."

"I have come," answered Zechar al Maghrib, son of a Berber woman, "because I was led here by the hand of God."

They spoke long into the night, the four men outside the mystery of the sphere, and the people of that enclosed and separated world. They spoke about families who were lost to them, about the remembered places of earth, cities and forests,

248

farmlands and protected wilderness, the vivid countrysides of their minds. Through the long night, Maghrib, Arthur, Phillip, and Tadeo huddled beside a campfire near the glass wall of the biosphere. They listened to the voices from their future speak of the world that had once been.

"I had begun to lose hope for what the future would be for those of us living within the shelter of the dome," admitted Paul Schefield. "Since the first days of the virus, nothing has happened which brought us any closer to regaining our freedom, or being able to leave this sphere."

"The virus may have mutated," said Arthur. "It's possible, you don't know for sure—"

"I *do* know," Schefield interrupted him. "My daughter believed that was possible. She managed to escape the dome."

"Your daughter?" Phillip asked. "What happened to her?"

"She died. Her death was painful and slow. She was alone, and I could do nothing for her. My own child . . ." Schefield was silent for a moment. When he spoke again, there was a hard determination in his voice. "The virus hasn't weakened. It lies waiting like a thief, to steal our lives from us. Nothing has changed, not in all the years since this began. We are still held hostage by its threat, and will be until we die."

Maghrib felt the man's hopelessness. The men, women, and children of Biosphere Two were captives. They had survived the worst pandemic in the history of mankind, but they would never be free to leave the prison of the dome. His heart was moved with pity for them, for Schefield, and for the daughter he'd lost.

Arthur had been quiet while Schefield was speaking. Now, his brow was set in troubled lines. "We tried to save them," he said, as if Schefield

249

had accused him. "We thought we were right, thought the cultures would work using blood," he went on, seemingly unaware of the stares from those listeners both inside and outside the glass dome.

"Blood gave no lasting immunity," he told them. "We found that out too late. If there had been more time . . . We needed time to complete the trials. But so many died." His voice became a hushed breath. The fire crackled in the burning silence.

"You worked in the labs?" asked Schefield.

"In London. I was a doctor."

"That's amazing! I thought all the scientists were—I mean, we heard a few things, in the beginning days. I thought the mobs had—"

"I stayed hidden," said Arthur. "Before the day of the killings, when the mobs tore apart the labs and burned the doctors and scientists they found there . . . someone warned me, and I escaped. I've been hiding ever since."

Maghrib was relieved that this secret had been revealed to those survivors in the biosphere, and that he had not been the one to tell it. It had taken courage for Arthur to admit to them that he was a doctor, and that he had known about Biosphere Two all these years, and done nothing.

"I was afraid that if I told anyone of your existence, both you and I—all of you within the biosphere—would have been burned to death like the others. I was afraid to let anyone know I was ever a doctor."

"Until he saved my wife's life," said Maghrib loudly. "She lives, because of him. Now, our people know, and you know. He led us here to you." It was important to Maghrib that they understood.

"You can do nothing for us," said Schefield. "If

250

the trials with the virus failed—"

"They failed with immunity through blood," said Arthur, "but not with bone marrow. We had success with that. It seemed to be working. The trials were promising, and then—"

"And then the patients died," Schefield filled in the words. "They died, didn't they? That's what happened?"

"Yes," Arthur conceded, "but not as a result of our experiments. There wasn't time to test anyone who hadn't already been exposed to the virus. Sickness spread through our population so quickly. Preparations needed to be made. The procedure to obtain matching marrow donors was more complicated. Tissue-typing had to be checked and because of the rampant spread of the virus to our population, there weren't enough donors available with matching tissue types."

"The point is," said Schefield, "you failed. The patients died."

"The tests didn't fail," Arthur insisted. He seemed stronger than he had been before, unwilling to give in on this point. "We never completed the study. I think . . ." He let the words go unspoken.

"You think what? Are you trying to say it would work? Is that it?" Schefield's voice was loud and angry.

"Yes, I think it would. Bone marrow transplant was the strongest hope we had," he told them, excitement burning in his eyes.

Schefield laughed bitterly. "It might have been a *difficult* thing, trying to give bone marrow transplants to everyone in the world." His voice was low and curt with ridicule. "How did you imagine you'd do that?"

"It was the only hope we had!" Arthur stood up and walked away from the campfire.

"The man's a fool," Schefield accused. "His plan would never have worked to save the world. It's too complicated, too huge."

Maghrib wanted to leave the confrontation surrounding the campfire, but he stayed. It was important that Schefield understand something. "Your mind is blocked with hatred, and you are not hearing what he says. We did not come here to save the world." He tried to keep his voice under control, but he was angry, and it rose louder with the words.

"Why did you come?" Schefield was on his feet now, a tall, ghostly apparition behind a shield of glass.

"To save *your* lives," said Maghrib, standing in answer to the threatening image of the other man. "We don't need the transplants; you do."

Maghrib turned and walked into the dark, following Arthur's track of footprints in the yielding sand.

Thirty

"I thought about it," Paul Schefield said to the two men sitting across the glass from him in the morning sunlight, Maghrib and Arthur, "and I realized I hadn't given you a fair chance last night to explain your theory completely. I was too hard on you, because of my daughter, I suppose. Because of the deaths of so many people. They weren't your fault," he admitted. "You were the only one I had to blame."

"I thought about it too," said Arthur, ". . . all night. If anything, I'm more convinced than ever that it might work, and that we should try it."

Schefield sighed deeply. His reluctance to act on Arthur's theory was obvious. "Tell me again why you believe it would work now, when it failed then. What has changed? The virus is the same, deadly as ever."

"We've changed," Arthur leaned forward with the words, his face suffused with eagerness.

"Dammit, my daughter died!" Schefield swore. "She hadn't changed."

"No," Arthur agreed quickly, "but *we* have . . . we, the survivors outside. We have immunity to the virus. We lived through it, and we can pass that immunity on to you.

"We couldn't have succeeded when the world was

so full of people," Arthur went on, "but we are far fewer now. Our immunity will be passed on to our children, and there's a chance we can save you, too. With all that has happened," he added, "I think it's a chance worth taking."

"It may be your only chance," said Maghrib, "for when we leave this place, who else will know how to do such a thing? Arthur is the only healer I have found since leaving the Berber lands. He may be the only one alive. Who else could save you?"

Paul Schefield's brown eyes glanced from Arthur to Maghrib, moving with the anxious motion of a pendulum, back and forth.

The eyes are the rivers of the soul, thought Maghrib. At this moment, he felt the current of Schefield's soul flowing over him, washing him with the man's doubts, questions, and desperate hopes. The moment was the edge of a sheer cliff, a choice of stepping over the chasm, or going back.

And then Schefield decided; Maghrib could see it in his eyes.

"I have to talk to someone about this," said Schefield. "There's another biosphere."

"Another?" Arthur's eyes widened in surprise.

"In North America," Schefield went on. "I have to talk to the leader there—Jessica Nathan. Their situation is more critical than ours. It might be that you could tell them how to do this. Jessica might be willing to try it on her people. If it succeeds with them . . ." the pause was drawn out, lingering between his words, ". . . then we'll see."

"How is it you can speak to people in North America?" Maghrib's curiosity overwhelmed him.

"By satellite hook-up over the computer channel between our two systems."

"You can talk to a world across the ocean?" The idea bewildered him. He had walked from the desert of the Sahara, across mountains and beneath an

254

ocean to come to this place. Was it possible that a man could talk to someone so far away by this computer?

"I can't believe it," said Arthur, his expression incredulous. "Two biospheres still exist. It's fantastic! After everything that's happened—My God, it's impossible, but wonderful!"

"Understand," warned Schefield, "you're risking their lives with this idea. If it fails, they have no escape from the dome. The virus will be with them, and all of their efforts will have been for nothing. Think how important this is," he emphasized, "and tell me again, are you confident that the transplants will work?"

Maghrib couldn't answer such a question. No one could, except Arthur. He waited, watching as Arthur lifted his gaze to the heavens, and Maghrib was reminded of another day, another vision of this Briton gazing toward the sky, standing in the sunlight within a circle of stones.

"Tell them how to begin," said Arthur. "God alone can be certain, but I believe it will work. I'm sure it will. With skill and luck, the transplants will buy their freedom. And yours."

"I'll tell them now." Schefield walked away, disappearing deeper into the hidden places of the glass cave.

That was how Maghrib saw the place, a wondrous cave built by man, into which the virus could not reach, but from which a human voice could carry beyond an ocean to a people a continent away.

He closed his eyes to set this image in his mind. He knew one day he would tell it to his sons and daughters. Around a campfire such as this one, he would gather the grandchildren of his nation and tell them the story of a glass cave, and the vision of a man called Arthur.

Bram Nathan, Jessica's youngest surviving son in the biosphere, spent the evening of his twelfth birthday struggling to breathe. His mother supported him in her arms as the terrible coughing seized him and his body convulsed with painful spasms. Now, as had happened earlier in the night, his skin was paled with a bluish flush, as he fought to draw air into congested lungs.

An asthmatic since birth, Bram's airways were choked by the ash particles and gas toxins remaining in the biosphere since the fire. In time, most of the heavier ash particles had settled to the ground, and the sprinkler system had soaked them into the earth of the individual biomes, but the toxic gases produced from the burning plastics and other substances lingered and were absorbed by every living organism within the sphere, plants and animals alike. They polluted the drinking water. They were present in every kind of food source. Now those gases were present in Bram's blood, and were causing his attack.

"Try to swallow some of this." Jessica held the mug to her son's lips. The drink was a blend of aromatic herbs and tea leaves. She hoped the rising wisps of steam from the hot liquid would help to open his constricted airways.

He sipped weakly at the drink, coughed, and sipped a little more. After, he slumped against her. The effort had exhausted him.

It was nearly morning. Late night was always the hardest time for Bram, especially when the temperature was cold, but this night had been the worst. Too close. He'd scared her. More than once, she'd seen that she might lose him.

One by one, she might lose all of them.

She had known the deaths of her children, first

256

Matthew, then Cameron. Their deaths had claimed part of her life, too. She was less without them. The biosphere was less, and so was their world. Her childrens' lives were too precious for her not to do everything possible to save them. To save all the lives within the dome. Whatever the cost might be to herself, she was more determined than ever to bring the people of Biosphere Seven out of the sphere.

When the satellite call came from Paul Schefield that morning, Jessica was ready for any option he might suggest.

"Paul says this doctor believes it will work if the tissue types match, and if the recipients don't reject the transplants. He said the research he and his lab team conducted before everything fell apart showed early signs of being successful. The virus interfered with those results. It stopped their study before anything could be proven with humans." Jessica was alone in the computer room with Quinn. She tried to explain everything she had heard from Paul in Biosphere Two. To Jessica, Paul's message had sounded like an answer from God. Now, they had a chance.

"Dammit, Jessica! Do you think I'm going to stand back and let you throw your life away? Forget it! You're not going Outside. Get it out of your head. I don't care what Schefield or anyone else told you. It won't work. You'd die out there like . . . like all the others."

She knew he was thinking of Cameron and how he had died. They shared that pain. She understood, but she couldn't let even this hurt stop her. "There's no one else. I'm willing to risk my life, if it could mean a chance to save us. We can't go on waiting, Quinn. The children are dying—Cathe's children, and Bram is so sick. He won't live much longer like this. We've got to do something."

Quinn pulled her close to him. "Do you hear what you're saying? Jessie, the virus is still out there. If you go Outside, you'll die too. How will your death help them?"

"I might become sick," she conceded, "but if I survive the virus, if I live through it, then I could give a bone marrow transplant to some of the others. At least it's a hope. That's more than we have now."

"Jesus, woman!" Quinn's hands closed too tightly on her arms, hurting her, but the pain was in his eyes, on his face. She was the one who had caused it. He'd been through so much, they all had.

"Quinn," she said softly, "it's all right."

He was holding her away from him, stern and forceful, but she leaned her head against his chest. The hard grip of his fingers slackened on her arms, and she felt the anger go out of him. She pressed her face against his neck, and her arms went up his back, holding him to her in love.

"It's all right," she said the calming words again.

His heartbeat was a pulse between them, as if she was a part of him, and he a part of her. Her lips tasted the salt of his skin, and she kissed his neck, his chin, his mouth.

"I'm scared of losing you," he told her, "so damn scared. I remember how it was when Brad . . ." He didn't finish the sentence, but let the thought die unspoken. "If you were the one alone Outside, sick and needing me, and I couldn't —"

"I'm right here." Her fingers were a gentle touch on his neck.

"Jessie, promise me you won't do anything foolish."

"I promise that I love you." Her hands slid to the back of his head and drew him down into a kiss. "I promise that I want you." She pressed her body closer to his. "And I promise that I . . ."

His arm went tight around her back, and his knees bent, lowering, lowering, as he pulled her down with him to the hard track of the floor. Their fingers tore at resistent buttons and clothing, the bright heat of his skin burning hers, his touch urgent.

She was part of it, this desperate need, part of all he wanted; it was all she wanted, too. She looked into Quinn's eyes, a shining blue path, and saw into his soul.

"Don't go," he asked her one last time.

But she knew one day she would.

Alone in the computer room, Jessica filed the latest entry of her journal. She had kept a record of their days within the biosphere. She had counted the births and deaths, noted the changes which had come to them over the years. Her journal would be a chronicle of mankind's struggle for survival in the world which had been left to them.

It was past midnight; the computer registered time as well as her thoughts. Bram had been able to rest tonight; that much was good. Quinn was with him, sleeping in the same room, giving Jessica this breathing space to be apart from her worry, from her fears for this child.

It was natural for her to have come here, almost as if the computer was a close friend, someone who understood. She had always felt a strong pull within herself to continue this journal. At first, it had been an account of the final days of humankind, of those Outside. She had kept accurate details of how efficiently the biosphere had functioned, what adjustments had been made to insure its continuance, and listed how well all forms of life had existed beneath the shelter of the glass dome.

Now, however, what she wanted to record was the personal connection between herself and the biosphere. This might be the last journal entry she would write. If she went Outside—and the thought was in her mind to do so—then she wanted to be sure that the children born within Biosphere Seven might someday read this journal and see her not only as the leader they had known, but also as a person like themselves, one who had known fears, and doubts, and joys.

She knew that what she was writing was a bridge, linking her to them. She wrote these words for the children, for Quinn, and the others of the original team. If she listened to the voice of her heart, Jessica knew she wrote for herself, as well.

She wanted to leave something behind that said she had cared. She had lived in this sphere of life, not just existed. She had known love, happiness, and sorrow. Her life had been more than an effort to leave this place, more than a struggle to survive. This closed sphere was where her span of life had been given to her. To them all. Now, with her time here coming to an end, it became important to touch the others through these final words, to leave the people of this world a human touch.

What matters is that we have loved. All else means little. Life is an exercise of nature, without it. We are, and have been, much more than that. Our feelings are what marks us as human. Caring for one another all these years, makes us a family of man.

It would be morning soon. The night had passed in stillness. Looking to the sky for the first light of the new day, Jessica saved the journal entry and exited the file.

Each dawn was a beginning. Each day, a hope. Alone, she walked back to her room . . . back to the people who loved her.

Thirty-one

As each night turned to dawn, Willow Gray Wolf would awaken, go out into the cold and stand alone facing the east, beyond the boundaries of any house of wood or adobe, to watch and feel the purple and yellow mornings rise and heat the earth, just as she had done as a child in the camp of her father. It was a habit she and Josiah Gray Wolf had shared, this personal dawn each day. She knew and witnessed every morning. Each day of her life was counted in this simple beginning.

Spring had returned. The seal of winter cold upon the earth was easing, and the colors of life beginning to show once again on the healing land. Willow felt a oneness with this, for she was healing too. Like the frozen winter earth, Jonathan's death had brought a cold stillness to her life. She had known what it was to be stopped and unfeeling. Her world had slowed until the life force beating in her was almost too small to be noticed. For a time she had not taken notice, like the earth that each winter grows quiet and seems to die.

But she had not died. She lived, and through her, another life came to be.

Points of grass marked the opening of the hard and thawing ground. Grass was the firstborn of the land, leading the way for other plants to lift their way into the light. Like the small green spears which broke through the barrier of cold and solid earth, a thin cry sounded, breaking through the quiet of this dawn and reaching the mother, as new grass reaches to the sun.

Called to this sound as clearly as she was called to each morning, Willow turned and started back to the wooden house beside Mirror Lake. Her steps were halting, and she leaned heavily on the sturdy cane her brother Yuma had made for her.

Since the nearly fatal attack by the wolf-dog, Willow had been left crippled in her right leg. Her ankle had been crushed by the dog, and had never completely healed. The pain from the shattered bone had been terrible; it was the only force that had kept her awake and alive through the dark days after Jonathan died. Strangely, this suffering had saved her.

Now, since the birth of her child, she was healing in body and in spirit. She knew her ankle would never be whole again. It was as though she had been marked by this great loss in her life, losing Jonathan Katelo, and would carry that loss until the day she died.

The child's small cry sounded again. Like the morning sun, it touched her undeniably, and Willow hurried to the warm room where her infant son waited.

With Andrew, Brad had crossed into Texas two days earlier, and now was following the wide trace of the Ware River. It had been spring when he left this land a year ago, and now it was spring again. He thought of the flash flood that had taken four lives: Josiah and Elizabeth, young William Wyse, and Skeet Hallinger. These people were strong memories here, like the terror of the flood.

Other memories lingered in this place. He knew it

would be painful to be back. What if he had been wrong? What if the dreams of a fire were only his own longing to be with Jessica again? Now that he was close, he couldn't believe that he had done this, that he had come so far on the strength of a dream.

He was afraid to see her. He had to admit that to himself. A year was a long time. A person could change in a year, could sicken, or die. Had she forgiven him for taking Andrew away? So much to wonder. So much to fear. The river had led him to this land. What would lead him home?

If he rode on, he would be at the biosphere before dark. If he rode on, he would see Jessica and know the answers to all his questions, know the meaning of his dreams . . . but he didn't ride on. He waited, uncertainty burning like a live coal within his heart.

He had crossed the snow-laden land with a young child to be with her. He had slept in the cold, eaten little, and driven himself hard to reach this place. Now that he had come so close, his courage was lost. He couldn't find the will to ride up to the glass walls of the biosphere and see her.

The day will keep, he thought. *Tomorrow. I'll ride in with Andrew tomorrow.* It was a promise he made to himself.

When night came he didn't sleep. The ground held remembrances that rose up like a mist and covered over him. He felt the memories crossing through the broken paths of his mind, twisting and rushing like some tormented beast. They weren't dreams. He lay awake knowing the torment was real, and so was this place.

When the last star of morning disappeared, Brad closed his eyes and drifted into exhausted sleep. There was no night in his dream, no bright stars to hold the heavens by, for the sky he saw was red with flames. Fire was the known reality. He had felt it searching in his mind all night, trying to find the dream. He had held it back as long as he had stayed awake, but now he could only watch.

She was there, Jessica, a muted image trapped by the garish blaze. Dark smoke curled toward her, and he felt the heat from the fire push at him, the sound of burning billow like waves in the air, like the flap of a sea bird's wings. She was the fire that had called to him. She was the flames that had haunted his dreams. *Jessie . . . Jessie . . .*

"Jessie!"

The coral and yellow sky of morning was like the fire, only softer. Softer. The pounding crush of Brad's heartbeat slowed at the sight of it, as the dream faded back into the skies of night and sleep.

Quickly, he fed Andrew and bundled him warmly into the backpack. Whatever doubts he'd had the day before were gone.

"It won't be far now," he said to his son. "We're almost home."

Jessica gathered the things Paul Schefield told her she would need. Diana Hunt's lab provided the eighteen gauge large-bore aspiration needle, a stylet to cut into the bone, and syringe. She wrapped them in a clean cloth, and put them in a box. Into the same box Jessica put a bottle of rubbing alcohol, sterile cotton packs, adhesive bandages, a handful of Demerol tablets, and two drawn syringes of Novocain.

The Novocain would only work until the needle hit bone. When the cutting stylet started twisting into the iliac crest at the top of her hipbone, and she had to keep pushing the narrow blade deeper into the bone cortex until she hit the soft marrow, it was going to hurt like hell. She knew that, but there wasn't any choice. Without anyone to help her, she'd have to do the agonizing surgical procedure on herself. On impulse, she grabbed another handful of Demerol tablets and hurried out of the lab.

She had spent time with her four children—Roarke, Bram, Meredith, and Rachel—during the night. That had been hard, being with them and not letting them know what she was planning.

She had wanted to see Trinity too, but he hadn't spoken to her since the day the Biosphere Four experiments were erased from the computer files. He blamed her for that, and he was right. Cathe had insisted, but Jessica had to admit that she was the one with the final say. Now, she wished she hadn't allowed Cathe to delete the file. Knowledge was always valuable. It was fear that had made her destroy it.

The world of Biosphere Seven was still asleep. In an hour, it would be too late. If she intended to go through with her decision, she would have to act now, before she lost her courage. Cradling the box of medical supplies in her arms, Jessica hurried to the docking chamber and pressed the button opening the sliding steel doors.

Her memories of this room were colored with sorrow. She put the box down at her feet, then stood for a moment at the center of the room, remembering . . . Josiah, so young and so long ago, leaving the biosphere in the sealed PAL vehicle . . . Mike York standing in this room waving goodbye to the little boy standing at Jessica's side, Trinity . . . and Cameron, standing with Sidra, their hands pressed on the glass, looking in.

Cameron. He had come here, her son. He had given himself a chance to live Outside. Whatever his fears had been at leaving the sphere, he had conquered them. Did she have less courage?

She looked through the triangles of glass. The morning sky was brightening to a silvered blue.

Everyone would be up soon. There wasn't much time.

Leaning forward, Jessica pushed the box closer to the glass outer door. She would go back to the entrance of the docking chamber and start the sequence that would seal off the chamber from the rest of the biosphere with thick, stainless steel doors, then would open the glass exit door from the chamber itself.

Later, when they realized what she'd done, Quinn could evacuate the air from the docking chamber and sterilize the area before opening this biome to the rest of the sphere. That would safeguard them from any exposure to the virus. By that time, it would be far too late to stop her. Once she left, she could never come back.

Jessica pushed the box level with the door, then straightened and looked out. The land stretched far into the distance. Outside. She would be there soon. She would walk on the grass and breathe the blessing of fresh air, not the smoke and toxic fumes of the biosphere. She would run to the top of the hill and—

She saw a man coming down the grassy slope toward her.

It was hard to see through the film of ash that clung to the glass. She rubbed at the pane with her hand, smearing the image. Moving over to a cleaner point on the wall, she looked out again. It *was* a man. He was riding one horse and leading another.

He was still too far away for her to see clearly, but something about him . . .

And then she knew. *Brad*.

For an instant, all she thought was that he had come home. He was back where she could see him, where she could talk to him. A fierce jealousy that had been a cold and living thing within her said— *He's come back to me.* She was glad. For that one moment, she didn't care about anything but that. He had come back for her.

But, if Brad was here, where was Andrew?

All that had been beauty a moment before turned to ashes. Had he come back to tell her that Andrew was dead? Their son. Would he have come so far without the child? In the terror of this thought she waited, watching him as he rode nearer.

When he was close enough for her to see his face, he looked directly at where she stood, and she knew that he had seen her, too. She couldn't read the message in his eyes. Too far away. They were years, and space, and a glass wall away. The biosphere had kept them apart. Only the child they shared had brought them together. And now . . .

She waited, afraid to move from this spot, afraid to feel anything.

Brad swung his leg over the back of the saddle and dropped down from the horse. He stepped closer, and pulled his arms free of the straps over his shoulders, taking off the leather and fur backpack he had been wearing, and lowering it to the ground in front of him.

The backpack moved. Out of it came a small hand and arm, and then the head of a little boy with dark, shining hair.

"Andrew!"

Brad told him something, Jessica couldn't hear what was said, and the boy started toward her, a two-year-old with sturdy little legs lifting and falling, slowly at first, and then running across the grassy plain to the biosphere. To his mother. To her.

Thirty-two

"I'll do it," Brad told her, after he'd heard the plan for the bone marrow transplants. "I've had the virus, and it makes much more sense than risking your life."

"It's a painful procedure," she warned him, "and there's a risk of infection to you. The conditions won't be sterile. I want you to understand—there's a danger of blood clotting, hemorrhage, inflammation of the bone, or the tissue surrounding the surgical site . . ."

"Jessica, stop telling me all the things that could go wrong. I knew you needed me and now I'm here. I'll do it, whatever it takes."

She sighed. He was right, of course. He was a better choice for the marrow transplant. He had survived the virus and would have immunity which he might pass on to the rest of them, if the tissue types matched. That was the first step. It required a simple blood test for everyone in the dome, but then they would know. Brad wouldn't have to be tested. She already knew what tissue type he was because of the blood transfusion for Cameron.

"If you're sure," she told him, still giving him the chance to back out of it.

"If I wasn't sure, I wouldn't have traveled through the winter with a two-year-old just to come back to you. I'm here because I want to be.

Tell me what needs to be done, and I'll do it."

"All right," she said, taking another deep breath. "I guess the next step is to convince everyone else. They have to understand what it would mean, and agree to take the risk."

"I know you're scared, Jessie." His voice was a soft, calming stream. She felt as if she was sliding into it, letting him carry her in the refuge of that soothing flow. "I'm with you, if that makes it any better."

"Any better! If you hadn't arrived when you did, I'd be Outside right now."

"That wouldn't have been so smart." He didn't list all the significant dangers. He didn't need to.

"I was desperate, Brad. We're way past the point of waiting for a change and doing nothing. Something has to happen, and now. The fire forced this on us. It made any other decision impossible."

In the few minutes they'd been together, Jessica had told him about Cassi and the fire set in the granary. He listened intently to everything she said, and when she was through, he stunned her by saying he'd known about the fire, and that was why he had come back.

"I dreamed it," he explained. "At first, I thought it was my reaction to missing you, worrying about you, but the dream kept persisting night after night, until I had to believe it was a warning and listened to it."

She was shocked. "You *do* have some sort of hotline to God, don't you?"

He grinned, and she remembered the way his smile always made her feel. She loved him; she couldn't deny it, and she was tired of trying to convince herself that she ever could.

"What about Andrew?" she asked. "What's going to happen to him if you get sick?"

270

"I'm not going to get sick," he promised, "but if the worst happens and I do, then you can come out of the biosphere the way you would have done anyway."

"I could take care of both of you."

"You could."

And now she was smiling back at him, because he made her feel so sure and so confident. "I would, you know—take care of you." The smile was gone now, and she suddenly felt as if she wanted to cry. "I stayed in here once, when you were sick and needed me." The words were painful for her, hurting, but needed to be spoken. "I could never do that again."

"Jessica . . ."

And then she said it, words she couldn't take back. Didn't want to take back. They surfaced from her, and she said them, her voice trembling. "I'm still your wife, Brad, whatever else has happened. That hasn't changed, and never will. I still love you. I could never watch you suffer again, and not destroy the whole world to be with you. I couldn't do it again. I wouldn't. Not again."

She was crying. The tears burned her eyes and ran down her cheeks as if unstoppable. She was crying for all they had lost, for all she had given up . . . and for all they still had between them. She was crying for love.

Our feelings are what marks us as human. She remembered the words of her journal. *What matters is that we have loved.*

In spite of everything, all that was gone, all that was forever lost, they had found love. Their lives had been a telling of that commitment to each other. Living it. They had found love, and in the final judgement, it was all that mattered.

* * *

271

Telling Quinn was the hardest thing Jessica had ever done.

"You were going to leave without a word to me? I thought we'd talked about this, Jessie, that we'd decided it was too dangerous."

"You decided," she came back at him, feeling hurt, feeling wronged by his anger, and feeling guilty at the way her emotions were torn between him and Brad. She felt as if her soul were being ripped apart. She loved Quinn. She loved Brad. The impossible thing was she loved them both, and couldn't imagine living without either one.

"You don't do things like this on your own, Jessica. You know that. Cameron did, and he died because of it."

"And Sidra lived."

Quinn looked for a minute as if he was going to hit her. She almost wished he would, then she could learn to hate him and not go on feeling this unbreakable bond to two men, but he didn't hit her. He didn't touch her at all. And that was worse.

"Quinn—"

"Just tell me," he didn't look at her when he spoke, "is it because of Brad? Is he the reason you want to leave? What are we dealing with, Jessica? Are you acting as a leader of this biosphere, or as a woman in love?"

She felt as if he had hit her, as if the words had been closed fists. It was hard to breathe. Hard not to cry out for him to stop. She felt crushed by the truth of his words, and by another truth just as strong, that what he thought of her mattered. The love she felt for Quinn was as undeniable as the love she felt for Brad.

She loved him, but she was also angry.

"I would have gone Outside to save our lives,

272

Quinn. Brad wasn't here. I didn't know anything about that. It wasn't for him. It would have been for you, and for our children," she said in words that were weeping mourners. "I would have put my life at stake for the people of this biosphere." She was angry enough to say what needed to be said.

"I'm tired of making excuses, pretending and lying to you, Quinn. I love Brad."

He looked up. Now, she saw his eyes, those blue pathways she had followed to his soul so long ago.

"And I love you, too. With everything I am, I love you, Quinn. You're always so ready not to believe that, but it's the truth. God help us all, I'm in love with both of you, and I'm always going to be. There's not a damn thing I can do about it."

Stronger for having said the truth at last, she walked out of the room and left him standing alone.

The emergency group meeting of Biosphere Seven decided unanimously to follow the procedures given to them by Arthur Penn. Even overly-cautious Cathe voted for taking this chance, and began tissue typing immediately. Jessica had been afraid they might say no. When the vote was taken, it was clear that they knew they didn't have a choice.

There were twenty lives in Biosphere Seven: Jessica, Quinn, and their four children; Cathe, Daniel, and their nine; Alix and Lara Hunter; Griffin Llewellyn, and Trinity. The hard fact was that a tissue match was much more complicated for bone marrow transplants than for blood transfusions.

As Arthur explained to them, it was a matter of histocompatibility antigens. These antigens, or proteins, were naturally present in the tissues and represented a role in the body's immune system. The most critical of these were the HLAs, human leukocyte antigens. These HLA *fingerprints* were present on the surface of a person's cells, an inherited pattern, and unique to that individual. A perfect tissue match was possible only in the case of identical twins, but siblings, relatives, and sometimes unrelated people could achieve closely matching HLA types.

They used antiserum containing antibodies of Brad's HLA blood proteins for the test specimens. Where the antigen was present, the color of the antiserum changed.

It wasn't possible that Brad's tissue type would be compatible with all of them. They knew that before the blood tests were done. It was like drawing straws to see which of them might live. The wait for the test results was agonizing. Cathe read them in the lab.

Jessica overheard the whispers among those who were waiting outside the closed door of the lab.

"It'll be the Innes kids, you wait and see," Lara Hunter told her sister Alix. "Cathe will say her kids matched, even if they didn't."

"Maybe someone else should be in there," agreed Alix, "to keep it honest."

Jessica thought about telling them that Cathe was as honest as they come. She thought about telling them a lot of things, but she didn't. Alix had been Quinn's lover not so long ago, and that fact put a wall between Jessica and both of these sisters. They weren't likely to believe anything she said, especially Alix, and there was an awkwardness in any confrontation between them that Jessica would rather simply avoid. On a bigger issue she would take it on, but for this . . . she let their comments go.

Everyone was nervous. Some were afraid. That was making them say stupid things. Jessica had heard nine-year-old Dalton Innes tell his brother, "I don't want them to transplant me. You gotta have a shot, and it makes you sick, and if it works, you gotta leave everybody. You gotta go Outside." The little ones were afraid, too.

When Cathe came out of the lab, the silence felt like a real presence. It ate at them. No one spoke, or even breathed. Instead, they watched Cathe Innes' eyes, and waited to read the sentence of death that might come to them in the meaning of her regretful glance.

"These are the names with a good possible match," Cathe told them bluntly. There was nothing subtle about Cathe. It was her way, thought Jessica. It always had been.

"I'm just going to say them. Nobody stop me until I'm through."

No one said anything.

"Maria Innes, Paige Innes," Cathe began.

"What did I tell you," Lara fiercely whispered.

Jessica wanted to scream. They were being numbered for life or death. Those on the right will live. Those on the left—

"Quinn Kelsey."

Jessica turned and stared at him, unable to stop herself from this act. It was unbelievable that it would be Brad who might save Quinn.

Cathe went on calling the names. "Rachel Nathan."

Quinn's daughter, thought Jessica. They shared more than personality. The thought came to her, tearing at her soul—*Would Cameron have been a match too, if he had stayed in the sphere?*

"Griffin Llewellyn," said Cathe, "and Lara

275

Hunter."

When she stopped calling the names, there was an audible gasp from someone in the hall.

"Only six!" Alix Hunter verbalized the number they all knew. Her name hadn't been called. "That can't be right. How can Lara be a match and not me? We're sisters. We have the same blood type."

"You have different fathers, different tissue types," Cathe tried to explain to the obviously distraught young woman.

"What about the rest of us?" asked Samantha Innes. She was twenty-two, the eldest of Cathe's children still living within the sphere. "What happens to us?"

Cathe looked unsure if she should speak. She glanced questioningly at Jessica, and then, as if making up her mind, declared what else she had to say. "There are four more possible recipients among us."

The room stilled again.

"They aren't as strong a match as the others, less chance for successful transplants." It was as if she was stalling, trying to decide how much to give, how much to keep. "The danger would be rejection. I don't know if we should attempt it with such minimal matches, but with immunosuppressant drugs such as cyclosporine, a good result might be possible."

"What are the names?" It was Cathe's husband, Daniel Urquidez, who had asked.

Jessica felt the tension present in the room, as if all of them were suspended by thin paper, waiting to fall through. "Tell us the names, Cathe. We'll ask Arthur Penn whether we should go ahead with them."

Cathe cleared her throat, straightened her back,

and read the four names from the list. "Alix Hunter."

"Oh, God!" cried Alix, and began to sob.

"Christopher Innes, Dalton Innes—"

"Mom—I don't want to do it," Dalton Innes cried out.

Cathe took a long breath, and read the last name. "Daniel Urquidez."

Not herself, thought Jessica. Her children, her husband, but not herself. Like me. She looked at Cathe, and what she saw in this good friend's eyes told her that Cathe understood what she was thinking. They had lived together for too long not to know the train of each other's mind.

"Don't make me go, Mama. I'm scared of Outside. I'm scared to be alone." Dalton ran into his mother's arms, and Cathe stood holding him, trying to calm his fears.

"What happens next?" asked Griff. He was a quiet man, who over the years had shown himself to be more interested in his study of bugs than in any people of the biosphere. It seemed strange, at first, that he should be the one to ask, but then Jessica remembered that his name was on the first list. He was one of the six.

"The next step is to give Brad the surgical pack," she said loud enough for all of them to hear, "and to wait for him to provide the marrow sample, if that's possible."

"If it's possible!" mimicked Alix. "After what we've just gone through? It damn well better be possible!"

Jessica wanted to choke her. Her fingers ached to wrap around Alix Hunter's slender, young throat. "If you don't shut up," she said, "I'm going to give your place for the transplant to Meredith. Understand?"

For a minute Alix looked really worried, then her face relaxed a little. "You can't do that. Meredith's test didn't match."

Jessica knew Alix didn't know enough about tissue typing to be really sure of her ground. She'd put the doubt in Alix's mind, and that was enough. The girl didn't say another word.

"Go on back to your room," she said to her. "All of you, go back to your work and leave the rest to me. When Brad's ready, he'll give us the sample, and we'll begin the first of the transplants."

The group broke up then, each of them going back to their families, their lives, their work here within the biosphere. Jessica hurried away, too. She walked upstairs to the viewing window, where she stared out through the clear pane of unlined glass.

The world Outside seemed frightening and unreal at this moment. She had been inside the biosphere for so long, over half her life, that it was more a home to her now than the other world. If it seemed so strange and fearful to her, how must it be to a little boy like Dalton? He had never known any other place.

"All right if I join you?" Quinn stood just inside the doorway.

"I'm lousy company," she warned him, turning back to the view beyond the glass.

"I'll take my chances." He sat beside her on the bench. "It's beautiful Outside right now, flowers blooming across the desert, green shoots everywhere you look."

"It's spring," she said flatly. "It happens every year."

He smiled at her attempt at sarcasm. "I remember. I haven't forgotten spring. I haven't forgotten

278

a lot of other things, either."

She glanced at him. What was he leading up to?

"We've been together a long time, my love. I've done a lot of thinking lately about us, about how this whole thing has come to be, the biosphere, the virus, and now us trying to take on one man's immunity, just to survive in our own world." He shook his head as if the concept were overwhelming.

"And what did you decide, after all this serious thought?"

There was no smile on his face now. The blue tracks were back, and she saw right into him. "One thing's for certain; I'm not leaving the sphere without you."

"Quinn, you have the tissue match."

"Maybe, but I don't care about that. There's nothing Outside that I need. My world's where you are. I've been with you too long, Jessie. I'm not leaving you, no matter what."

The words were hard to hear, beautiful, but hard for her. She looked away from him, back at the land Outside. It drew her, too. The land, and the man who was waiting for her there.

"The other thing I wanted to tell you," he said slowly, turning the words over like a gift, "is that I've done some thinking about you and Brad. I understand the way you feel about him," he let out one short breath, "and I guess I'd be feeling the same way he does about you, if I were him."

She turned to face him. "What are you saying? That you want me to go to Brad?" She felt the tears pulling at her, chest swollen with hurt, eyes stinging.

"No," he closed his eyes when he said it, as if the thought was too hard to picture, "not that. I wouldn't give you up." He was working up to the words, shifting his position on the bench, glancing away. "This is going to sound strange, I guess."

She waited.

"If we get out of here," he began at last, "I don't see why we can't all live together—the three of us."

She hadn't been expecting that.

"We're not teenagers, Jessie. I know you were with him first; he knows you've been with me all these years. Hell, for that matter, you and I have been with other people in this biosphere. That's not what counts."

"What counts?" she asked him.

"Love. When all the games are over, that's the only thing you take home as a winner. I don't want to ever lose that, Jessica, and I don't want to ever lose you. So I say we become a triangle, me and you and him. What do you think?"

She wasn't thinking; she was feeling. The earth was outside them all, as if the three of them were apart from it. They were their own world, and made it the way it was and would be, only for them.

"Jessie, say something. I'm going crazy wondering what you're thinking."

"Come closer," she told him.

He slid over on the bench.

"It might not work," she said.

"I know."

"I mean, the immunity might not take, and even if it does, I might not ever find a way to leave the biosphere."

"I know that," he said, "but if we do, I wanted you to know that this is what I want for us. This is the life I see."

"You've made it happen, Quinn."

"What?"

280

"You've made us that triangle."

"Oh, I don't know about that."

"For me, it already is," she said. "I feel it; it's real."

He nodded. "We'll have to see what Brad thinks of the idea. It's not a notion that would appeal to most men. But Jessie, we're in a new world now. We can make our own rules. Who says we can't be together if that's what makes us happy? Who's going to stop us?"

"Quinn."

"What?"

"God, how I love you!" She put her hand on his cheek, touching him, drawing him closer, "But you're Irish, and you never know when to quit."

"I don't?" He leaned closer still.

She shook her head. "Stop talking, Quinn, and kiss me."

Thirty-three

Sidra knew the way from here. She recognized the scarp of land as it sloped from the foothills toward the high desert floor. This was the hunter's trail she had walked with Shepherd, Willow, and the others when they'd searched for Sagamore, found him so badly injured, and carried him home to the People.

The memory of that day flooded through her, and she thought of her father, this man the others called Sagamore. What would he say when he saw her? What would he think of the fact that she had left Seth and come home? How would she explain it to him, the feelings that had driven her apart from Seth, apart from Parker, and back to the seared earth of this place?

The land was welcoming, a carpet of desert flowers, the blossoms pressing their tiny faces to the sun. The day was full with sounds of life: the cry of a brown-winged hawk overhead, a soft wind blowing wispy plumes of grass, and the steady thud of the horse's hooves against the yielding ground. She listened, drew it all in, and settled it in her memory.

This time, she had found her way, alone.

I've changed from the girl who left this place, she realized. I'm stronger now, able to have come back here alone, because that was my choice, and not to please anyone else. Able to stand on my own.

All of life was a change. Since the day she'd left

the biosphere she'd traveled across the distances of the Outside world, lived with three men, and found her way back to this place she called home. She had become a survivor, like the rest of those who called themselves the People. She hadn't been one of them when she left the Outsider's camp with Seth, but she was one of them now. She was a daughter of this land, these people, and she was coming home.

Up ahead of her, she saw the small rise where the ground crested before it leveled to the desert floor below. From there, she would be able to see the camp, and the glass walls of Biosphere Seven in the distance beyond it.

She hesitated, full of doubt. *Only a few more feet.* Part of her wanted to pull back on the reins and wait. *Wait.* Part of her wanted to rush ahead, to gallop down the hill and into the camp. *Into the arms of her father.*

Instead, Sidra nudged the mare gently with her knees, then let it trot forward at its own pace, carrying them to the top of the rise.

"Oh, God," she said. "What happened?"

The words escaped her, as Sidra stared down at what had once been the camp of the Outsiders . . . adobe houses and storage huts, planted fields, and rows of trees . . . where now there was nothing. At first, she thought this had to be the wrong place, she'd made a mistake, but then she saw sunlight glinting off the glass walls of Biosphere Seven.

In the river valley, it was as if the campsite of the People had never been there. *Even the trees!*

Everything was gone.

Brad took the bag of surgical implements and supplies from the docking chamber. He'd had one good look at the syringe, the size of the needle, and the stylet that would twist into the bone, then he'd

283

put it all back into the bag. Out of sight, but not out of mind.

The thing was, even if he could manage it by himself — and he wasn't at all sure that he could — what was he going to do about Andrew? He couldn't let his two-year-old son run around in the desert alone while he was busy drilling holes in his own hipbone with a cutting instrument that looked like it ought to be mining for ore in rock.

The thought struck him as funny. They were mining for ore, in a way. His body held a value that was greater than any gold deposit ever found on earth. This was the payload that might save their lives. If that fellow Arthur Penn was here, this whole thing would be a lot easier. But, he wasn't. It wouldn't be easy. In fact, he wasn't sure he could do it.

That was what scared him most. What if he tried and couldn't stand the pain? What if he couldn't go on with it, once he started? If he quit, he would be responsible when the people in the sphere began dying. Jessica had been ready to come Outside, to contract the virus, and if she recovered from that, then do even this to try to save them. She had been willing to risk everything. Now, he needed to be willing to risk everything too. Including pain.

But what about Andrew? Brad watched his son for a minute. The boy was playing with a handful of pebbles, throwing them high into the air and racing away from them as they fell. He was laughing the way only a two-year-old laughs, irrepressible giggles, delighting in all the things of life that were new. Watching him took Brad's attention off everything else, and he started laughing too.

"Watch out, Andrew!" he joined in the game. "Run that way. Look out. Over there. Run back, run back!"

He had been watching the boy, chasing after him

and watching the way the pebbles fell. Andrew had raced five or six feet away, toward the escarpment where the land broke and banked to the river valley below. Brad ran a few steps after him. "Not too far," he warned.

The sunlight was in Brad's eyes, a glare so bright he couldn't see where the child was standing until he moved to the side a couple of steps and the blinding brightness eased.

Then he saw her.

The woman was standing at the crest of the ridge. She was young, tall and slim, long dark hair . . .

"Willow!" he cried. He ran across the high plain toward her. She was running, too.

She *was* Spirit Woman! She had known. Somehow she had known how desperate he was and she'd come here to help him. Now, it would be all right. Now, with her help, they would find a way to save them all!

"Prophet!" the woman called.

Brad stopped. Hearing her voice, he knew. It wasn't Willow, wasn't Spirit Woman, but Sidra.

Andrew came racing after him. His arms wrapped tightly around Brad's leg, and his face pressed hard against the cloth.

"It's all right. She's a friend," Brad told him, realizing how much these sudden actions had scared the child. He picked him up.

Andrew burrowed his face against Brad's neck, turning away from the woman who was very close now. He wouldn't look at her.

"Sidra. I never thought I'd see you again. Where are the others?"

"I came alone." Her face was streaked with tears, her eyes red and swollen. "What happened here? Where's my father?" She was sobbing. "Where are the children? The houses? The trees?"

285

"Don't, Sidra." Brad put one arm around her, and she moved into his embrace as if she were another frightened child, like Andrew.

"Are they all dead?"

"No, they're not all—"

"My father? Is he . . . ?"

Brad couldn't lie to her. "I'm sorry. Your father and Elizabeth are dead."

She pulled closer to him, as if the pain of his words was too great. For a moment, he said nothing. He stood with her, the child between them, and held her while the pain became tolerable. He heard a hawk cry in that space of time, and thought of Sagamore, his friend.

"Tell me," she said at last, and stepped away. Her eyes were dry.

"It was the rainy season, in the spring, over a year ago. We had heavy rainfall for nearly a week, and then . . . a flash flood," he said. "It washed out of the hills and carried everything in its path away. We lost Skeet Hallinger that day, and young William Wyse."

"Everything's gone," she breathed the words. "It's like a hand came and scraped it all away."

Brad nodded. "It's like it was before we came. We didn't make much difference here."

Sidra stood straighter. "Where are they, everyone else?"

"They left."

"Left?" She acted as if she couldn't believe it.

"There was nothing to keep them here," he explained. "The fields were gone, the houses, everything. Life was too hard. This high desert was never good for farming. We decided to head north to someplace where summers didn't burn the crops in the fields, where the children could grow up seeing trees and rich farmland, where life would be easier."

"We?" she asked. "You went with them?"

He nodded.

"But you came back. Why?"

His glance met her eyes. "You came back too. We both had our reasons. Maybe we should leave it at that."

She seemed to think about it for a minute, accepted what he'd said, and then asked, "This is Andrew?"

Brad smiled, and tried to get the boy to turn around. Andrew was wedged against him like a sea urchin to a rock. "Right now, I think he's a rabbit, hiding."

"Not a rabbit," said Andrew, his voice muffled.

"I think he's a little wolf cub," said Sidra.

The boy lifted his head and peaked beneath the fringe of his dark bangs at her.

"I was a wolf cub like you once," she said. "My father was Josiah Gray Wolf, leader of the People."

Andrew looked at his father questioningly.

"It's true, little guy," Brad told him.

The boy pushed back and wriggled his way out of his father's arms. He walked to where Sidra stood, and put his small hand in hers.

"I think you've made a friend," Brad told her.

It was good to watch them together. Andrew needed other people. And Brad—

He suddenly realized what Sidra's coming here could mean. He had been so unsure of himself. Now, if she would help him, it might make the difference.

"Come on," he said, excitement carrying in the timbre of his voice. "Follow me up to the biosphere. Talk to Jessica and the others. There's a lot we have to tell you."

They walked toward the sphere, the sunlight at their backs, and the hope of a new beginning ahead of them.

* * *

Before the day was over, Sidra had not only agreed to help Brad obtain his sample of marrow by performing the arduous surgical procedure for him, but had insisted on donating her own bone marrow, too. A sample of her blood was drawn and tested for tissue typing with the others. Her tissue type was a close probable match for several members of Sidra's immediate family: Cathe, Samantha, Anne, and Thomas. The match was less perfect with brothers William and Dalton, but with the option of the immunosuppressant drugs, the decision was made to try the transplants anyway, and hope that they might take.

"It's incredible that both of you have come here now," said Jessica, "when only days ago, things were at their most hopeless."

"How could you not be one of the tissue matches?" asked Brad. "How could that happen? Of all the people here I wanted to help . . ."

"With what you and Sidra are willing to do for us, there are fourteen out of twenty people who will be given a chance. That's more than I ever hoped for."

"It's you I wanted to save," he told her.

"I know."

Sidra thought that they might want to be alone. She left them and wandered up the outer staircase to the observation window platform, where she waited to talk with Trinity. She had asked that he meet her there.

Waiting for him, she had some time to think. Trinity's name wasn't on the list. Even with the drugs, his tissue type wasn't a possible match with either hers or Brad's. Like Jessica, Trinity would be one of those left behind. It seemed so wrong.

She had come back because she was drawn to this place, because her parents were here, and this was the world she was familiar with. That much was true, but if she was honest with herself, she knew that she had come back mostly for one reason—to see Trinity again.

When he walked into the observation room she felt her breath draw in, for he had changed more than she'd expected. She'd been gone for only a little over a year, but Trinity looked years older. Something had changed in his eyes. Some sorrow had marked him, and she saw the scar of it at once . . . in the *aloneness* that he wore like a mask over his skin. She saw it in the way he looked, and in the way he looked at her.

"I've come home, Trinity. I'm not leaving here ever again." These were her words of greeting to him, telling him that she wouldn't go away. Too many people had left him; she saw that at once. Too many people had left them both. She understood.

"It's good to see you again," Trinity said. "I never thought I would, once you left here."

"That's what Brad told me, too." She was nervous with him, scared of what she might say wrong. It surprised her, feeling this way. She had always been good friends with Trinity. Now, she was unsure of herself, and unsure of him, as well.

"You're going to do the transplant for them?"

She nodded. "I wish it were for you."

"Do you?"

"What is it, Trin? What's happened to you? I came back here thinking . . ."

"Thinking what? That I'd be the same? That this place would be the same? Well, nothing is. You left, and that changed a lot of things. It changed me, for one."

She knew then that he loved her. Maybe she'd known it all along. Before, she hadn't let herself think about his pain, what leaving the biosphere with Cameron had done to so many people—to her mother, to Jessica, to Trinity. Now, she saw it.

"I thought of you when I was away," she told him. It was the truth. She'd thought of him more and more in the last few months, when she was with Parker, and when she was alone and on her way back. "I thought of how it was when we were kids growing up, and how you were always there for me."

"That was a long time ago."

"Not so long. I remember it. Don't you, Trin? Don't you remember?"

"What do you want from me, Sidra? Why did you come back?"

"To see you again," she said, and didn't know why she was crying. "I wanted to help you, if I could."

"You can't," he told her. "Not you. Not Brad. Get somebody else for your game. I don't understand the rules, and I don't want to play anymore."

"Why are you so angry? Do you hate me that much?"

He pressed his hands on the glass. "Hate you? Yes, sometimes I do. My God, Sidra. My God." He shook his head. "I wish you luck with the transplants, with all of it. At least you and Brad are doing something to try to get them out. I tried, but they . . ."

"They what?" She knew he was getting ready to go, and she didn't want him to leave.

"Doesn't matter. I hope this Arthur Penn knows what he's doing. After what you'll have to go through to get the stuff, I hope to God it works. You and Brad might save our world yet. Hell, maybe in a few years you can get Andrew in on it, too. He's little, but who knows. Maybe when he's nine or ten—"

"What did you say?" The thought was making her heart race.

"I said, maybe in a few years—"

"No, about Andrew. Why didn't we think of him before? He's been right here in front of us the whole time."

"Wait a minute. Andrew can't be more than two. You couldn't get enough from him to do anything. Could you?"

"According to Penn, it doesn't take much. If Andrew's a match for the rest of you . . ." she jumped up and started down the stairs.

"Where are you—"

"I'll talk to you later. I've got to get that blood test and check it out right now. If we're lucky, maybe all of us can come home."

She hurried down the stairs and raced across the hardened ground of the high desert, shouting, "Brad! Andrew!"

One thing she knew for certain. She wasn't going to give up on Trinity. Not now. Not when there was a chance of future for them both.

Thirty-four

Parker had walked all the way from Cheyenne Mountain, Colorado, to this peak-ringed valley of Montana. The journey had retaught him about the necessities of living, basic needs he had forgotten while remaining in the NORAD caves: finding food, warm clothing and sturdy shoes, protecting himself from predators.

If he wanted to eat, he had to kill or take from the land. If he wanted to survive the cold night, he had to build a fire and sleep beside it each evening when the hunters' eyes stalked the dark. If he wanted to find his way to where he was going, he had to observe the land, notice the gradual rise of the ground, the name of a creek, and the places Sidra told him he would pass on his way to Mirror Lake. To all things, Parker became observant once again, as if he had woken up from a long night of exhausting sleep.

The voices of his wife and children had left him. For the first time since their deaths, and since Sidra left him, he was completely alone. In that solitude of mind and spirit, he had traveled toward the promise of other people, toward Montana, and the future he hoped would be there.

His clothes were nearly dry from the late morning sun. He had crossed the Missouri River at dawn, and walked so fast to warm himself that a heat rose off him in wisps of steam. Now, he had come to the crest of the foothill and the valley floor lay cast like a green net below him.

Parker ran rough fingers through his hair, pushing the coppery strands back from his eyes. Mirror Lake was just as Sidra had described it to him, a silvered medallion shining on the land. Framing the lake was a jagged range of black mountains. A wide stretch of grassland was enclosed by thick woodlands to the north, east, and south. To the west, the grassland broke free of the ring of mountains and continued in a green and unobstructed plain.

The house and smaller outbuildings were scattered within close distance of the lake. From where he stood, it seemed to Parker as if the house and buildings were a child's toys, and he was the only one to see them. None of it seemed real. It was too much like the memory of other images in his mind . . . of his wife at home, or his children playing on the farm. He almost turned away. And then he saw her.

The tall, dark-haired woman came out of the barn. Her step was slow and halting. He could see, even from here, that one leg was crippled. She dragged that foot behind her, and supported herself with a cane. Parker watched as she drew handfuls of grain from the sack slung over her shoulder, and dropped the dried kernels to the chickens gathered at her feet.

In that moment, all was still hidden. He was the watcher, unobserved. She was a stranger to him, but there was an instant familiarity, as if he'd seen her before, known her. He watched, captivated by her simple actions, and would have gone on staring, except in that instant, she glanced up and saw him.

Her reaction was immediate and strange. She dropped the bag of grain she was holding, and as if afraid, hobbled quickly into the house.

Willow had known him at once. The memory of that long-forgotten day came back to her, clear and vivid in her mind. She was eight years old, and the man called T. J. Parker was leaving the People. She could see him now in that sharp recollection, Parker walking away from the camp, his broad, square back moving away from her, disappearing into the blurred landscape of the desert.

In that day of childhood, she had first learned of grief and mourning. He had given up his right to live among the People, and had chosen to be alone in his sorrow. He had walked away, out of her life, but the memory had left a scar of sadness in the child. It was a scar that still marked the woman.

"A man is coming from those hills," she told her brothers, Yuma and Jared.

"Where?" asked Jared. "Show me."

"You will see him soon enough," she said, and made no effort to show Jared where Parker stood. "I know this man," she told them. "Once, he was one of the People. He lived among us for many years, and then he chose to leave."

"Who is he?" asked Yuma.

"He will be here soon," she said, ignoring Yuma's question. "I don't know why he came, but I know that the image of this man was burned into my mind long ago, when I was still a child. I knew him instantly," she said, glancing quickly at her brothers, "and I think he knew me."

"Willow," said Yuma, "what are you trying to—"

"Shhh," she warned.

The silence was broken only by the sound of footsteps approaching the house. Three loud knocks rapped at the door.

Yuma was his father's likeness. He was Josiah in the way he strode across the room, in the straight line of his back, and in the steady glance of his eyes as he pulled open the door.

"I'm T. J. Parker," said the man whose large frame filled the space of the open doorway. "I've walked all the way from Colorado to come here."

"Let him in," said Willow.

He turned toward her, at the sound of her voice. "Sidra?" he asked. "Is that really you?"

And then Willow understood why it had seemed that Parker knew her. She and Sidra were sisters of the same father, but their looks were as close alike as that of twins. Parker had mistaken her for Sidra.

She stared at him now. He was older than the man she remembered. There were streaks of white in his hair, and his eyes said that he was long past her memory of him as a young man. He looked confused and tired.

"My sister, Sidra, is gone from this place. I am Willow Gray Wolf," she told him, "and these are my brothers. Come inside where it's warm. You are welcome here, T. J. Parker."

His gaze never left her face as Parker stepped into the center of the room. Behind him, Yuma Gray Wolf closed the door.

In the hours which followed, T. J. Parker told Willow and the others about how he'd come to know Sidra, and how he'd found his way to Mirror Lake. He told them of the long days of travel, of crossing rivers and walking through deep snow.

He told them of the things he'd seen along the way, the stark cities and the empty land.

They listened, but many things were left unsaid, like why Sidra decided to go back to the camp of the Outsiders, and why Parker had lived for so many years alone in the caves of NORAD. Willow held the questions within her, and wondered. She would ask him these things when she knew the man better. For now, she let him rest, and she kept her brothers and the Wyse brothers from asking too many questions, either.

Salena found a place for Parker in the house. He was given the room Seth had shared with Sidra. Salena eyed this stranger with distrustful glances.

"How do we know he's safe to bring among us?" she whispered to Willow. "He might be dangerous. A man who lived as a hermit for so many years," she added fearfully, "should we trust him so quickly?"

"He's safe," said Willow. She was very sure of that.

"How do you know?"

"I know," Willow assured her.

Salena wouldn't let it drop so easily. "I thought Jack Quaid was safe," she said. "I was wrong about him, and that mistake nearly cost me my life. This man is a stranger to us, after all."

"He's not a stranger, Mother. I know him." Willow had begun calling Salena "Mother," after Jonathan's death. It made her feel closer to Jonathan, and closer to this woman who was her baby's grandmother.

"I don't know," Salena said. "I'm going to watch him. What would John have done? I don't know anymore. Tell me, Willow."

Salena had seemed to have become frail since

296

her husband's death. The loss of John Katelo had marked them all. In his absence, Jonathan had become the leader of the family. Seth had never wanted such responsibility. Now, with both Seth and Jonathan gone, Willow had assumed this role. She decided what was needed for all of them.

"You know that I am sometimes given pieces of the future to see, Mother?"

"You saw him?" Salena asked. "Like the dream that told you of Jonathan's death?"

The mention of that dream, and of Jonathan's name, opened the wound in Willow's heart. She had seen it clearly and known it would happen—that Jonathan would give his life protecting her—only she hadn't known how to stop it.

"No, this is not the same," she said to Salena. "Jonathan's death was a part of my future I could not change. T. J. Parker is a part of my past. I think I have carried the vision of him with me all my life, since the day he left the Outsiders. That memory has stayed with me, clear and strong."

Salena listened to her son's wife as though Willow knew the answers that she had forgotten. "But, why has he come here? What does he want with us?"

"Maybe Parker is searching for a future that he lost long ago, Mother."

"Are you part of that future, Willow?"

The question surprised her. Salena had become nearly childlike in her thinking during the last few months. Yet now, there was a seriousness Willow saw in Salena's eyes that was nothing of a child. It was as if a strong woman was still there, buried deep within the spirit of this seemingly frail widow.

"The Inuits believe that life is not accidental," said Salena. "He told me this, after the way we had found each other. So unlikely," she told Willow. "He was alone, living in a cabin in Canada. In the middle of a winter storm, with the man Jack Quaid, I found my way to that cabin." She shook her head, remembering. "It was no accident that I came there."

"What are you telling me?" asked Willow.

"Not telling you," said Salena. "Only wondering. Is it an accident that this man, Parker, has come to us now when you are alone, without a husband?"

Willow was angry at the thought, angry that Salena was betraying Jonathan by such a question. "That's not why Parker came here. It wasn't because of me."

"Wasn't it?" Salena's eyes were solemn, calm lights in a storm. "You feel something for this man; I see that. Whatever it may become, don't close your mind and heart to such feelings, Willow. Jonathan wouldn't want that. Maybe the Inuits are right. Maybe the paths of our lives are not an accident."

"Let it go," Willow told her. The pain of hearing Jonathan's name was too great. When Willow thought of him, of the way it had been when his arms were around her . . . of seeing him standing in the field with the sun on his face . . . she couldn't breathe. A hurt came to her that was so profound, she felt unable to move, as if all her strength was in that pain, and she would die.

Only, she hadn't died. She had gone on living without him. She had given birth to their son, and watched the days follow one another in an endless line. *Endless.* Life was blank without him. That was the truth she had learned to feel. That was what the future held for her, a blank space of days, without him.

Salena did let it go, as Willow had asked. They spoke no more about the man, T. J. Parker, but the old mother's thought had seeded itself into Willow's mind. *Was it an accident that Parker was here now?*

Like his father, Jonathan Katelo had believed in the Inuit way. He had spoken of the dead as "spirit guides," to lead those among the living.

Willow felt strongly that Jonathan was with her still, that he knew her pain, and his spirit remained near, protecting her. Was it possible that Salena was right? That nothing was an accident? That Jonathan knew of Parker, and that he had led him here?

Long after the light had faded from the fire in the room, Willow stayed awake and saw into the shining dark. For the first time since Jonathan's death, she looked closely into the visions of her mind . . . and saw the future.

For her, the future was a long and happy life with this man, Parker. She saw their many children, sons and daughters, and the days without end that would fill their lives. She saw a love that would find their souls and heal them both. That love was the vision Willow watched as a promise unfolding. It was the path to which Jonathan's spirit led her.

At dawn, when Willow walked outside and stood in the open field to greet the morning, she felt the warmth of the new day touch her. It was a trust she had in the dawn—that each day would bring a new beginning, that each morning was a time of birth, and death. One must be let go in order for the other to begin.

That dawn, Willow let go of Jonathan. He had remained with her because she needed him. He had led her to this point. Now, she would be strong enough alone. She watched the brightening colors of the sky as the day lifted into being, and with the death of the night and the new hope of the dawn, she said a final goodbye to Jonathan, and felt his spirit leave her.

It was another morning, a time of beginning. Willow turned away from the past, and followed the track of sunlight back to the house by Mirror Lake . . . to the people there, and to all the mornings of her tomorrows. Like a lost child who had found her way home, Willow followed the bright path that would lead her to her future. It was morning; the day had just begun.

Thirty-five

Andrew's tissue type was a close match with his mother's, and his half-brother, Roarke. It was a less perfect match with siblings Bram and Meredith, and only a possibility with Daniel and Trinity. With immunosuppressant drugs to improve the odds against transplant rejection, the chance was worth taking, even for them.

Everything was ready for the recipients: a sterile environment for the surgical procedure, antiseptic solution to bathe the injection sites, and prepared bags and needles for the intravenous transfusions. After aspirating the bone marrow from the donor, the soft, red tissue would be transfused intravenously to each recipient. If all went well, the marrow cells would then find their way through the recipient's circulation into the marrow cavities of their bones, where they would begin to grow. If the transplanted marrow was not rejected, the marrow cells would begin to produce the needed immunity to the virus in those persons, and the transplants would be considered successful.

All that was needed now was to begin the aspiration of the donor marrow. For this, Brad volunteered to be first.

They waited until Andrew was asleep. It would be easier without worrying about a two-year-old running around by himself, or letting Andrew stay with them and watch what was happening.

Sidra injected the Novocain into the soft muscle above Brad's right hip. He was lying on his back within the sterilized field of the docking chamber, staring at the dome ceiling, and waiting for the local anesthetic to take effect.

"Don't look so scared," he told Sidra, trying to lighten the mood. "I'm the one who's getting the needle."

"I'm not scared. I just don't want to hurt you."

"From what Arthur Penn has explained to us, I don't think we can avoid that." He touched his finger to the flesh above his hipbone. "The area's numb. We should start."

"All right," she said, and picked up the syringe. Her hands were shaking.

"Wait a minute."

"What's the matter?" She stopped immediately. "You're not numb yet?"

"No, I'm ready," he told her. "I want you to look at me, Sidra."

She had been staring at the instruments, fear glazed on her face like theatrical make-up. When he called her name, she glanced up at him.

"However bad this whole thing might turn out to be," he said, "I want you to remember how much worse it would have been for me, trying to do this by myself. I would have done it, too. Remember that when it's hurting me, Sidra. You're helping. Okay?"

"Thanks," she said. Her trembling stopped. This was as calm as either of them was going to get.

He laid back and closed his eyes. "Go ahead. Start."

He felt a pressure, but no pain, when the needle punctured his skin.

"Tell me if you want me to stop," she said. Her voice was shallow, nervous sounding.

"No, don't stop," he said, "no matter what I tell you. Just get the marrow sample. I want this over as fast as possible."

"All right, Brad," she agreed. "We're at the hip bone."

He didn't need her to tell him this. The instant the needle make contact with the bone, he felt an electric charge go straight down his leg. He gasped, and all his muscles locked into a rigid barrier, trying to force the needle out.

He couldn't force it out.

When the stylet bit into the bone, and Sidra twisted the thin lance deeper and deeper into the hipbone's cortex, Brad felt pain flood over his mind in bright, hot colors. He ground his jaw closed, and tasted the heat of those colors, reds and blood-orange, silver, and white. He tasted stark and excruciating white.

"Brad, I'm finished cutting. We're at the marrow. I'm going to start aspirating into the syringe. Hold on a little longer."

He felt the extraction of the marrow from his hipbone. It felt like a tooth being pulled from his spine, the roots deep within him, the pressure building as the syringe filled with the soft, fatty tissue.

The loud groan escaped from between his teeth which were crushed together in a tightened vise.

"It's over," said Sidra. She held up the syringe, reddened with Brad's blood, and the thicker tissue of the marrow. "Oh, God," she said softly, "it's over."

He tried to speak, tried to tell her of the relief from pain, but words wouldn't come. His body began to shake, and all he could do was sob.

While Brad recovered within the adobe shelter he had built for himself, Sidra, and Andrew, the six first recipients of the bone marrow transplants received Brad's immunity-producing cells through intravenous transfusion.

They were lined up on tables in Diana's lab — Quinn, Rachel, Paige, Maria, Lara, and Griffin — the IVs hanging from steel arms and hooks over the lab tables. The volume of Brad's marrow had been enough to provide a small donor sample for each of them. The red cells and platelets from Brad's marrow fed into the narrow tubing of the IV bags, and slowly entered the bloodstreams of the six.

"Daddy," said Rachel Nathan, "can this hurt us if it doesn't work?" Rachel was Quinn's daughter with Jessica, the only biological child left to them.

"I don't know the answer to that, Rache." He didn't want to lie to her. "This is new to us. We aren't sure what might happen. One thing I do know," he told her. "I'm staying with you all the way. Okay?"

"Okay." She had Jessica's eyes, and she looked at him with such love.

"Did I ever tell you the story of my mother and the night visitor?"

Rachel shook her head.

"No? Then it's time you heard it."

The slow measure of the red cells released into the circulation of the six recipients of the transplants. The marrow dripped, and to the metered rhythm of the sound, Quinn told them the story.

"My father was a man who was away from home a lot of the time," Quinn spoke directly to his daughter, but everyone could hear. "Sometimes, he worked at night. My mother and we children were often on our own at the house. We didn't mind too much. It was a small enough house, and there were six of us."

"What was my grandmother's name?" Rachel asked. She wasn't looking at the IV drip anymore.

304

Her attention had shifted to Quinn and the story.

"My mother's name? Sweet Jesus, girl. Have I never told you that? Your grandmother's name was Siobhan Roarke Kelsey—Roarke before she married my dad."

"What was he called?"

"He was Cameron, like your brother." Saying his son's name was a hurt to Quinn, but he went on with the story quickly, so Rachel wouldn't notice. "My mother was a strong-willed, independent woman, Irish to the core, but a free thinker if there ever was one. I never was afraid as a child, for I knew that if my mother was there, nothing would have had a chance at hurting me. She would have fought any danger like a tiger to protect her children." His throat tightened with emotion, telling the story. He remembered the small house where he and five brothers and sisters had grown up, and the image of his mother, still young in this memory. Telling it, took him back to the feelings of that day, still fresh and vivid within his mind.

"Your own mother is the same," he said.

Rachel nodded, and smiled. "Did something happen that night?" she asked

"We were sitting in our living room—that was the gathering place of the house—" he explained this unfamiliar term to Rachel, "me watching a program on television, and Roarke eating a late night bowl of cereal from a tray on his lap. My sisters were doing their homework, I think. From out of nowhere, we hear this noise. It's at the back of the house, like a door opening."

He had their attention. The only sound in the lab except his own voice was the steady drip of the IVs down the plastic tubing.

" 'Turn that noise off', my mother said of the television. I did, and we listened with our ears up like little wolf cubs for the sounds coming from the dark of the house. And it came again. A door was shutting, and we heard heavy footsteps coming toward us."

"What was it?" Rachel leaned closer to him, as if she could see the answer in his eyes.

"We didn't know, but we were sure it wasn't only the wind blowing the door shut. Wind couldn't make the sound of those slow steps coming closer, or the creaking of the floorboards. Wind wouldn't have bumped its leg on the table and groaned. We knew someone was in the house."

"What did you do?" Rachel's eyes were wide with interest. "Did you get a weapon?"

"We did," said Quinn. "My mother rushed into the kitchen and brought back the only weapons she could lay her hands on in our house."

"What?"

"Potatoes. My mother handed us each two big-sized ones, hard as bricks, and said that if anyone came into the room, to throw a crack at his head with the spuds, and run."

Quinn could hear the sound of Griffin laughing from the far table at the end of the room. "Oh, you might not have had such defenses in a Welsh home," said Quinn straight-faced, "but we were poor Irish. Siobhan Kelsey's where they got the term *the mother of invention*. She was thinking on her feet."

Lara was laughing too, and Rachel was smiling from chin to cheekbone. They knew he was playing with them, and they were having fun with it.

"Nobody warned the poor man who was coming into this barrage. He didn't know the kind of battle he'd have walking through that door."

"Stop, please wait a minute," pleaded Griff. He was laughing so hard, he couldn't catch his breath.

Quinn took no pity on him and went on relent-

306

lessly. "The door swung open and a dark-haired head poked out, looking . . ."

"Stop! Oh, my side," cried Griff.

"And twelve hard lumps of potatoes went shying through the air, not counting the two bigger ones in my mother's hands, hitting the poor man fourteen good cracks to the braincase. We were good at pitching stones, we kids. None of us missed our shot."

"Did you run?" asked Rachel. There was water standing in her eyes from laughing.

"We did—to pick up our poor dad. He didn't know what hit him, creeping in late like that, after a night of too much drinking at the pub."

"Was he all right?"

"Oh, he slept it off. We told him next day that his terrible headache was from falling down drunk. I don't think he was quite sure of what had happened, which was so much the better for us, but he never came home late to my mother's house again."

"I would have liked your mother," said Rachel.

"You would have," Quinn told her. "And she would have loved you."

The IVs were flat and empty. Cathe and Jessica moved among the tables, removing the IV needles from the recipient's veins and applying bandages to their mercurochromed arms. The first phase of the experiment was completed. Now, they would have to wait and see what would happen.

Thirty-six

Two days after Brad's surgery, he recovered his strength enough to draw the marrow sample from Sidra. Carefully following Arthur Penn's directions to reach the iliac crest — the top of the hip bone — he aspirated thirty c. c.'s of soft marrow tissue into the syringe and left the sample in a sealed container within the docking chamber.

Both after the first transfer, and now, the docking chamber was resealed, the air forced from the closed unit, and sterilized with a solution of bleach disinfectant from ceiling and wall nozzles mounted around the room. Only after this was done was Jessica, or any other member of the biosphere, allowed into the docking chamber.

For Brad and Sidra, the worst was over. Tomorrow, Brad would perform the last surgical procedure, this time on Andrew. He was dreading that, the pain this would cause the boy. Andrew was a child and couldn't possibly understand why Brad would be hurting him.

Fortunately, in Andrew's case, his bones were thinner and softer than an adult's. All of a child's bones contained red marrow, the kind rich in red blood-producing cells. That changed when a child reached its teen years. From then on, most of the marrow in the body became a yellow fatty substance not suitable for transplant. After the teen years, the principle sites for red marrow remained the iliac crests, the sternum, the spine, ribs, clavicle, the shoulder blades, and skull bones.

Brad had decided to risk drugging Andrew. He'd use the same chloral hydrate blend that Diana Hunt had produced in her lab and put in the breakfast coffee to immobilize the team of Biosphere Seven, so many years ago. The idea to use the narcotic had been Jessica's suggestion.

"Andrew's too young to endure such a thing for our sake. I won't let that happen to him. Giving him the drug is dangerous, but doing this to him without it is inhuman. I'm asking you to take the chance and put him out."

It wasn't a chance Brad wanted to take, but he agreed with Jessica. They checked with Arthur Penn about the right proportions, and would mix that amount of the liquid into Andrew's drink tomorrow morning. At this point, Brad, Sidra, and Andrew were living off the provisions of the biosphere. For the first time in a long while, Andrew had milk to drink, and fruits and vegetables to eat. Food was left in the docking chamber each time the outer door was opened for the next marrow sample to be collected.

"Will it work, do you think?" asked Sidra. She was lying on a layer of blankets covering the floor of the adobe shelter. The blankets and a few other items needed for their survival, had been given to them by those within the biosphere. They had become vitally important to the welfare of the people inside the sphere, and it was critical that they stayed alive and healthy.

"If I didn't believe there was a strong possibility of that," said Brad, "I wouldn't be putting Andrew through the transplant surgery tomorrow. This is the best chance they've got. Yes, I think it might work. God help them if it doesn't."

"What do you mean?"

"I mean, we've introduced our blood cells into their bodies. You and I have been exposed to the virus. I've had it; you've been around it. If they don't acquire our immunity, we may well have given them the virus."

"What about Trinity? There's nothing to protect him. He hasn't had the transfusion yet."

"Tomorrow," said Brad. "It's as much as we can do. Jessica will be one of the last ones to receive the transfusion. I'm afraid for her, too. Afraid for all of them."

"If they die," said Sidra, "if we were the cause of their deaths . . ."

Brad couldn't answer her. The same thought had been tormenting him. *If Jessica died*—if he was responsible for bringing her the virus—*could he go on?*

In the distance, he heard the sound of a coyote howling at the black overhanging sky. The future was a mystery, dark as night. He couldn't pull it from him, or push it away. All he could do was hope to move it in the right direction.

Brad closed his eyes. In the solitude of that seal of blindness, like the coyote beneath the forbidding sky, he felt like howling to the heavens, too.

Jessica knew this was the morning Andrew would be given the drops of chloral hydrate. She was afraid for her son, afraid for the others in the sphere. Today the last group would receive the marrow transplants: she and Roarke, Bram, Meredith, Daniel, and Trinity.

Jessica tried to pull her scattered thoughts into one connected line of consciousness. So many concerns claimed her attention: the survival of Quinn and the other recipients who were recovering from

310

the transplants; the danger and pain from the marrow donation for Andrew, Brad, and Sidra; and what would happen to the twenty lives within Biosphere Seven if the experiment failed?

The concerns had faces — Quinn's, Brad's, Andrew's. It was possible that she could lose them all. The end had come to the people of the Outside world. Good people, loving, kind. Because of these transplants, would the end come to her world now?

A knock sounded softly at the door of the computer room.

"Come in," she called.

The door opened, and Trinity stood in the hallway. "We have Andrew's marrow sample in the lab. Cathe says they're ready for us now."

"Is Andrew . . . ?"

"He's all right. Brad said he slept through the whole thing."

"Good. That's good. I didn't want him to feel — I didn't want to cause him any more hurt. I couldn't stand that."

Trinity started to walk away.

"Wait. Could you come into my room for a minute? I want to talk to you."

He seemed to hesitate.

"Please."

"All right," he said. He stepped inside and closed the door. "We have a few minutes."

"Trinity," she began, "there's something I want to show you." She switched on the computer and accessed her file.

"What is it?"

"It's my journal. I kept a record of our years in this sealed world, a listing of events, birth, deaths, and the way we changed. It's all here, in this file. No one has ever seen it except me. I wrote it for myself. It was a kind of companion for me when I needed a friend, someone to talk to."

He looked at her blankly.

"Sometimes I was lonely, too. I want you to have this," she said, and held out the box of disks.

He didn't reach for it. "Why?"

"Because if we don't survive these transplants, I want to know that this will be read — and not remain hidden, as if it didn't exist. It's important to me that one person sees it, to make it real. You understand?"

"Why me?"

"You're my eldest child," she said. "Of all of my children, you're the one most like me. I want it to go to you."

Slowly, Trinity reached out and took the box from her hand. His fingers touched hers, and for a moment he didn't move them away. "I'll read your journal," he said. He didn't look at her, but at the box in his hand.

"Thank you. It means a great deal to me."

"We'd better go now, Mother." He glanced up, and his eyes were wet.

"Trinity, I —"

"Come on," he said, stopping the words she might have spoken. "After the transplants do their work, we'll have years Outside to talk about everything."

She nodded, and started out of the room.

"I hate needles," he told her. "Maybe I could hold your hand?" He reached across the space between them and took her hand in his. Together, they walked down the hall and to the lab.

While those within Biosphere Seven waited, those within Biosphere Two waited, also. The results from the bone marrow transplants were almost as important to Arthur Penn and the people within the glass dome in Wales as they were to the families within the sphere on the high desert of Texas. If the transplants took, and the people of Biosphere Seven were free to walk Outside and survive, then a freedom would be gained for the people of Biosphere Two, as well.

"What have you heard from them?" asked Arthur. In the last few days, his question was put to Paul Schefield almost hourly. Events were moving quickly. Change could be sudden, and dramatic.

"Two members of the first group of recipients, Griffin Llewellyn and Maria Innis, are experiencing mild symptoms of rejection. The child has a rash, and the man's becoming slightly jaundiced. They're treating them with cyclosporine."

Penn accepted this news without comment. "Everyone else is all right?"

"So far," said Schefield. "It's early yet, only a few days since the first transplants. I don't think we should get too optimistic. Even if they don't experience massive rejection, how do we know if it worked? What kind of test is going to tell us if they've acquired the immunity?"

"None," said Penn bluntly. "The only way we'll know for sure is when they go outside—and live."

"Great. Russian roulette," said Schefield.

"That's right," said Penn, "except in this case, all the chambers are loaded. Our only hope is that the gun is firing blanks."

Like Arthur Penn, Paul Schefield waited anxiously for word from the American team. If Jessica Nathan and the others died, Schefield knew that his own people would be so disheartened, they might not have the courage to go on. More was resting on this experiment than the twenty lives within Biosphere Seven. Their own lives were in danger, too.

He pressed his fingers to the glass partition between himself and the Briton. "It had better work,"

313

he told Penn. "God damn you to hell if it doesn't! It had better work!"

"Tell me when you hear from them," Arthur said to him, not visibly reacting to Schefield's words. He walked away and sat beside the campfire.

"That man scares me," Schefield told the dark-haired woman beside him.

"Why? He seems to care about what happens to them. What has he done that you don't trust?"

Schefield couldn't put a name to the feeling. It lived in him though, and was growing more uneasy by the minute. So much depended on the knowledge of this one man. Could Penn really know so much? Had they been right to believe in him?

"I don't trust anything I can't see," said Schefield, "and his words are just that—words—until I see the proof of them."

"Give him a chance, Paul. Right now, he's the only hope those people have." The woman walked away, leaving Schefield standing alone before the glass.

He'd better be right. The thought wriggled like living snakes in his brain. *Goddamn him! He'd better be right.*

On the fourteenth day of May, in the year of the Earth 2021, the doors of the sealed structure known as Biosphere Seven were opened. The sheltering environment of this autonomous world had sustained life for over twenty-three years, since the date of the biosphere's closure on December 25, 1997.

Jessica Nathan walked out of the sphere and onto the hard, white ground of the desert. With her came her children. Beside her walked Quinn Kelsey. In all, twenty lives were freed from the confines of the biosphere, twenty lives reborn into a world the people called Outside.

314

On the crest of the hill overlooking the dome, Brad McGhee stood and watched as the glass walls unfolded like the petals of a flower, and released the human seeds of promise into the future.

He waited as the woman walked up the hill alone, opening her arms . . . to him.

Thirty-seven

"We're leaving," Jessica told Paul Schefield, through the satellite communications system linking their computers.

"But you don't know yet whether the experiment worked."

"It doesn't matter," Jessica told him. "We're claiming life, Paul. Live or die, we've decided to see as much of this world, and do as much as we can, in whatever time we have left. Some of us may live because of the transplants, and some may reject the donor marrow. It might be months before that happens, as it was for Cameron. We're not going to wait that long. Each day is a whole life, if you put living into it. We've decided to live."

Schefield's face on the screen reflected his concerns. "If you're gone, how will we know what we should do? Whether we should take the same chance? How will we know if the transplants worked?"

"I'm not in charge of this world anymore," she told him. "I'm not the Lady of the Sphere. I don't have answers for you. I can tell you that my son, Trinity, has chosen to stay on in the opened biosphere, with Sidra Innis. They'll live here to maintain the survival of the individual biomes, and to keep the satellite computer operational."

"They'll keep in communication with us?"

316

"Trinity wants to keep the computer links open, both with Biosphere Two, and with the larger systems in NORAD, if one of us chooses to live there."

"It's something," said Paul. "At least, we'll be able to monitor how well the two of them survive the transplants."

"Sidra was a donor for the marrow, not a recipient," Jessica corrected him. "She has an inherited immunity to the virus through her father, Josiah Gray Wolf. I'm afraid your only test case will be Trinity."

"One person?"

"One life," said Jessica. "It's as much as any of us are given. One chance."

Paul Schefield's mood seemed to change into an acceptance of her words. The anger that had been evident in his eyes and in the hard lines of his face became a question. "What will you do, Jessica? Where will you go? What's going to happen to the rest of them?"

For the first time since she'd taken on the commitment as leader for the biosphere, Jessica didn't need to know the answers. She was one of them still, but no longer responsible for them. A profound sense of peace had come to her with that realization.

"Brad, Quinn, the children, and I will all be heading west. Quinn wants them to see the ocean. I want them to see a forest. I don't know what the others will do," she told him honestly. "Many will go their separate ways. The fourteen born within Biosphere Seven are anxious to see as much as they can of our world outside the dome. It's a new earth to them, Paul. Like being released from Eden."

"Allowed into Eden, you mean."

"Yes, I guess it's that, too. The earth is a biosphere, isn't it? We're just travelers, moving from one home to another."

"I wish you well on your journey home, Jessica," Paul Schefield said in parting.

"And I wish you well on your journey," she told him, "wherever it may lead."

They left the biosphere three days after the doors were opened. In separate families, and solitary travelers, they moved away from the place that had nurtured their lives.

Trinity and Sidra stood before the open doors of the biosphere, watching the others leave. Together, they would remain here, claiming this land as their home.

Trinity thought of the documents for the CXT experiment, still hidden in the planter in his room. A time might come when he would look at them again. He was glad he had saved the experiment. There was new hope in the world. If he lived, it might be that he could bring an end to sickness through the knowledge gained from the work in those hidden documents. The scientists of Biosphere Four had been close to a breakthrough, Trinity felt sure. Their knowledge had been passed on to him. With luck, he would carry it forward, into the bright hope of the future.

Trinity watched the brothers and sisters he had loved, and the family he had known within the biosphere, move away. He raised his arm and waved goodbye to them all. They were part of him, children of the same world.

At the rise of hill where the land swept up and out of his sight, Jessica turned. For a long moment, she looked back at him. She had been his mother. Maggie Adair had been his mother. The sealed world of Biosphere Seven had been his mother, too. Like the meaning of his name, he had been the child of all three.

Framed by the sunlight above her, Jessica waved to him one final time. She pulled at the reins of the white horse, turning it toward that which was to come . . . and rode away.